Symphony of Monsters

ALSO BY MARC LEVY

If Only It Were True
Finding You
Seven Days for an Eternity
In Another Life
London Mon Amour
The Children of Freedom
All Those Things We Never Said
The First Day
The First Night
The Shadow Thief
The Strange Journey of Mr. Daldry
Replay
Stronger than Fear
Another Idea of Happiness
P.S. from Paris
The Last of the Stanfields
A Woman Like Her
Hope

Symphony of Monsters

A NOVEL

Marc Levy

Translated from the French by Tina Kover

HarperVia
An Imprint of HarperCollins*Publishers*

Without limiting the exclusive rights of any author, contributor or the publisher of this publication, any unauthorized use of this publication to train generative artificial intelligence (AI) technologies is expressly prohibited. HarperCollins also exercise their rights under Article 4(3) of the Digital Single Market Directive 2019/790 and expressly reserve this publication from the text and data mining exception.

This novel is a work of fiction. Any references to real people, events, establishments, organizations, or locales are intended only to give the fiction a sense of reality and authenticity and are used fictitiously. All other names, characters, and places, and all dialogue and incidents portrayed in this book are the product of the author's imagination.

SYMPHONY OF MONSTERS. Copyright © 2023 by Marc Levy. English translation copyright © 2026 by Marc Levy. Note from Cover Designer copyright © 2026 by Pedro Viejo. All rights reserved. Printed in the United States of America. No part of this book may be used or reproduced in any manner whatsoever without written permission except in the case of brief quotations embodied in critical articles and reviews. For information, address HarperCollins Publishers, 195 Broadway, New York, NY 10007. In Europe, HarperCollins Publishers, Macken House, 39/40 Mayor Street Upper, Dublin 1, D01 C9W8, Ireland.

HarperCollins books may be purchased for educational, business, or sales promotional use. For information, please email the Special Markets Department at SPsales@harpercollins.com.

harpercollins.com

Originally published as *La Symphonie des monstres* in France in 2023 by Robert Laffont / Versilio.

FIRST HARPERVIA HARDCOVER PUBLISHED IN 2026

Designed by Elina Cohen
Maps © Springer Cartographics

Library of Congress Cataloging-in-Publication Data has been applied for.

ISBN 978-0-06-346500-8
ISBN 978-0-06-348074-2 (Intl)

25 26 27 28 29 LBC 5 4 3 2 1

For my mother

It began long before February 24.

—The Group of 9

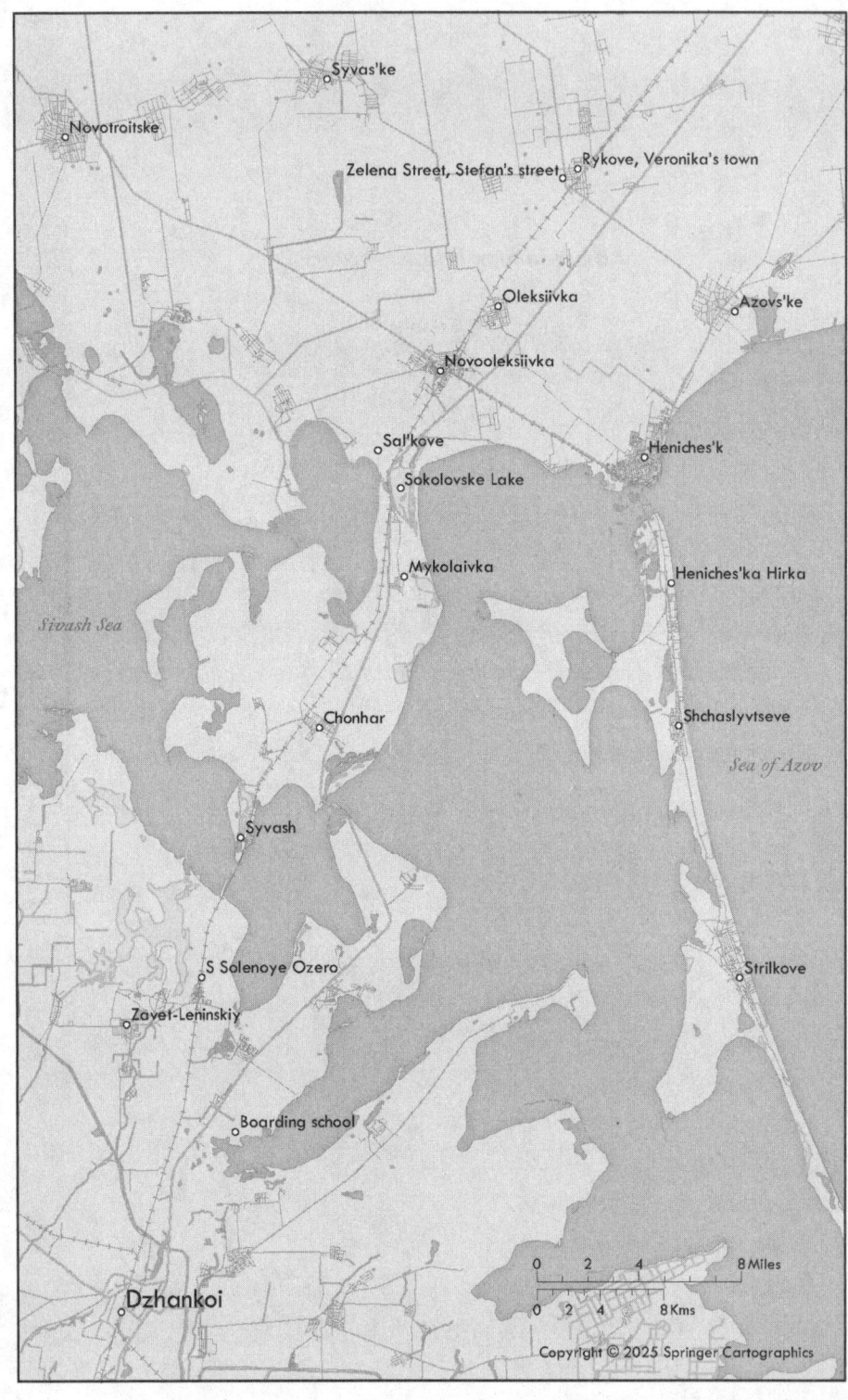

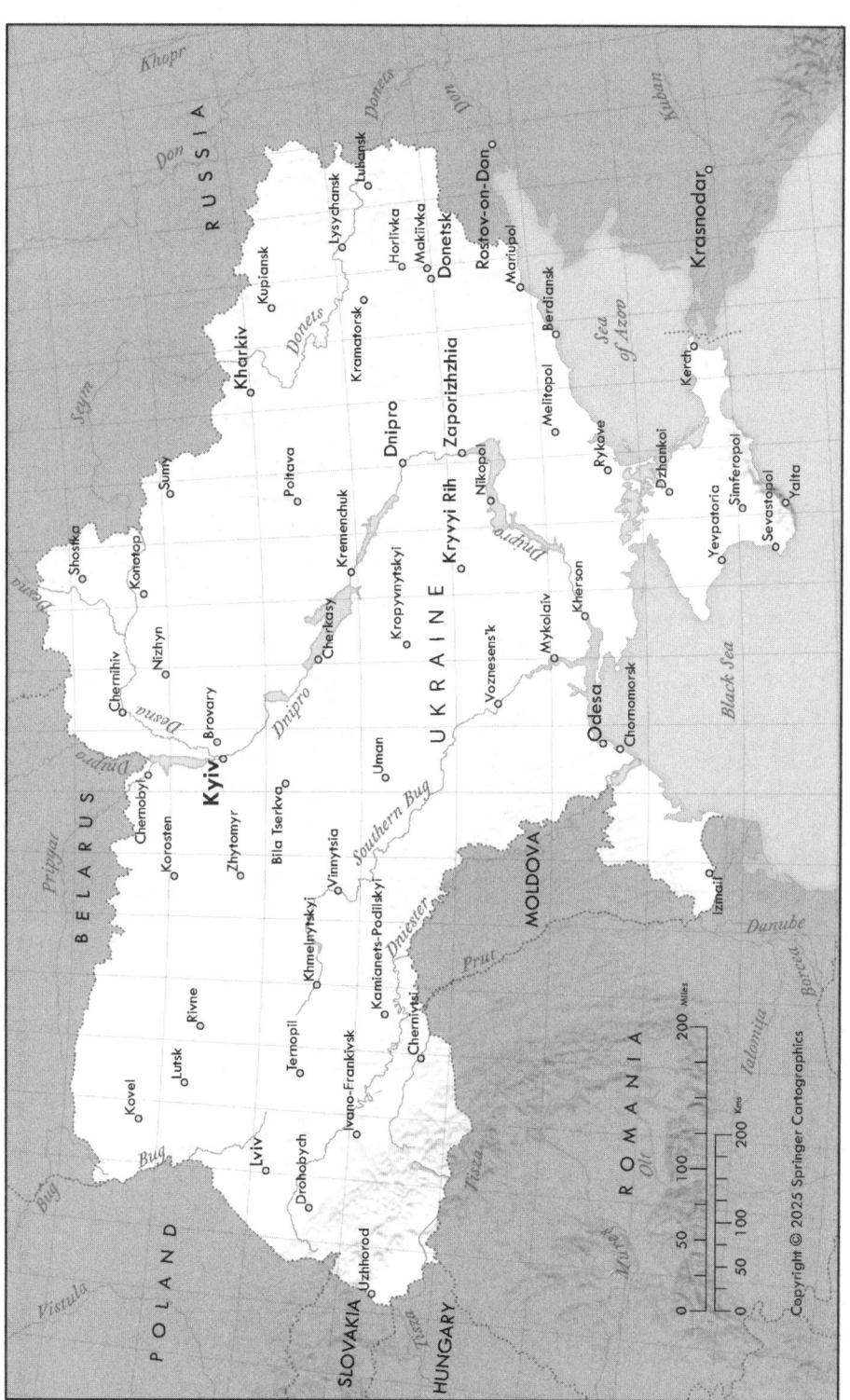

You disappeared today.
I know you're alive, because I feel it with everything in me.
Mom doesn't know they've taken you yet.

It was before everything changed. Dad had come home from work exhausted, as he all too often was. Mom looked just as tired as he did, and the mood at the table wasn't exactly light. You and I looked at each other, waiting for one of them to say the word, the phrase, that would trigger the eruption. It was almost a game between us, to be the first to wink when the moment had definitely come. There was a jar of candy in your room, and whoever won the competition could help themselves. It was our way of reconnecting with happiness, our way of forgetting, when we went to bed, about what we thought at the time were adult wars. Now I'd give anything to hear them shouting, Mom sighing, to see our father fleeing the battle by taking the dog for a walk. Now, all I want is for everything to be the way it was. Before one man's madness cast a bloody fog over our land.

When you didn't come home at the usual time, I knew something had happened to you. I knew the monsters had snatched you up in their claws. I ran as fast as I could, promising God that if I was wrong and I spotted you in the schoolyard, sitting alone on the bench as you sometimes do when the day's been too hard, or in the nurse's office because you'd skinned your knee again in some scuffle you'd lost, I'd never doubt His existence again. I passed Mrs. Blansky's house, the shutters closed, and sped up. Running past the ruins of the building where Mr. Zillig, the pianist, used to live, I couldn't remember whether it used to have seven or eight floors, and the uncertainty filled me with a terrible rage. How could anyone forget a detail like that so quickly? As if the happy days had been swept away forever.

1

Head cocked to one side, Valentyn eyed the man. When he was observing someone, this position gave him an interesting perspective, an angle from which he could see more. Maybe it was just an excuse to justify his precocious quirkiness. When you're nine years old, that's the term people use for anything about you that's out of the ordinary: *precocious*. Valentyn was as precocious at chess as he was at the piano, and he was equally precocious in mathematics, but the *most* precocious thing about him was his intuition; he had an uncanny ability to guess what people were thinking. The only area in which he lagged behind was speech. Valentyn's parents had been assured by Dr. Zablonsky that his was merely a case of childhood mutism, that it would pass, but by the time Valentyn was six years old, he still hadn't uttered a word. Dr. Zablonsky, an excellent pediatrician, wasn't one to settle for a hypothetical diagnosis, especially when it came to tricky problems like this one. He'd investigated every possible lead, looking for the slightest correlation between symptoms, and he wasn't too proud to ask his colleagues for their opinions. After having his young patient examined by a speech and language specialist and sending his file to a neurologist, he'd been able to say with certainty that the boy's hearing was impeccable, his intellectual development above average, and his brain, as confirmed by an MRI scan, absolutely normal. Had Valentyn been able to speak, he would have asked Zablonsky what a "normal" brain was, exactly. At least his silence kept him from asking stupid questions.

That day, Valentyn saw an odd man who seemed to be pretending to shop for cereal. He could have sworn that the man was following him. Two weeks earlier, he'd noticed him on the sidewalk in front of the pharmacy. The man had taken a ridiculously long time to open a pack of chewing gum, which wasn't exactly a complicated maneuver; stranger still, when Valentyn had neared him, he'd put the pack away in his pocket without taking a piece out.

A few days later, he'd thought he saw the same man again, this time standing at the bus stop. But the buses hadn't been running for a long time now—everyone knew that—so why hang around there? In any case, he wasn't local to the area. Valentyn knew just about everyone, and few faces in the neighborhood were unfamiliar to him. He should have shared his concern with his sister, he thought, but Lilya had enough on her mind as it was, and maybe he was just imagining things. Valentyn had his own world, which he filled with imaginary beings whenever he was bored, and where he could string extraordinary adventures together like beads, one after the other, if the boredom lingered—like in class, for example. It was while he was thinking about this, and to reassure himself, that he recalled an important detail. Three days earlier, he'd seen two other men standing on the sidewalk, not directly in front of the school, but twenty yards on either side of the entrance, in such perfect symmetry that he'd found it strange.

The memory made his heart beat a little faster. He opened

his backpack and took out his speech book, a spiral notebook he used to communicate with those around him. Grabbing the first ballpoint pen he could find in his pencil case, he pretended to be writing out a shopping list. He jotted a note for his math teacher, whom he'd see for the first lesson of the day, put his things away, and headed for the canned-food section at the very back of the supermarket he had just entered, acting as if nothing were wrong. Glancing back to make sure the man hadn't followed him, he quietly opened the back door and slipped out. Home field advantage, as the father he hadn't seen in months would have said.

Outside, he broke into a run, dodging down a narrow alleyway and ducking under the fence enclosing the vacant lot, taking the shortcut to school he used on mornings when he'd stayed in bed a little too long.

Reaching the schoolyard, Valentyn didn't slow down, but ran past his classmates without a wave, hurrying into the old brick building and up the stairs. On the second floor, he stopped in front of his classroom door to think for a moment.

If he shared what he'd written, people might think he was just looking for attention. Suspecting a man of being up to something because he had trouble opening a pack of chewing gum and then seeing him again at the supermarket, or two other men because they stood on a sidewalk for too long . . .

But Valentyn's instincts weren't wrong; he was sure of it. Nature might have condemned him to silence, but in return it had given him unusual powers of perception. Summoning up his courage, he carefully recorded the latest findings of his investigation in his notebook, entered the room, and set the book on his teacher's desk.

Mrs. Jaruski read what he'd written, then looked up at him,

her gaze intent. Valentyn shrugged, steeling himself to receive a lecture. But he'd misinterpreted the serious look on her face.

"You did well to bring this to my attention. I'll mention it to my colleagues. Don't dawdle on your way home tonight. If you like, I can call your mother to pick you up."

Valentyn shook his head.

"All right, it's up to you. But be very careful. And if you see any of those men again, let me know right away. You can sit down now," she added, handing him back his notebook. It was almost time for class to begin.

Valentyn's instincts had been spot on. This wasn't going to be just another day at school.

At a middle school four blocks away, Lilya sat at her desk, rolling the pencil she'd been chewing between her fingers and staring at the peeling paint on the walls of her classroom. The windows, caked with pale dust made clumpy by the rain, were still intact. A miracle, as there weren't many buildings with windows left in the area. The principal kept insisting that schools were safe places, that the barbarians who were bombing civilian homes wouldn't wage war on children. It was clear to Lilya that he was naive. A dreamer. The barbarians had already shelled a maternity hospital in the west of the country and, in Marinka, a shell had burst through the ground-floor wall of a preschool and exploded in a playroom—though, fortunately, the attack had occurred at lunchtime and the cafeteria was on the second floor. No one had been killed, but there were many injuries. How do you explain to a four-year-old child that men hiding dozens of miles away had deliberately targeted them? No, the principal was wrong. Schools were not sanctuaries.

Lilya's gaze moved from table to table, flitting like a sparrow unable to fly. Eventually, the bird came to a stop on the nape of Stefan's neck, there in his seat in the third row.

There was something thrilling about this boy. The others swaggered through the corridors in groups, while his tall figure moved more languidly, with a casual grace she found elegant. He was older than his classmates, having been held back a year. His presence made Lilya feel new sensations, a lump forming in her throat anytime she came near him. But what unsettled her more than anything was how attentively he listened to her. As if every word mattered. At the end of the day, he sometimes walked her silently home, and Lilya, normally so proud of her independence, had to admit that she found his presence comforting.

Their first real meeting had taken place one evening when Stefan approached her outside the school after class.

"Are you going home?" he'd asked.

"I have to pick up my little brother first."

"Want me to come with you?"

Lilya was dying to say yes.

"You don't need to," she'd replied.

"Suit yourself."

"Wait," she'd protested. "It's not what you think. My brother's . . . well, he's different."

"Aren't we all?"

And before Stefan could ask another question, Lilya had told him the truth.

"He doesn't talk."

"I don't talk much either."

"Yeah . . . but he *never* does."

Stefan had shrugged, and then surprised Lilya with his answer. "Well, that's his right, isn't it? Can we talk to him, though?"

"Of course. He answers with hand gestures, or by writing in his notebook."

"Your brother's a poet, sounds like."

"Something like that, yeah."

Two days later, Stefan had waited for Lilya at the same place. As they walked through the ruins of what had once been a shopping mall, he'd taken a small book out of his pocket.

"For your brother," he'd said.

Lilya had looked at the cover of the book, a collection of poems by Serhiy Jadan.

"You know," Stefan had said, "the most precious thing . . . it's not a voice, but freedom. More and more people are realizing that lately, I think. The people invading us have never known freedom, that's why they hate us so much. The ones who do hate us, I mean."

He'd stopped walking then, and smiled at Lilya, and turned back the way they'd come. And she'd held the book of poems in her hands, feeling as if it were warming them, and watched him walk away, her heart full of a completely unfamiliar emotion.

It was during those evenings they'd spent together as teenagers, without ever telling anyone about them, that a friendship had sprung up between them. One tinged with love.

During the lunch hour, while her pupils were in the cafeteria, Mrs. Jaruski looked out of her window at the two buses parked outside the building. She hadn't been informed of any school trips, which in these times would have been inconceivable anyway. The presence of a curtain-sided truck parked not far from the buses worried her even more. Suddenly, the buses started up, the rumble of their engines rattling the window where she'd rested her forehead against the glass. How stupid of me to be afraid, she thought. But how could you not be afraid when there were always explosions ripping through the night, when sirens blared without warning and you had to lead the children for whom you were responsible to the shelters, keeping your voice down so they wouldn't be worried, because your calm tone was the only thing that reassured them? Just a few months ago, Mrs. Jaruski had been complaining about changes in the school menus, which had caused problems in the cafeteria, and now she was raging against servants of hatred and oppression.

The curtain-sided truck passed the school again, ahead of the buses. But why did it go around the block, Mrs. Jaruski wondered, if not to keep from attracting attention too soon? Something is wrong. She left her classroom to notify the principal, quickening her pace in the corridor. She still had to climb to the second floor and her lungs were already on fire. She hesitated as she reached the stairwell. Time was of the essence, and if she was going to save the children from what seemed to be imminent danger, she'd to have to push herself.

Instead of climbing the stairs, she headed down toward the ground floor, taking the steps as fast as she could. A coughing fit seized her as she reached the landing, doubling her over. She was struggling to breathe now. Her doctor had begged her not to exert herself, but now wasn't the time to obey him. Twenty more yards. She wrapped her arms around her torso like a marathon runner at the end of a race and kept going, her legs wobbly. She could hear men shouting in the distance, doors slamming. Reaching the cafeteria, she flung the door open wide. Breathless, unable to utter a word, she cast a despairing glance at the cafeteria attendant, whose job it was to make sure the pupils ate their lunch quietly. The cook, busily washing dishes, took one look at Mrs. Jaruski's distraught face and understood the situation immediately. She ordered the children to stand, while the math teacher began to recover herself a bit.

"Leave your things, run to the gym, and go out through the emergency exits. Once you're outside, go straight home without stopping and don't come back until you're told to, is that clear? Now go, go, go!" the cook shouted.

But the children didn't move. They were confused. The sirens announcing an air raid hadn't sounded, and why were they being told to go to the gymnasium instead of the basement, as they usually did? Mrs. Jaruski clapped her hands, pushing those who had risen to their feet toward the exit. The cook broke the fire alarm glass and pulled the handle.

As soon as the bells rang, the cafeteria finally emptied, the children rushing down the corridor toward the swinging doors of the gymnasium.

Cosima lagged behind. Not because she didn't want to obey, but because she too was different. Her prosthetic leg made her limp. The orthopedist had promised that, when she reached her adult height, he'd give her a more up-to-date prosthesis that would allow her to walk and even run like everyone else, but that would have to wait. Until Cosima grew up, and until her country was free again.

Valentyn refused to abandon her. But Cosima wouldn't allow herself to be taken by the arm; she hated to be helped around at all. So he simply walked beside her, matching his step to hers. Hearing voices behind him, he turned. The sight that greeted him was a bizarre one. The cook and Mrs. Jaruski were trying to use their bodies as a barrier to keep the men from coming after them. Mrs. Jaruski was matchstick thin, but the cook's physique was truly intimidating; even the principal was no match for her. Her whole being radiated rigid authority, and when she planted her hands on her hips, anyone facing her was in for serious trouble. So, when Valentyn saw her fall heavily backward, roughly shoved by a man in uniform, he couldn't believe it, and if he'd been able to talk, he would have shouted at Cosima to hurry. As it was, he broke the rule and grabbed his best friend by the hand to hustle her into the gymnasium.

The cook might have lost the battle, but her and Mrs. Jaruski's ruse had worked all the same, as all the other children had managed to get out. In the deserted gymnasium, Valentyn pointed Cosima toward the emergency exit behind the basketball hoop.

Cosima was shaking, paralyzed with terror. They'd never get out in time, Valentyn realized. He thought of his father, whom they hadn't heard from since he left for the front. What would *he* do in a situation like this? The answer seemed obvious. Pointing again to the basketball hoop, he smiled at Cosima and pushed her gently but firmly toward the exit, then turned back. He would hold off the enemy as long as possible.

When the soldiers finally seized him, it was only after he'd put up one hell of a fight, leading them on a merry chase up and down the bleachers. As he felt their hands close on him, he managed to turn his head again, just in time to see the line of sunlight on the floor diminish and vanish as the emergency door fell shut again.

The two buses intended to take a hundred children to an unknown destination would end up carrying only two: Valentyn, and a classmate who'd made the mistake of lingering too long in the bathroom.

How can we understand what motivates people to feed on lies? Veronika wondered. Perhaps it was because, more than God, they were afraid of facing their own truth. During her break, the head nurse of the Rykove clinic had come, however reluctantly, to accept a truth of her own. If the occupiers won the war, it wasn't just her country that would disappear; even the *memory* of it would be lost. The invaders needed to delete the past, to rewrite history in a way that would justify their ideology and erase their crimes. Putin's historians had already seen to it that the crimes of the Soviet system, to which millions of Russians had fallen victim, were forgotten, the mass deportations transformed into mere internments or resettlements. *It's in the general interest*, proponents of forgetting were fond of saying, *for the victims to live in peace with their executioners*. The duty of remembrance had too much power to prevent atrocities from happening again. But history is made up of the everyday lives and stories of ordinary people. Veronika had already seen so many witnesses end up under a sheet in the clinic's emergency room. Two hundred bodies had been buried on the outskirts of town since the invasion began. So many lives lost, parents and grandparents who wouldn't pass anything more on to their children and grandchildren. Nothing grows in the graveyards of lost memories but thistles of hatred.

Veronika's pager vibrated on her belt. She snatched it up just in time to check the message.

"We've got a new arrival, in bad shape," said a fellow nurse, entering the staff room. "You know there's no smoking in here, not even at the window."

Veronika stubbed out her cigarette, dreaming—as she did every day around this time—of a new Nuremberg trial, this one to be held in Simferopol, in the liberated Crimea.* But meanwhile, her break was over and, with a surgical operation looming, her shift wouldn't be ending anytime soon, unless the patient died. She glanced at her watch: two hours until Lilya would be picking Valentyn up from school. Her children didn't make her life easy; her nine-year-old son, walled in by his silence, and her fourteen-year-old daughter, forced to grow up too fast. She felt a stab of guilt at having almost wished for the surgery to end prematurely and resigned herself to the fact that she wouldn't see the children until after dinner, as had frequently been the case since the war began. She'd go into their rooms and kiss them in their beds when she got home, praying with all her might that there wouldn't be an explosion to disturb their sleep. Nights were quieter now that the city had been captured, but everyone was watching out for the counteroffensive.

She stopped in front of the washbasins, taking care not to use any more disinfectant than absolutely necessary, then slipped on her gown and secured her mask before entering the OR. Two casualties lay on the table, a man in his fifties and another who couldn't be any older than twenty, if that.

"They were on their way home from the fields when a mercenary opened fire on their car," explained the surgeon.

---

* The trial that took place in a Nuremberg courthouse between November 20, 1945, and October 1, 1946, tried the twenty-four leading figures of the Third Reich for war crimes and crimes against humanity. It represented the first step toward the establishment of an international criminal court and the first application of sentencing for crimes against humanity.

"Why?" asked Veronika sharply.

"No reason. Wagner's men love killing, that's all. They love it so much they've made it their profession. Yevgeny Prigozhin sold Wagner Group's private militia services to Bashar al-Assad to help him massacre Syrian civilians; in Africa, he makes his fortune by associating himself with bloody coups d'état. When his men run out of work, he sends them to plunder the continent's riches. From blood diamonds to cobalt. Putin is by far his biggest client; with the number of Ukrainians he's murdering, I imagine Wagner's thugs must be getting some hefty bonuses. I wouldn't be surprised if, one day, Prigozhin ends up killing the czar too, to sit on his throne. In the meantime, I can't take care of both these patients at the same time; the father looks worse off than the son, so I'll start with him."

"But the other one is much younger," Veronika objected, "and he's got a bullet in his lung."

"We have to make choices right now, and I might be able to save both of them if you help me instead of arguing."

The anesthetist had done his job, and the two wounded men were asleep. The surgeon suggested that Veronika watch over the young man while he operated. He'd call on her if necessary.

The young man's condition appeared stable, although the condition of a patient with a penetrating thoracic injury could deteriorate rapidly. If air accumulated in his chest, his lung would be compressed and quickly collapse. Veronika preferred not to think about what would happen next. In the absence of an ultrasound machine, the only preventive measure was to watch his chest and listen to his breathing, and at the first wheeze, or any indication of shortness of breath, to check that his lips and fingertips weren't turning blue.

She prepared the decompression equipment, just in case. A long needle that she'd have to insert between the ribs with meticulous care, because the slightest misplacement could have devastating consequences. This young man's only chance of survival would rest on her shoulders.

Thirty minutes had gone by when the surgeon let out a long sigh. Sweat had beaded on his forehead. He wiped it off with a cloth and sighed again. Two bullets had pierced the body of the man he was operating on, one in the left leg and one in the stomach. A seasoned physician, he'd already seen his share of war casualties during the invasion of Crimea, and now he delivered his version of the facts with the detachment of a forensic scientist.

"The bastard shot them like rabbits through the car door. The father was driving and shouted at his son to lie down. The bullet went through the father's stomach and came out again, lodging in the boy's body," he said, tracing an imaginary trajectory with his finger. "How's he doing?"

"He's holding his own," replied Veronika. "And he's not necessarily his son," she added. "He could be a nephew or a farmhand, or just some country boy he'd picked up in his car. I don't think they look alike."

The head nurse had only contradicted her boss in order to take her mind off the savagery men were capable of; better not to think that it only took three seconds, an instant of gunshot and hatred, to destroy a family—while here in this room they'd spend hours trying to repair the damage, to save two lives. And if they failed, it would be up to her to break it to a wife, a mother, that her son and husband wouldn't be coming home.

The principal of Lilya's middle school entered the classroom, his expression crestfallen. The students stared at him in silence. Stepping behind the podium next to the teacher, he announced that classes were over for the day. There'd been an incident at a nearby elementary school. He instructed the pupils to leave immediately, not to make any detours on the way, and to lock their doors as soon as they got home.

Lilya sprang to her feet and asked what had happened, and at which school.

"The one closest to here," replied the principal, struggling to find the words to tell her it was the school her brother attended. "The Russians carried out a raid," he continued. "Fortunately, with the exception of two children, all the others managed to escape."

"Who are the two students who didn't get away?" asks Lilya insistently, her voice trembling.

"I'm sure they'll be released before the end of the day . . ."

Lilya was out of the room and running down the corridor before the principal had even finished his sentence. She'd never run so fast in her life, never been so scared, not even when the mercenaries first entered her town, shooting from all sides. Reaching the small house where she lived with her family, she rummaged through her backpack with clumsy fingers, searching for her keys, banging on the door, and shouting her little brother's name. When no one answered, she turned her backpack upside down and emptied it on the stoop. Finding her keys underneath a notebook, she unlocked the door and burst into the house. She shouted down the hall, into the living room, up the stairs to the second floor. Valentyn couldn't answer, obviously, and the idiot probably hadn't appeared yet because he was in bed with his headphones on, playing video games. She was going to yell at him—no, she was going to hug him, kiss him like never before, and then they'd laugh together about how lucky they were...

But her brother's room was empty. And he wasn't with a friend either. Lilya knew it, because she had the gift of sensing when something bad was about to happen. She'd been the first one to notice that her brother wasn't speaking, and she'd known her father was going to leave for the front well before he told her.

Falling to her knees, she let out a terrible howl, like an animal in agony. She pounded the floor with her fists, screaming, "Not him! Please, not him!"

But crying wouldn't solve anything. She got up, ran down the stairs, and headed for the school. If she saw him there on the playground, sitting alone on a bench as he sometimes did when he'd had a hard day, she promised herself she would never doubt the existence of God again.

She passed the Blansky house. Since her husband's death, the widow had always kept the shutters closed. She ran past the ruins of the building where Valentyn's music teacher used to live. Rage burning in her gut, she lengthened her stride until she reached the elementary school playground.

On the bench, Mrs. Jaruski was comforting the inconsolable cook.

An exchange of glances was all it took for Lilya to understand.

2

"The father's out of the woods for now," the surgeon said, washing his bloody hands.

He should have swapped out his gloves for clean ones, but their stock was running low.

"Or the uncle, or the Good Samaritan," the nurse corrected.

"You're really getting on my nerves, Veronika. And what's worse, I'm beginning to think you enjoy it."

"We have to take our pleasures where we find them, Doctor."

"How is the young man doing?"

"Oh, he's in tip-top shape, as you can see," she replied.

The surgeon glared at her but refrained from taking the bait. All she wanted was for him to lose his patience and yell at her. Saving a life had put him in a better mood than usual, even if there was nothing routine about stitching up civilians with bullet wounds. Putting in the stethoscope's earpieces, he listened for a long time to the lungs and the heartbeat, then checked the young man's blood pressure and frowned, an expression that looked to Veronika more like a strange sort of grimace. Kneeling down and positioning himself on eye-level with the wound, he studied it carefully, then inserted a finger.

"In another life, I was probably a ballistics expert," he said, a touch of pride in his voice.

"I don't think that discipline existed in your previous life, because that would take us all the way back to the end of the nineteenth century," replied Veronika, cheekily.

"Joke all you want. It doesn't change the fact that the bullet, after passing through the car door and the father's body fat, entered this young man's body at very low velocity. It's a miracle it didn't hit his lung. It's stuck between two ribs; I can just feel it with the very tip of my finger. If you'd be so kind as to hand me a pair of forceps instead of looking at me like I'm crazy, we might even be able to remove it and sew this young man up."

Veronika handed him the forceps she'd been holding at the ready since he first bent over the injured man. Naturally, the privilege of telling the family the good news fell to the surgeon, and as if that weren't enough, the old salt turned out to be doubly right: not only had he managed to save both patients, but they were indeed father and son.

"Assuming fate plays a nasty trick on me and we work together in your next life, I've asked to be a ballet dancer, so I thought I'd warn you . . . I'm having a hard time imagining you in a tutu."

Circumstances had forced Danylo to become the clinic's de facto handyman. Before February 24, 2022, his duties had been limited to maintenance, which was already a mammoth undertaking. Despite his lack of formal training, he was a skilled repairman, maintaining, fixing, and tinkering with anything he could get his hands on. The boiler gave him a hard time every day of the winter, and Lord knew how long the winters were in this part of the world. The moment the temperature dropped and you pushed the boiler just a bit too hard, it stalled, coughed, and the burner went out. "What a nightmare," he'd grumble, every time he had to find the part that would stave off the inevitable, if only for a little while. He was a surgeon too, in his own way, and his hands were frequently just as bloody as the doctor's when he'd finished an operation. He was responsible for cleaning too, these days. Between those who'd died and those who'd left, the clinic was cruelly short-staffed. It had been an hour since his shift was supposed to end, and since then he'd been hanging around outside the OR, periodically peeking through the porthole-style window. Finally, taking a chance, he pushed the door open a crack.

"And have you finished?"

His habit of beginning sentences with "and" was a source of amusement to many. Some people in the clinic mimicked his tic to make fun of him, and a few even called him "And."

Veronika was above such pettiness. She simply asked him to fetch a stretcher and come back to help her transport their patients to the recovery room.

"Your daughter called, and it sounded urgent," Danylo said.

"When did she call?" Veronika asked anxiously.

"Uh... a little while ago, I guess," grumbled the maintenance man, not too pleased about having to play stretcher-bearer on top of all his other duties.

He hadn't looked at his watch, but it wouldn't have made a difference anyway, since access to the OR was prohibited during surgery.

The surgeon suggested that Veronika leave; he'd look after the patients and inform the family that they were out of danger. Taking off her surgical gown, Veronika wondered what the call had been about. Lilya never disturbed her at the clinic. Maybe she had one of those teacher's notes for Veronika to sign for the next day, or maybe she'd had an argument with her brother again? When Valentyn's thoughts were racing too fast for his pencil to keep up, he sometimes lost his temper. A child who couldn't use words to express his anger showed it in other ways, sometimes by slamming doors, occasionally by breaking things.

A light rain mingled with the wind whipping her face. In the darkened parking lot, Veronika pulled the collar of her coat tighter around her neck. It was a good ten-minute walk to her house, but gasoline was too scarce for her to drive her old car to work.

She began to walk up the street, exhausted but looking forward to seeing the children—even though, judging by Lilya's call, it might not be a peaceful evening. She walked slowly, savoring these few moments alone, however brief. Crossing the roundabout, she reflected that the day, though difficult, had turned out rather well. Life had become even harder since the father of her children had gone. Their married life had long since dwindled to little more than a cohabitation, but even so, his absence had left an emptiness greater than she could have imagined.

At home, she found her daughter sitting on the floor in the middle of the living room, hiccuping and red-eyed with weeping.

"What's happened?" Veronika demanded.

The news of Valentyn's kidnapping brought sudden, excruciating pain, as if the bullets that had cut down the two farmers were suddenly piercing her own chest. She felt as if she were suffocating, her own heartbeat thundering in her ears.

Lilya burst into fresh tears. Veronika looked at her. She wouldn't let panic get the better of her. She had to keep going. Even in the worst moments, she was still a mother, with a daughter to protect. So she knelt down beside Lilya and gathered her into her arms, giving her all the love she had left, all the tenderness she'd held back without knowing why—perhaps because life, and exhaustion, had walled it up inside her.

It had been so long since Lilya had taken refuge in her arms that Veronika felt as if she'd stepped back in time. Her top grew damp with the tears of the little girl she'd soothed when she had nightmares, who'd shared everything with her, her laughter and her sorrows. Her son had been taken from her, and now she had her daughter back.

"We'll look for him tomorrow," she promised. "You can sleep with me tonight, or I'll sleep with you. Anything you want."

On the bus, Valentyn felt full of strength, proud to have saved Cosima, or at least to have spared her this forced excursion. He had no idea where they were heading. Perhaps they were being taken to a Russian village on the other side of the border, so that on the way back he and his friend could tell everyone how much better it was than back home. He'd heard people say that children could always be relied on to tell the truth, but that wasn't always the case. Cosima, who was still on his mind, was the queen of fibs. She invented a new one every time she was late for school. Like the time she'd claimed her grandmother was very ill, even though her granny had been dead for ages.

As they turned onto the road leading to the border, he wondered what foul play the Russians had planned. With the way the old bus's engine was rattling, things weren't going to turn out as they'd hoped. He knew a thing or two about mechanics. Back when his family still lived in Irpin, on the outskirts of Kyiv, his father had taken a shine to an old Volkswagen Beetle, and during the weekends they'd spent refurbishing it, he'd taught Valentyn almost everything he knew. The rest the boy had learned from books and service manuals. He knew the names of most engine parts and could tell by ear when something was wrong. One summer, when the family had taken a few days' vacation in the countryside, the Beetle had made the same kinds of noises the bus was making now, and then broken down. Valentyn was sure it wouldn't be long before the bus driver pulled over to the side of the road. Meanwhile, his friend was having a hard time of it, and couldn't stop sobbing. Being caught with his pants down had been so humiliating. He'd yelped when the stall door had been flung open and had had just enough time to clean himself up before being grabbed by the shoulder and dragged away. It was bad enough to be yelled at when you'd done nothing wrong, but the fact that he'd been innocently going to the bathroom made it even worse.

Comforting his friend made Valentyn feel even stronger. He opened his notebook and wrote that everything would be fine, that there was nothing to worry about, and that they'd probably be home before dark, because it wouldn't be long before the bus broke down. Wanting to show off his automotive knowledge but unsure how to spell the word, he wrote that a connecting rod would soon give out. Unable to hide his satisfaction when the driver, seeing a cloud of thick smoke billowing from the hood, let out a string of expletives, he turned to a blank page and wrote in big letters, *They're screwed, we'll be home in time for dinner.*

But on that point, Valentyn was wrong.

Veronika and Lilya left home as soon as it was light outside and headed for the town hall, where the Russian command had set up shop. Veronika was already notorious for her temper, but no one had ever seen a tirade like the one she was about to unleash. Invading a country, bombing cities, and decimating entire populations to serve the megalomania of a fading dictator wasn't enough? Now they had to kidnap children? Had they really been reduced to this, these swaggering thugs commanded by incompetent generals? Mercenaries, corralled into an army without honor?

When it came to bravery, the soldier on duty in front of the town hall didn't have much left. They didn't know what the hell they were doing here, in this remote corner of the world so far from home. The soldier was young, barely twenty-five years old, just happy to have taken a small town without too much resistance, and even happier to be alive. He directed them to the office of his superior, the officer in charge of the occupied population. "The town's next mayor, once we've finished denazifying Ukraine," he explained proudly.

"Great news, so you'll be going home soon," Veronika replied curtly, dragging her daughter along with her.

They walked down the corridor at an almost military pace, their heels clicking so loudly that no one dared ask where they were going. Lilya pointed out the commander's office. Veronika took a deep breath and opened the door.

"Where is my son?" she demanded, striding into the room.

The officer, who'd been dozing with his head on his desk, gaped at the two women, startled.

"Who is your son?" he asked, yawning.

"Valentyn Khodova!"

The man sat up straighter, sighing, and reached toward a shelf for the binder listing the names of soldiers captured or killed at the front.

"Don't pretend to look for his name. He's nine years old, one of the two children you kidnapped from their school at lunchtime yesterday. Are you really going to act like you don't know?"

The man's expression changed. It was he who'd been ordered to carry out this mission a week earlier, despite its value seeming questionable at first. It wasn't as if he didn't have enough problems to deal with already. But the call had come directly from Moscow, and more importantly, from the Kremlin. Few officers of his rank could claim such an honor. The call had lasted only a few minutes, but he would never forget the soft, benevolent voice of the Children's Rights Commissioner, who'd made no bones about the power that came with her proximity to the president. Instead of employing the threatening tone he was used to from his superiors, she had quietly, carefully explained the importance of what he had to do. What nobler cause could there be than protecting orphans and minors from the dangers of the Ukrainian rebellion? From people who accused Russia of the worst evils, yet couldn't be bothered to worry about their children's future? "Saving the orphans is a priority," she repeated before hanging up.

"Orphans." He might have left that term out of the instructions he'd given to his unit. But come to think of it, why should he have mentioned it, when he'd been told that the facility in question was an orphanage?

And yet, here was a mother claiming that her child had been taken; his sources of information must not have been as reliable as he thought. He resolved to find out who was responsible for the error. Thinking back, it seemed to him that the Children's Rights Commissioner had also mentioned children "in precarious situations." That was enough to reassure him of the legitimacy of his mission, since, after all, the entire town was living in precarious conditions.

"You call that dilapidated building a school?" he said now, rattling his binder.

"You've been dropping bombs on us, and most of the time we live without water or electricity. Are you going to blame us for cracked walls and broken windows?"

"Nevertheless, children need care that your institutions aren't able to provide, least of all in this region. We're showing infinite kindness and spending precious money to help them. You should be grateful and thank us; the Russian government's mission is to protect minors, whatever their nationality."

Veronika wanted to ask him how many children had been killed by the bombs his government had dropped on schools, maternity wards, hospitals, and public parks, and how many other children were now orphans, but she forced herself to hold her tongue.

"My son doesn't need any care, especially not from you," she replied icily. "On the other hand, the civilians your men are shooting at point-blank range are in desperate need of care from *me*."

"Then get back to work," the officer retorted.

"Where is my son?" asked Veronika again, ready to commit murder.

The man stepped to the window and looked out into the street.

"On the way to a reception center. Our specialists will interview him and, after assessing his condition, decide what's best for him."

"My son won't answer your questions. He can't talk."

"And you said he doesn't need any care? What kind of parent are you?"

Lilya saw her mother's eyes flash dangerously. She grabbed her hand to remind her that she was there by her side, then spoke to the officer herself.

"We don't want to cause any trouble. We just want to find my brother and know that he's okay and where you've taken him. Please."

The officer was surprised by the teenager's restraint. She might be easier to deal with, he thought. She might even help him convince her mother to leave him alone.

"Your brother is fine, and we haven't stolen him. We've simply taken him away from the fighting, so that he can have the childhood he deserves, the healthy food he needs to grow, and the support he needs to complete his studies properly. Even during a special operation like this one, he deserves those things, don't you think?"

"A special operation?" cried Veronika. "It's a war you're waging against us!"

"The use of misleading terms like that carries an eight-year prison sentence, you know! We're not at war with anyone, we're liberating Ukraine," protested the officer, outraged.

"And in your country, is it a crime to talk about rain when it's raining? Do you have to call a thunderstorm a drizzle?"

"When calm returns and his safety is assured, we'll send him back to you, I promise," the man said, in a voice that made it clear his patience was wearing thin.

Veronika's steely composure had made him feel rather small, his sense of superiority slipping through his fingers like the sand he'd played with as a child on the beaches of Odessa. His own mother was probably about ten years older than this woman, and if she'd come face to face with him in similar circumstances, she'd have kicked his ass right out of the room. This time, though, he wouldn't take it lying down. He'd show her exactly who he was.

"One more word out of you and I'll have you arrested!" he said, his tone stern. "Your daughter needs you, and if you can't look after her, I'll be forced to take her to safety too."

"Where is this center?" asked Lilya.

"I don't know which one he's been taken to yet; we've got a lot of them. There are so many kids in precarious situations in your country. Come and see me in three days. I'll know more then, and I'll be able to tell you where your son is. I might even be able to give you some news about him, as long as you don't make a fuss in the meantime."

Afraid of being kidnapped herself, and hoping that the officer would keep his word, Lilya seized her mother by the arm and begged her to obey. There was nothing more they could do today, except make their situation worse.

Outside, mother and daughter paused, dazed, not knowing what to say or do. Finally, Lilya shrugged and started walking, not even sure of where she was going. Veronika hurried to catch up with her.

"He's alive, that's the most important thing," Lilya murmured.

"Just imagining how afraid he must be, spending the night alone, so far away from us . . . it breaks my heart," her mother said, her eyes glistening with tears.

"If they've sent him to a center where he's with other children, that must be making him feel a little better."

"You think so? If I'd come home earlier, we could have . . ."

"There was nothing we could have done," said Lilya, cutting her off. "He was already on the bus by the time I called you."

"Is the other boy a friend of his? That would be comforting for him."

"Yes," said Lilya, although she didn't have a clue.

"I'm not saying it makes me happy that they kidnapped another child—it would be horrible to think like that—but—"

"Yes, it really would be horrible," Lilya said, speeding up.

"Where are you going?"

"Where do you want me to go? School's closed. But you'd better get to work, because if we both have to sit around the house worrying, we'll end up fighting."

"Will you be OK on your own?"

"Isn't it kind of late in the day for you to be asking me that? What do you think I've been doing since Dad left and you're always at the clinic?"

Veronika went to her daughter and stroked her cheek.

"Your father didn't leave because of me, you know."

"That's your business, not mine. See? I was right. If you don't go to work, we'll just argue."

"I know you're angry, I know you're afraid for Valentyn, but we're both going through this, and we have to stick together, because arguing, even if it's merely to let off steam, will only make things worse."

"But you're blaming me for this, aren't you? I was in class when it happened. Do you think I can't take care of him?"

Lilya walked away quickly, before bursting into tears. Veronika watched her daughter until she disappeared around the corner. Then, shoving her hands into her coat pockets, she turned in the direction of the clinic.

3

Valentyn and his friend sat on a rock by the side of the road for two hours. The man in civilian clothes escorting them gave each of them cookies, a bottle of water, and a candy bar. As the wait dragged on, he introduced himself to put them at ease and even allowed them to pee against a tree, provided they didn't wander off. Dimitri looked authoritative, but he didn't seem threatening, even if the scar on his cheek made Valentyn uncomfortable.

Finally, a military vehicle arrived to pick them up. Seeing that they weren't going to be taken back the way they'd come, his friend looked discouraged. Both of them knew that their chances of being home for dinner were diminishing as the day wore on.

They were pushed onto a battered bench seat. The wind coming from behind made their hair fly in every direction. They bounced a little in their seats at every pothole, which made them smile. From time to time, Valentyn winked at his friend, who didn't unclench his jaw. He picked up his notebook and wrote that if the men had been planning to harm them, they wouldn't have offered them candy.

Once they'd crossed the border, Dimitri came to sit between them and struck up a conversation. There'd be a good meal waiting for them when they arrived, he promised, and a bed with clean sheets, and days full of fun activities. Valentyn's silence quickly began to get on his nerves, so his friend piped up, explaining that Valentyn couldn't help it, that he'd always been like this, and that he'd never heard the sound of Valentyn's voice himself. Valentyn raised his eyebrows, and Dimitri, who didn't know it was possible to be mute and still have perfect hearing, learned something new.

Twelve miles farther on, they stopped at the entrance to a village. Dimitri helped the children get out and pushed them toward a black sedan waiting at the curb, its lights off. Valentyn felt like he was in a spy movie, but the comparison ended there; he was in no mood to travel to an imaginary world. Since nightfall he'd been missing his mother and sister terribly; his throat was tight, his head full of dark thoughts.

They drove in a straight line that never seemed to end. Then, abruptly, the car turned onto a path that ended in front of a large wrought-iron gate, black and ominous. The driver, who hadn't said a word for the entire journey, honked twice, and the gate opened as if by magic. They then drove into a courtyard surrounded by fences so high that no child could climb them. The car's headlights illuminated the facade of an ancient cloister. There was small bell tower with a clock on one side.

Dimitri rubbed his hands together, pleased that his workday was over. He told them to get out and, as soon as the door had closed behind them, the sedan drove off, leaving them alone at the foot of the steps.

A heavy rain began to fall. Valentyn saw this as a bad omen and wondered what awaited them inside the cloister.

The woman who greeted them in the hall wore a brown

uniform and a smile that was meant to be reassuring, although nothing could reassure Valentyn and his friend. They were safe now, in their new home, she told them. It was already late, she continued, but tomorrow she'd explain the rules and give them their class schedules and a list of the sports they'd be able to play here. Leading them to an open gallery overlooking a garden, she told them that there was food ready in the cafeteria; the cook had stayed up late just for them, knowing they'd be starving after their long journey. Then it would be time for a shower and bed. There was no shortage of hot water or soap in Russia, she assured them with pride in her voice; in fact, there was no shortage of anything.

If he'd been able to speak, Valentyn would have told her that hot water and soap were the least of his worries.

The first thing Valentyn did upon entering the deserted cafeteria was to count the empty chairs around each table and multiply them to deduce that there must be three hundred children living behind these walls. The realization only added to his terror. A friend had once told him about the summer camps in Crimea. As crazy as it sounded, Ukrainian families had sent their children there on vacation, and those who were there before the invasion had never been able to return home. What had these parents not understood about the words "occupied territory"? His own mother would never have believed in such a fool's bargain, even before the war. If this was one of those camps, he and his friend were in big trouble.

As he finished his applesauce, Valentyn had only one thing on his mind: escape.

The surgeon was drinking a coffee in the staff room, his feet propped on the table where the nurses ate their meals. Veronika shot him a dirty look as she opened her locker.

"It's very quiet this morning," he said.

"Not for everyone. I've got patients waiting for me," she replied, putting on her smock.

"We're in a good mood, I see. Something happen last night?"

She clenched her teeth and slammed the door.

The two men they'd operated on the day before had been moved to the ward, and Veronika had made sure they were in beds next to each other. The young man had regained his color, but the father's face was twisted with pain. The clinic didn't have enough painkillers left to administer them in sufficient quantities. Where they'd typically given a dose every eight hours, now they had to manage with two doses a day, thus saving a third of the supply but leaving patients to suffer for four long hours before their next dose. The clinic was waiting for the Russians to approve a new supply, but they had to make do in the meantime.

Despite his pain, the farmer noticed the tense expression of the nurse who'd approached his bedside.

"That bad, is it? Am I going to die?"

"Not this time," replied Veronika. "But I'm afraid you're going to have to bear the pain. Tomorrow we'll try to get up and walk around a little bit."

"You or me?" he quipped, forcing a hint of irony into his voice.

Veronika didn't smile back, just continued changing his bandage in silence.

"When my wife gets a look like that on her face, I know the score. I have to ask her ten times before she'll tell me what's wrong. Considering the state I'm in, would you give me a discount?" the farmer whispered.

They entered the dormitory dressed in the long underwear they'd been given when they got out of the shower. The matron shone a flashlight on the floor so they could see where they were going in the darkness, signaling them to be quiet so as not to wake the other children, and led them to their beds, which consisted of a thin mattress on a wooden frame. Dimitri hadn't lied: the rough sheets smelled freshly of washing powder. The matron waited until they'd tucked themselves beneath the covers before leaving the room. Valentyn followed the flashlight's beam across the floor with his eyes until the door closed. Now it wasn't only terror that overwhelmed him, but loneliness too.

"It's okay," his friend whispered. "Get some sleep, and we'll see what it's really like in the light of day."

Valentyn wanted to argue that it really wasn't okay at all, and things weren't likely to be any better tomorrow, but in the dark, his mutism was all the more pronounced. Unable to fall asleep, he searched his mind for an imaginary world to escape to. Anywhere but home, because whenever he thought of his mother, his eyes filled with tears and his throat tightened with sobs. He'd never missed his father as much as he did right then, and even if Papa were dead and no one had told him about it, he still couldn't possibly miss him any more than he did in that moment.

Valentyn was immediately angry with himself for having the dark thought. To make amends, he allowed his mind to wander to the shed where the Beetle sat beneath a gray tarp, but that too sent a shiver down his spine. He had to go further away, to a place where his parents didn't exist. And, more importantly, where his sister didn't exist. Putting his hands behind his head, he brushed a nail in the headboard with his fingertips. A nail he could use to dig a hole, a hole that would eventually become a tunnel. A tunnel that would extend far beyond the gates of the courtyard. Then he'd escape, on a night as black as this one. Of course, he'd have to think of a way to hide all the dirt he would be digging up. He remembered seeing something similar in an old movie when his father had taken him to the cinema, back when they lived in the suburbs of Kyiv. It had been set during a war in the last century. At that time, the bad guys were Germans. Some prisoners—he couldn't remember if they were English or American—had managed to escape from a camp. Summoning into his mind the images he'd seen on the big screen, Valentyn began his journey. He was on the back of a motorcycle that backfired as it sped along a dirt road; he was admiring the incredible azure sky, the peaceful, mesmerizing landscape; his hair was blowing in the wind, tickling his face. The motorcycle sped along a path up a hill and he drifted off to sleep.

"Do you have any idea where they've taken him?" the farmer asked.

Veronika's silence had touched him, and he was thinking very seriously about her situation. He'd been born in this part of the world and never left. They'd experienced a few setbacks here and there, but they'd recovered; they always chased away the Russians in the end. But to kidnap children was to lay hands on what was most sacred. He'd forgotten all about his wounds; this woman who'd saved his son needed real help, not a bedridden old carcass. He insisted on sitting up in bed; it was a matter of honor.

"I know what we'll do," he said. "We'll gather as many people as we can and organize a march on the town hall to demand the return of our children!"

Veronika found herself deeply moved by his reference to *our* children.

"You seem to have forgotten something. Right after they occupied the city, the Russians photographed everyone who took part in any protests. Two days later they arrested a hundred people. Only ten came back. I refuse to put the people here in such danger."

"Then we'll pay the commander's office a little visit. A heist!" exclaimed the farmer, delighted at the prospect. "He obviously knows more than he's letting on. They're all lying. We'll find out where they've taken your son—it'll be somewhere in his paperwork."

"But there are too many men stationed at the town hall—some even sleep there."

"Hmm," murmured the farmer, thinking. "There must be someone we can bribe for information."

He was silent for a few moments, concentrating deeply. Everything Veronika had told him suggested a tightly run operation, and none of the soldiers he'd crossed paths with in the past few weeks had seemed anywhere near busy enough to be part of it.

"You're right," he said at last.

"I didn't say anything."

"You've said quite a few things, actually. Now all we have to do is rearrange them a bit. I don't think we're going to find a solution to our problem here in town. We have to find out where the original order came from. Just think, without the intervention of the school staff, who by some miracle understood what was going on, the Russians would have kidnapped a *hundred* children. Everything was planned, from the precise moment to act—when the children were all gathered in one room—to the means of transporting them. But where to? That's the question. You said two buses were parked in front of the school; well, I'm telling you that two buses driving through the countryside don't go unnoticed these days. I'm sure other farmers must have seen them. I'll pass on the information, use the radio if necessary. We'll find them sooner or later. Trust me."

Veronika wanted nothing more than to believe him. Her patient, she'd discovered, had the soul of a detective—and for him the prospect of being useful seemed to be as effective as painkillers.

"With this job ahead of us," he continued, "I'll need to go home, of course. I won't be able to organize everything from this hospital bed."

"Nice try," Veronika replied, "but you'll have to set up headquarters here. I can try to get you a room, but there's no way I'm letting you leave before that wound is healed. You'll have to delegate some of the work to your son—his wound is superficial and he'll be able to leave soon."

The father looked over at his son, who was fast asleep, and sighed.

The surgeon, who'd been examining an injured man in the next room, hadn't missed a word of the conversation. He continued his rounds as usual, but the next time he passed Veronika he requested to see her in the staff room immediately.

She already knew what he was planning to harangue her about: that it was her job to save the patients, not the other way around. And that she shouldn't have promised to find the farmer a room of his own, which was impossible. But she was sick to death of the surgeon's reprimands and had no intent of being cowed by them. The farmer had given her some hope. And if his plan seemed far-fetched, well, at least he was taking a real interest in her, instead of asking meaningless questions like "Something happen last night?" She'd had enough of his treating her with arrogance because he was a surgeon and she was "just" a nurse. There was nothing simple about her life. She did just as much work as he did. She was bringing her children up on her own, teaching them not to put their feet on tables. And she'd had her son taken away from her last night, so, yes, "something happened," something serious enough to entitle her to a little comfort, even if it meant breaking the rules.

"Why didn't you tell me?" the surgeon asked as soon as she entered the staff room. "I can't imagine the night you've had. It's awful. You should have told me right away."

"What difference would it have made?" she replied wearily.

"It would have reassured me that you feel closer to me than to a patient you only met yesterday, for one thing. Even if that man is making a lot of sense. We need to find out who ordered these kidnappings and why. I don't think the mercenaries prowling around town would stoop to using children as bargaining chips—although you never know what people like that are capable of. Before accusing them, we've got to find out whether this whole thing was their idea, or if it came from the Russian military command occupying the region, or . . . ." he paused. "Or an order from Moscow."

"How would kidnapping children from this small town serve the Kremlin?"

"They don't just want to conquer our country; they want to make it disappear. Putin is rewriting history to get people on board with his crusade. I may be wrong, but turning our children into little Russians could be part of his mission. And the only way to know for sure is to find out if this has happened in other places."

"But how?" asked Veronika, her anger forgotten.

The surgeon stood and began to pace the room; he clasped he hands behind his back, as he always did when he was thinking. After a few moments he stopped and stared at Veronika, struck by a revelation.

"If these abductions have been occurring on a larger scale, I'd be surprised if our own government didn't know about it. If such information exists, it must be centralized in Kyiv."

"That's a lot of ifs, and they've got bigger fish to fry in Kyiv than investigating missing children."

"No they don't. This is about the future of our country."

Veronika thought the last remark was a little overblown, but given her situation, she wasn't about to tease her boss for being supportive.

"But I don't see how we can get to Kyiv while we're still blockaded."

"That's the hard part," the surgeon agreed. "I may have a way. It's risky, of course, but it's your son, so it's worth it."

He sat down again, propping his feet on the table. She couldn't hold it against him this time.

"Why are you doing this for me?"

"You're a real pain in the ass, but I've gotten quite attached to you. Or maybe I'm just a masochist."

"Stop talking nonsense."

"What can I say? War brings death and misery, but it also reveals the humanity in us that we thought we'd forgotten. Like the need to help others. Isn't that why we spend our days and nights holed up in this dingy clinic? Trying to save lives? And please, spare me the smirk! It's your fault that I'm waxing lyrical, and it's ridiculous. Let's say I'm doing it to get away from you for a few days. The patient you were talking to earlier, on a scale of one to ten, how would you rate his courage?"

"To get out of here, ten out of ten."

"In that case, he might just be fit for the job."

"What kind of twisted idea do you have in mind?"

"Not that twisted, my dear, don't worry."

Getting out of an occupied city was no easy task. Those who succeeded, usually with the help of professional smugglers who knew the safest routes and which border crossings would be unguarded at particular times of the day and night, generally didn't intend to return until the city was liberated. This wasn't the case for the surgeon, who, as the only emergency physician in the area, would never abandon his post—and since the invasion, his acts of service hadn't been limited to surgical interventions anyway.

His plan was simple. They'd claim that the farmer needed bypass surgery, and quickly, otherwise he'd die. This meant that they required medical evacuation to a city with a hospital that had a cardiology unit—a city on the other side of the demarcation line, naturally. It was the perfect cover story. After all, the commanding officer Veronika had spoken to had brazenly talked about the local children needing care that the region couldn't provide, so surely his reasoning would apply to someone with a serious injury. Unless, of course, he preferred to provoke the wrath of the farmers, who were already feeling hard done by. Even under artillery fire, they continued to sow the land with wheat, rye, and barley, plowing at the risk of their lives, land mines lurking beneath their tractors. All this, only for the Russians to confiscate two-thirds of their crops. If word got out that one of their own had been wantonly gunned down on his way home from the fields and *then* denied the evacuation that would have saved his life, there would be plenty to whet their appetite for revenge.

"It's tempting, isn't it?" said the surgeon, proud to have come up with such a plan in such a short time.

"What if they offer to transfer him to a Russian hospital?"

"Too far. I'd tell them he wouldn't survive the trip."

"All right. And then what?"

"Well, once we're in the free zone, I'll drop off our patient and drive to Kyiv to get some information. I'll pick him up on the way back, treat him as needed, and then we'll all go home."

"This is all very generous, and I appreciate it, but you're talking nonsense."

"Do you have a better idea for getting your son back?"

Veronika did not.

"Then we'll have to convince the others. I'll leave the patient to you, since you get along so well with him. You can explain my plan to him and I'll take my request to the commander this afternoon."

Veronika left the staff room and headed for the ward. She was fonder of the old so-and-so than she'd wanted to admit, she realized now, and the thought of something happening to him was unbearable. The pain of missing her son abruptly flooded her whole being, like a vice clamping down on her heart. She stopped in the hallway to lean against the wall, breathless, and then slid down the wall. Burying her face in her hands, she burst into tears.

She felt someone put a hand on her shoulder. Without saying a word, the surgeon sat down next to her and put an arm around her. She hadn't even heard him approach. Feeling ridiculous, she wiped her tears with the back of her hand; he silently handed her a handkerchief. Then he stood, grunting softly as his knees cracked, and continued on his rounds.

It took every ounce of strength she possessed to pull herself together again. At the farmer's bedside, sitting on the edge of the bed, she leaned in to whisper to him, wary of spies. Sleeping with the enemy was no guarantee against health problems. There were very likely a few people on the ward who'd bought their safety by becoming informants, by denouncing those who resisted in one way or another, or simply by proclaiming the benefits of living under the Russian flag.

The farmer agreed before she could even tell him the details of the expedition. Whatever it took: the moment he was out of this place, he'd be up for anything—except to be brought back when the mission was over. On that point, whatever the state of his wound might be when the time came, he wouldn't budge.

"When do we leave?" he said, enthusiastically.

She pressed a finger to his lips, urging him to keep his voice down. He clutched at his heart, pretending to have chest pains already.

"Your wife must never get bored with you around," Veronika said, laughing, unable to think of a better way of showing him how grateful she was.

"I do what I can. I'm probably more of a clown than she'd like, sometimes, but a marriage without laughter is like a field in winter."

4

Jolted awake by the sound of a bell ringing, Valentyn rubbed his eyes, wondering where he was. Opening his eyes, he sat bolt upright in bed. The dormitory was huge; he couldn't begin to count the beds. The high ceilings and blue walls resembled those of St. Michael's Cathedral, which he remembered visiting with his parents in Kyiv on a day when he'd otherwise been thoroughly bored. The windows seemed just as large, but there was no stained glass here.

The other residents were already up, meticulously making their beds, tucking in their sheets, folding their itchy blankets into tight squares. Some had already taken off their pajamas, which they carefully tucked under their pillows before dressing for the day. His friend urged him to hurry up; it wouldn't look good to be late on the first day. Valentyn realized, his heart sinking, that the other boy had already accepted their fate. Still, he copied him, resolving to go along with the new routine.

The matron appeared in the dormitory, and the children immediately lined up in pairs, arms at their sides, and followed her to the cafeteria. To Valentyn the room seemed bigger than it had the day before, maybe because it was even more crowded than he'd expected. A whole wing where the adults sat had completely escaped his attention the previous night. Children his age occupied the center tables, while the youngest sat near the entrance. Except for the sound of cutlery on dishes, the cavernous space was totally silent. Women in gray blouses walked up and down the aisles, each pushing a cart. They passed out breakfast: buckwheat porridge, a glass of milk, a bowl of semolina, and a slice of toasted bread with a thin layer of strawberry jam.

"It's not bad," said his friend, wolfing down his porridge. "More than we get back home."

He was hungrily gobbling up everything that was served to him. If he'd dared, he probably would have asked for seconds. Valentyn gave him a dark look, then pushed his plate away, motioning for his friend to help himself. The boy hesitated for a moment, then grabbed the toast and took a greedy bite. While he gorged himself, Valentyn scanned the room, searching the sea of faces for an expression, a look, some sign that he wasn't the only one who hadn't resigned himself to staying here.

The bell rang again. The children all stood up at the same time. Like a battalion of robots, Valentyn thought, obeying a signal from a distant control room. The matron, posted in front of the door, counted her flock as they passed by. Every now and then, she put her hand on a head, and the one who'd been chosen stepped out of line, letting the procession continue. Both boys were given this strange blessing, and when the room was finally empty, Valentyn realized what the ten chosen ones had in common: they were all new arrivals. The matron led the small group on a tour of the premises, speaking to them in a gentle voice, explaining the use of each room and the rules to be followed. After breakfast, it was time for class. The first lesson of the day was always preceded by the Russian anthem, during which they were required to stand. And they'd have to forget everything they thought they knew, because what they'd been taught so far was a pack of lies, she said, still in the same even, almost expressionless tone. Here, they'd be taught real geography, real history, and of course, they'd perfect their only true native language, Russian. It was forbidden to speak any other language—which didn't make any difference to Valentyn, of course. As for math and science, there were no major changes in the program. Recess would be at ten thirty in the morning with classes resuming at eleven, then lunch at one, and after that they'd gather in the gym for a lesson in patriotism, followed by two hours of sports. Mornings may have been devoted to study but, she promised, they'd have all kinds of fun in the afternoons. PE, soccer, basketball, handball, table tennis—plenty to keep them entertained, she said, lingering on the point as if to make them aware of how lucky they were. The rules didn't allow for questions; none of the children tried to ask any. The matron then escorted them to their respective classrooms.

Valentyn was reprimanded within the first few minutes for not being able to sing the Russian national anthem.

Ever since the invasion of Crimea, Vital and Malik, twin brothers living in their parents' old mansion they inherited, both formidable strategists and active members of the Group of 9 hackers dedicated to fighting autocrats, oligarchs, and dictators, had never doubted that sooner or later a rain of fire would descend on Kyiv. Two months before the invasion, when much talk and military preparations suggested that war was imminent, the twins had relocated their mansion's computer room from the attic to a more secure location, the basement, which was large enough to accommodate their equipment. Moving the server racks, pulling the communication cables, and installing electrical equipment and temperature controls had proven less complicated than extending the ramp that ran along the staircases so that Vital could move from floor to floor in his wheelchair.

Three days before the invasion began, the Group of 9 dungeon, headquarters for the squad's large-scale hacking operations, was up and running again. The technicians who'd done the work had had to deal with Ilga and her temper more than once; the housekeeper regarded disorder as the worst of all evils. She'd made countless trips into the city and back to stock up on food, enough to feed a regiment for months. The pantry shelves sagged under the weight of all the jars of food she'd canned in her kitchen. She'd also stocked the freezers, demanding that they be hooked up to the generator. Her two young geniuses needed to be able to withstand a long siege. And as it turned out, her foresight was twenty-twenty. The invaders were still trying to capture Kyiv, and the siege had already gone on for far too long.

But it wasn't the bombs, or the need to rush to the basement when the sound of sirens pierced the night, or living like a hermit in that big house that affected her the most. Since Malik's departure, Ilga's life had seemed over. She'd been caring for the twins even before their parents died, and hadn't stopped since. Of the two brothers, Malik was undeniably the one who'd given her the most trouble. His run-ins with the law, his illegal dealings of all kinds, his love affairs that ended in tragedy, the late-night calls when he'd had to be picked up at the police station or the emergency room because he'd gotten into a fight—she'd dealt with it all without batting an eyelash. But knowing that he was at war was something else entirely.

Every evening, in her bedroom, Ilga drew a pencil stroke on

the wall. She did it out of superstition, so that when he returned, they could count them together.

It was coming up on noon when she heard the doorbell ring. She bent to look out the window. The sky was black, the trees bending in the wind, rain lashing the windows so hard she could hardly see the front steps. Who would go out in such weather? They hadn't had a visitor in months. Her blood running cold, she crossed the living room, pausing in front of a mirror to ward off bad luck, and took a deep breath before opening the door.

A woman stood there, hair soaked with rain, silent and exhausted as if at the end of a long journey. From the looks of her, she must have walked all the way through the woods, on the path from the main road. Ilga silently prayed that the woman hadn't put herself through such an ordeal in order to bring her bad news.

Veronika introduced herself and said she had an appointment with the person who lived in the house. Normally Ilga would have asked her a thousand questions before letting her cross the threshold, but as long as this stranger wasn't bringing news of Malik's death, she was welcome.

"Don't stand out there, you'll catch a cold."

Jostled by the wind, the chandelier hanging above the grand staircase swayed slowly. The housekeeper asked Veronika to wait, then fetched her a towel. Veronika stood, watching the puddle spread over the flagstones at her feet. Ilga reappeared after a moment, this time to offer her a hot drink. Veronika thanked her, then asked again to see the master of the house—it was urgent, she said.

A term that made the housekeeper's stomach lurch with worry once again.

"Has something happened to Malik?"

Veronika frowned and replied that she didn't know anyone named Malik.

Ilga sighed. "That's a relief."

She looked at the stranger closely, then her eyes lit up.

"How could I forget?" she exclaimed. "I must be getting old. You don't remember me, and I'll admit I didn't recognize you either; it's been so long."

"I'm sorry, I don't understand. Please take me to him. We're running out of time. I have to leave soon."

Ilga led Veronika into the adjoining room, promising not to keep her waiting much longer.

A few minutes later, Vital wheeled himself into the room—and stopped in his tracks, stunned to see Veronika rise from the sofa. She stared back at him, eyes equally wide. Ilga hadn't lied. It had been a very long time.

5

"Miss Vlasenko?"

"It's Khodova, actually—I'm married now . . . at least, I hope I still have a husband . . ."

"What are you doing here? How did you find me?"

"That goddam surgeon didn't tell me *who* he'd made my appointment with. I guess he must have forgotten that I was already working at the hospital when you were admitted. I'm so happy to see you. You've changed, of course, but not that much. Still that same lost look. Do you live here, in this huge house?"

"I've always lived here, except for the two years I spent in your hospital. A part of my life I'd like to forget."

Vital had been a teenager when he was admitted to Veronika's ward. He'd been sitting in the backseat of his parents' car, waiting at a railroad crossing for a train that would never pass. Two men hiding in a thicket had fired at them three times. The bullets from their Kalashnikovs had hit him in the stomach, lungs, and spine. The surgeon had saved his life—a miracle, he said—but shrapnel had struck the spinal cord, costing Vital the use of his legs.

Talking about the hospital in Kyiv took Veronika back to that whole chapter of her youth. Her hours as an intern were hellish, the stipend barely enough to get by, but she'd loved her room in a guesthouse in the center of Kyiv and the hectic buzz of the neighborhood. When the surgeon who had trained her took a teaching position at Jytomyr University Hospital, she'd followed him there, taking with her the man who would become her husband. As the years went by, with two children to support, life had become too expensive, and it was hard to make ends meet, especially with a husband who was an artist still searching for his true calling. One day, the surgeon had offered her a promotion to head nurse of his department, on the condition that she move with her family to the small town in the east of the country where he planned to settle. It was an offer she hadn't been able to refuse, seeing in it the promise of a fresh start for her family. Why had her boss chosen such a rural clinic? This was still a mystery to her.

"It would have been better if we'd said no," she mused now. "Rykove has been taken by the Russians."

"There's nothing left of Jytomyr but ruins," Vital said sadly. "How did you get out of the occupied zone?"

"That's a long story. Did the surgeon tell you why I was coming?"

"He explained why *he* wanted to visit me, actually."

"I refused to let him leave the clinic, even for a few days. His absence would have too many consequences; not a week goes by without someone coming in for emergency treatment. Besides, it's my son, not his, so I had to take the risk. Can you really help me?"

"I owe you my life. You got me back on my feet—well, almost," Vital joked, gesturing to the wheels on his chair. "It's the least I can do."

"It was the surgeon who pulled you back from the brink of death. I wasn't good for much back then."

"It took him eight hours to operate on me. You spent *two years* on my physical therapy."

"You were one of my most difficult patients."

"I had nothing against you, but your exercises hurt like hell. I don't even like thinking about it."

"When you first came into my department, you were a skinny teenager. Look at you now—a grown man, full of strength. Despite the awful circumstances, I'm happy to see you doing so well."

"Half-paralyzed in this chair? It must not take much to make you happy."

"You're alive, you can get around, you live in a beautiful house—it seems to me that things could be a lot worse."

"You haven't changed much either. Still always with something soothing to say."

"Soothing words are liars' weapons."

"I'm sorry for what you're going through," said Vital.

"I'd rather have your help than your sympathy."

"I started researching as soon as I got the surgeon's call. I'm not quite finished, but he was right about one thing—your case is far from the only one. The operation began a few weeks before the invasion."

"What operation?"

"A plan to deport Ukrainian children, designed and headed up by Maria Lvova-Belova, a woman close to the Kremlin. Putin himself is said to have given his approval and allocated substantial funds."

"Why target children?" asked Veronika, appalled.

"For the same reasons they use to justify their war. According to my sources, they target five categories of minors. Those they consider to be orphans—all it takes is for their parents to have joined the front line; those in occupied zones, allegedly to protect them from attacks from our side; wards of the Ukrainian state or those hospitalized and in need of care that only Russia can provide. Then there are the children whose custody situation is precarious and who are at risk of being left to fend for themselves, who are then placed with foster families."

"And the fifth category?"

"Well, they've stopped even bothering with excuses at this point, and they're simply kidnapping them from schools, like they did with your son," Vital sighed. "It's just another way of terrorizing us. The unofficial aim of the program is apparently to reeducate them—in other words, to brainwash them—to make them develop patriotic feelings toward Russia, not to mention venerate Putin, who's offering them a new life full of promise. The older ones are given military training; they'll be packed off to join Russian battalions as soon as they come of age."

"What about the younger ones?" asked Veronika.

"They have no scruples when it comes to age. The younger the prey, the easier the indoctrination. They even raid nurseries."

"How could a *woman* come up with such a monstrous project?"

"If it had been the work of just one person, none of it would have been possible. Large-scale atrocities require a collective commitment. It was a man named Miller in the United States who came up with the idea of separating migrant children from their parents and holding them in American detention centers, to deter others from crossing the border. If the men and women in positions of authority, from senators to government agents who took babies from their families in the middle of the night, to those who sent them to foster homes—if all those people had refused to take part in such an abomination, it wouldn't have happened. It's the same in Russia. The government is involved at every level. We'll start by putting together a roster of the people in charge. The day will come when everyone involved in this barbarism will have to answer for their actions."

"'We'?"

"Like I said, mass atrocities require a collective commitment, and it takes the same thing to fight them. Don't worry about that, though; this isn't the time or place. Right now, the only thing that matters is finding your son."

"How did you find out everything you just told me?"

Vital wheeled his chair behind the desk at the far end of the living room.

"The solution to a problem can sometimes be found within in its own structure," he muttered.

"What? What do you mean?"

"Nothing, I was just thinking out loud."

"You haven't answered my question. Where did you get all this information? Did you hear about this Moscow program from reliable sources? Please tell me. I'll go crazy if I don't get my boy back."

"Mrs. Vlasenko, I swear I'll do everything I can to help you find him. But I'm going to need you to help me find the answers to a lot of questions, not to ask more questions."

"How can I tell you anything useful? I don't know anything. Would I have come all this way if I did? What do you want me to do?"

"Get your strength back, for a start. When was the last time you had a proper meal?"

Out of shame, or maybe pride, she didn't answer.

Vital nodded and asked her to follow him. As they passed through the library, Veronika was struck by the sheer number of books on display. The library in her town no longer had anywhere near this many; the Russians had confiscated two-thirds of the books. Ukrainian writers and poets had disappeared from the shelves, their books burned. To wipe a country off the map, you had to eradicate every trace of its culture. The Russians had even amused themselves by bombing cemeteries where illustrious writers were buried, including some who'd been shot by the Soviet authorities. Their bones were remnants of a culture that the invaders would not tolerate. If Russia won its war, many others would suffer the same fate, along with countless philosophers, painters, and sculptors who, like the writers, had committed the crime of being free.

But Veronika's amazement didn't stop there. She'd never seen a dining room so large and beautiful. The kitchen her family ate their meals in at home would have fit into a third of this space. When her husband was still there, Lilya had had to squeeze painfully behind his chair to get to the sink. Here, there were eight chairs surrounding a long, oblong mahogany table, on which the housekeeper had already put out two place settings.

Vital settled into the place reserved for his wheelchair. Inviting Veronika to sit next to him, he served her a generous helping of *zharkoye*, Ilga's famous beef stew, the recipe for which only she knew. Veronika wolfed down several mouthfuls before putting down her fork, embarrassed, thinking how appalled her host must be.

"I can't stay much longer," she said, dabbing at her mouth with a corner of her napkin. "My daughter is home alone and I have to pick up a patient on my way back."

"Are you planning to take him back to the occupied zone?"

"It's not what you think. He volunteered himself; without him we'd have never gotten out. He's a brave man. I owe him a lot."

"If he's your patient, I think the two of you are already even."

"It's nice to hear you tease me. Nobody's brave enough to do that at the clinic anymore. For my boss to have called on you, especially being as proud as he is, you must be someone very important. Do you work for our government?"

Vital rolled his eyes, chuckling.

"I didn't think it was possible, but you're even nosier than she is."

"The housekeeper?"

"No, Cordelia."

Vital's smile was not lost on his guest.

"And who is Cordelia?" she asked.

"Eat," replied Vital, serving her another helping of stew. "You have a long road ahead of you."

"I see," she said, devouring a piece of meat.

She hadn't eaten anything so tasty since the war began. It almost made her feel guilty, and if the food could withstand the journey, she'd forget her pride and beg another portion from the housekeeper to take to her daughter.

Vital took a cell phone out of his jacket pocket and placed it in front of Veronika.

"Call me as soon as you have any information," he said.

"What information? Anyway, where I live the networks are down most of the time."

"I know. But this is a special kind of phone. It doesn't need a network; it's connected by satellite. Careful, though; it mustn't fall into the wrong hands."

"What do you want me to do with it?"

"If any child manages to get word to you of where they are, by any means whatsoever, make a note of everything they tell you; if they know where they are, the name of a village, a town, make a note of that. If they recognized anything while they were on the bus, if they've spoken to a friend, write that down too. A place, a first name, a last name—the slightest detail, however insignificant, could be a clue to their whereabouts."

"But—other than Valentyn, why would any child get in touch with me? I mean nothing to them."

Vital hesitated, then gently covered Veronika's hand with his own.

"Soon you're going to be put in touch with other parents who are in the same situation as you, and I'm not only talking about the family of the boy who was abducted with yours."

"You know other parents in my situation?"

Vital's silence spoke louder than words, and the look in his eyes reminded her that he'd asked for only one thing in return for his services: not to add more questions to the ones already on his plate.

"Gather all possible clues," Veronika repeated.

Ilga came into the dining room carrying a tray. She set down two bowls of fruit salad—canned, but Veronika still marveled at the sight. Ilga poured coffee for them both and departed without a word.

"Why do you live in this old house? Is this woman your only company?"

"I'll admit it's lost a little of its splendor—the house, I mean, of course. Before the war, it used to be full of life. It belonged to our parents. Ilga was already working here when they bought it, and she was here when we were born. Our father worked in business and politics. It was probably his involvement in politics that led to their deaths, or my mother's work as a journalist. In those days, in our country, it was difficult to know why people were murdered. Business, corruption, power struggles, sometimes it was just for a piece of land, a few acres of forest . . . in any case, the result was the same."

"You've never left?"

"Yes, I spent several wonderful months in London, but I don't want to say any more about it than that."

"Because of this Cordelia?"

"You're very perceptive," replied Vital. "I didn't want her to join me because it was much too dangerous, and I think she's terribly angry with me for it."

Vital wrote out a number on a napkin and handed it to Veronika.

"Memorize this: the cell phone I've given to you doesn't store anything, not even the most recent call. If you find out anything at all, call me."

"Will you do the same? Call me, I mean?" Veronika asked anxiously.

"No," he said. "We'd be putting you at too much risk, say, if it were to ring at the wrong time."

Veronika memorized the number. She drained her coffee, put the phone in her pocket, and rose to leave.

"I don't know how to thank you. For the meal, and for everything you're doing for me."

"Then we're even. I never knew how to thank you for everything you did for *me*. I hope you don't mind if I don't walk you out. I'd only slow you down."

Veronika kissed him on the cheek and turned to leave. In the dining room doorway she paused and looked at him, alone at the end of the table.

"You've changed," she said.

"Do you know anyone who *hasn't* changed since February 24?"

"I'm not talking about that; I've known you in hard times. But your pain seems different now."

"They've taken your son. Your heartache is worse than mine," he said.

Ilga, who'd been waiting outside the dining room, accompanied Veronika to the front door.

It had stopped raining. The earth was still soaked but the sky had cleared.

"Here, just in case," said the housekeeper, handing her an umbrella. "You're not planning to walk to Kyiv, are you?"

"No," replied Veronika. "A *marshrutka* stops two kilometers from here around 3:00 p.m., but I'm sure you know that."

"I didn't know they were back in service."

Ilga held out a small shopping bag. Veronika opened it and had to fight back tears when she saw that it held two jars of preserves.

She looked up to thank Ilga, but the housekeeper had already eased the door of the manor house quietly shut.

6

Valentyn sat on the gymnasium bleachers. He'd refused to join in with the basketball game. The teacher hadn't insisted, instead giving him the task of keeping score.

"There's no point in sulking," said his friend, who'd joined him during a break. "I hate sports as much as you do, but it's not so bad when the other team sucks. What's the score?"

Valentyn communicated it to him with his fingers.

"See? We're winning. Come on, it's kind of fun, really," his friend urged.

A whistle blew, signaling the resumption of play, and Valentyn grabbed his friend's arm to show him what he'd written in his notebook.

"Will you cut it out with that already? How the hell would we possibly get out of here?" grumbled his friend, standing up.

Before rejoining the game, he warned Valentyn to be more careful about what he wrote. If someone were to steal his notebook, he could be in serious trouble.

His friend was right. He resolved to use loose sheets of paper for important messages from now on and destroy them as he went along. Now, though, he turned to the sketch he'd started during their first class of the day and finished in bits and pieces in the afternoon. The boarding school was a square building with the austere charm of an old monastery, but the stones were too new for it to be genuinely ancient. The four long wings were three stories high. The children didn't have access to the top floor, which was probably where the staff lived. The middle level contained the dormitories, showers, and the large auditorium where students gathered in the morning to sing the Russian national anthem before going to class.

The classrooms, cafeteria, and gymnasium were distributed along the three galleries surrounding a courtyard and central garden on the first floor. Access to the fourth gallery was blocked by a gate on either side, and Valentyn wondered what might be inside. He'd found out that the matron's office was behind the windows at the top of the four-cornered structure that jutted out like a bell tower. Studying his drawing, he scratched his head. Something was missing. What had he seen in St. Michael's Cathedral that he still needed to add to his sketch?

The answer came to him near the end of the basketball game, a long-lost memory resurfacing. It was from a story his sister had told him one evening after their father had taken her to see the mummified monks in glass coffins resting in the catacombs of the Holy Monastery of Pechersk Lavra. She'd described the visit in detail, trying to scare him before he fell asleep. Valentyn didn't recall what he'd done to make her so angry, but he remembered lying in the dark with his eyes open, afraid that a mummy would appear in his bedroom. The next day, he'd told his mother all about it, and Lilya, who was given quite a dressing-down, didn't speak to him again all that week.

Here too the foundations must extend under the gym, the classrooms, and the cafeteria. And maybe the basement hid a tunnel like the one Lilya had described hoping to scare him even more; she'd even sworn that was where the mummies came out at night.

The gym teacher blew his whistle to signal the end of the game. Valentyn, despite not really paying attention to what was happening, had managed to count in his head the shouts that erupted with each goal. He called the game for the opposing team, just to piss off his friend. No one disputed the score he announced, because disputes weren't allowed in the boarding school.

He put his notebook in his backpack and took out his history and geography books, certified by the Russian Ministry of Education, for his next lesson.

The children lined up again in the hall. Valentyn paused on his way to join them to sneak a peek at the garden beyond the gates. His gaze wandering toward the forbidden fourth gallery; he spotted a trap door in the floor, similar to the ones often seen on sidewalks that concealed stairways leading down to sewers or abandoned subway stations.

A hand landed on his shoulder, startling him.

"Are you coming?" his friend asked. "You're so out of it, it's nuts!"

Valentyn shrugged and joined the others.

It wasn't the most boring lesson of the day. The history teacher talked as much with his hands as with his voice, which livened things up a bit. When the bell rang, Valentyn stayed behind to ask him a question: *Is there a library where I can get books other than the ones we've been given?*

"What kind of books?" the teacher asked.

Valentyn scribbled down the answer, confident that he'd get what he wanted. *Ancient history books*, he wrote. The teacher asked if he was interested in any particular era, and Valentyn replied that he liked *old centuries*, a phrase that made the teacher smile. *When big churches, monasteries, and even cathedrals were built—but I also like castles*, he wrote.

"So you like architecture, then?"

Valentyn nodded, and the teacher explained that there were no books in the study room other than those corresponding to the school's curriculum, but that he might have a few things at home to satisfy his pupil's curiosity. If he could find them, he said, he'd bring them in.

"Now run along, or you'll be late," the teacher concluded, intrigued by this boy who was always silent and yet chattier than the others. An unusual boy.

The marshrutka stopped a hundred yards from the hospital. Veronika glanced at her watch. She was two hours late. Traffic on the outskirts of Kyiv had been hellish due to military convoys clogging the roads.

She ran to her destination, afraid the nurse who'd very kindly admitted the farmer to her ward would have ended her shift; without her cooperation the chances of her patient being discharged after 6:00 p.m. were slim. As she reached the emergency room, breathless, a voice stopped her in her tracks.

"Finally decided to show up, have you?"

Danylo stepped out from behind a column, taking a last drag on his cigarette. He flicked the butt away and stepped over to her. Veronika feigned a confused look and babbled an apology.

"And it's a good thing I took care of the paperwork. And thanks to me, he's already on a gurney. And thanks to *you*, he's been waiting in the lobby for ages."

"I know," Veronika replied. "I did my best."

"And this is your best?" asked Danylo. "And I think we should hurry up, because we still have a long drive ahead of us; and we're going to have to stop and eat something, somewhere, too."

Danylo went inside through the double doors and reappeared almost immediately, pushing the gurney.

The previous day, Veronika had been about to get behind the wheel of an ambulance parked in the clinic's parking lot when Danylo had called out to her from the bench where he was sitting. He'd flicked away his cigarette the same way he always did, then asked if she was expecting to drive a long way in that old clunker of an ambulance.

An hour before that, Veronika had lied to Lilya, leaving her a note on the kitchen table and slipping out of the house at dawn.

> *Sweetheart,*
>
> *A colleague is ill and I have to cover her shift tonight. I'll do my best to come back tomorrow morning and give you a kiss when you wake up. If I can't, I'll sleep there for a few hours and then get on with my day.*
>
> *There's everything you need in the fridge, and I'll leave you some money in case you need to buy anything. Four hundred hryvnias—it's all I had in my wallet.*
>
> *See you tomorrow, honey.*
>
> *Be careful and please, don't leave the house.*
>
> *Your mom, who loves you, but you already know that*

She'd been so drained by having to make an impossible promise to her daughter, even if simply to explain her absence and spare Lilya even more worry, that when Danylo challenged her, Veronika had found herself at a loss, unable to tell him anything but the truth.

"And you're planning to make a trip like that alone, with a wounded patient? Have you gone completely mad, or are you just oblivious? And if the ambulance breaks down, are you going to repair it by yourself on the side of the road? And when you keel over from exhaustion, will the farmer drive the rest of the way? And do you know the safest roads? And do you know how to get through the checkpoints?"

"I hadn't thought about any of that," Veronika confessed.

"And she's the one giving *me* orders all day long!" Danylo muttered, shoving his hands in his pockets and going inside.

By the time Veronika started the engine and pulled up in front of the entrance, he was coming back out, pushing the farmer on his gurney. With a kick, he'd retracted the wheels and wedged the stretcher onto the rails as if he'd been doing it all his life. Then, wordlessly, he climbed into the passenger seat. Veronika, her hand on the ignition key, looked at him questioningly.

"And are we leaving now, or sitting here until tomorrow?" he asked.

Anyone who focused too much on Danylo's language tic should have paid attention to his remarkable practical skills instead. At the roadblocks, of which there were three, the soldiers in charge seemed to care little about Veronika's papers; the commanding officer's signature ended up being less useful than the cigarettes that Danylo slipped through the window. By the time they crossed the border, he'd gone through a whole pack. Later, when the ambulance's hood began to vibrate, he ordered Veronika to stop immediately. He tightened the V-belt before it tore, and as soon as it was repaired, they set off again.

When Veronika's eyelids had begun drifting shut, Danylo seized the wheel and steered the ambulance back into the correct lane. Then he'd driven for six hours, smoking his cigarettes, while his two passengers slept.

Tonight, getting back into the occupied zone would be even more dangerous than getting out. The outward journey had been made in daylight. Most of the combat took place at night, so they'd have to drive with the lights off.

Veronika had hated driving at night ever since she'd been requisitioned to take part in an operation that had traumatized her for life. The invaders had agreed to a body exchange. A dead Ukrainian soldier for a Russian one. The refrigerated trucks all had special identification marks: a sign affixed to the windshield with the number 200 in big type. Veronika had never understood the reason for this symbol, but she was told it was there to keep the trucks from being targeted by missile attacks. The Russians had agreed that there wasn't much point in firing at dead people.

A medical professional had been required to accompany the convoy, to monitor the bodies as they were transported to various cities where the remains would be identified before being released to their families. Veronika had been that designated medical professional.

Haunted by this memory, Veronika found herself unable to turn the ignition key. Her hands trembled. Danylo immediately understood that something was wrong.

"How about I drive until dawn, since I've spent most of the day on a bench? And, in the meantime, you can rest and regain your strength. And you can take the wheel when the sun starts to come up."

The farmer, who'd slept better in the Kyiv hospital than on the crowded ward at the clinic, thought this was a capital idea. He looked very well; maybe it was the prospect of returning to his farm tomorrow that had put him in such a good mood. "A promise is a promise," he reminded his nurse as she settled into the passenger seat.

"My wound is almost healed," he told her.

He's a better liar than I am, Veronika thought. I should ask him for lessons.

"So, was the trip worth it?" asked Danylo as they set off.

"I haven't found much, apart from this," replied Veronika, holding up the phone Vital had given her.

"And to think we came all this way for a worthless mobile phone! And have you heard the terrible news?"

Danylo told them that the Russians had bombed the Kremenchuk shopping center. Hundreds had been killed or wounded. Most of them women and children, of whom nothing was left. Not even enough to warrant body bags.

"And the locals are lining up to give blood, and the government has declared three days of mourning," Danylo sighed.

The farmer felt ill with rage. He'd rather not have known. The ambulance headed east, and the sun headed west, the sky already tinged violet with dusk.

7

On his first day at the boarding school, Valentyn had been put through a series of assessments. The matron was determined that her school would be a model of its type. She wasn't the only one managing an orphanage like this one; there were thirteen others in this region alone and four times that many in the self-proclaimed republics, with more popping up by the month in almost every oblast. Fifteen in Moscow alone.

Here, academic failure was not tolerated. To avoid it, children were grouped in classes by aptitude, not age. It was better for their performance and better for the matron's chances of being noticed by the governor. The matron had high hopes of being officially recognized by Moscow one day. A medal would be proof of her virtue. The president had recently honored a teacher from a rural school live on television. He'd even pinned the ribbon to her chest himself. The same honor could be in her future, she knew it; with all the trouble she was going to, it would be only fair.

Sitting behind her desk on the top floor of what looked like a small bell tower, she studied the assessment reports, making a pile on her right of the names to be demoted, who'd need to be given more work than the others. One student had scored twenty out of twenty in every subject. This was good news; she had little tolerance for anything but excellence. She would follow this boy's progress with particular attention, and tomorrow she'd go and have a closer look at him. Thanks to her, young Valentyn Khodova might go very far. This, the matron thought, was the whole reason for her mission: the reeducation of young Ukrainians, to turn them into great Russians.

The cafeteria was filled with the sound of children's voices, accompanied by the clatter of cutlery. At dinner, they were allowed to talk at the table. Valentyn's friend was complaining about the shower. He hated getting naked in front of people. *It's not just the showers that are horrible here*, Valentyn wrote.

Hunger had finally won out over resistance, and he was gobbling everything on his plate. Roast beef, along with mashed potatoes so thick he had to cut them with his knife. The women serving the meal were cheerful and smiling, taking care to heap extra food on the plate of anyone they thought was too thin. The monitors, though, were less friendly. They kept an eagle eye on the room, and order was strictly enforced. *This place will never be home for us*, Valentyn scribbled. He was going to *come up with a plan*, he added, lifting his gaze toward the tall, night-black windows. His friend wasn't against the idea of escape if it meant not bathing in front of a bunch of other children; it was that he lacked the courage. Even thinking about a possible attempt made his blood run cold with fear. He knew he was weak in both mind and body, perhaps because his mother had repeated it to him so many times. Physical education was an awful ordeal for him, especially ball games, because of his glasses. He'd broken the frames once, and his mother had wept with rage. He wished he could cry now—he missed his family so much—but if he gave in to the urge, the others would see it and make fun of him. Being here might be his chance for a fresh start. It wasn't escape he dreamed of; it was not being the class laughingstock anymore.

There was crème caramel for dessert. The caramel was bitter; the cooks must have doubled the amount of sugar in the custard. Valentyn's friend nudged him, demonstrating that if you mixed the caramel and the custard together with your fork, it wasn't so bad. Then, to amuse the rest of the table, he repeated the maneuver with his finger.

Valentyn didn't give a damn about his dessert. While his friend was clowning around, he'd dropped his knife on the floor, unnoticed by anyone. The blade was so close to his foot that it was all he could think about. Impulsively he bent to tie his shoelace.

Bent double like that, it was impossible to see if any of the monitors were watching him, and there was no time to assess the risk. Picking up the knife wouldn't be a crime, but hiding it in his sleeve ... he preferred not to think about the humiliation if he were caught, much less the punishment he'd face for stealing a bladed weapon. Valentyn was afraid, but the opportunity was too good to pass up. Stretching out an arm, he grasped the knife by its blade and slid it into his shoe.

Cheeks crimson, forehead sweaty, he sat back up. His friend wondered aloud how Valentyn could be so warm; he was freezing, himself. "You're probably just tired," his friend went on without pausing for breath, the flow of his chatter seemingly unstoppable. He was ready for bed too, he added, yawning to prove it.

The other boy's outpouring of words made Valentyn chuckle to himself. He was trying to show off for the others. Talking made him seem confident and composed, when in reality he was anything but.

The matron rang the bell, and the students lined up to exit the cafeteria. Passing through the doorway, Valentyn felt a disagreeable sensation: the matron had laid a hand on his head, and her smile reminded him of the evil characters in the horror films his sister loved. Of the predatory rictus they'd wear just before they turned into a monster.

No sooner had the lights been turned out, plunging the dormitory into darkness, than Valentyn felt the terror taking hold. Yesterday his friend had been even more afraid than he was, and even though it wasn't a nice way to think, he'd found that kind of comforting. Tonight, however, his friend was breathing deeply and regularly, already off to dreamland. To soothe himself, Valentyn went over the events of the day. He felt proud of himself; he'd made good use of his time. Not only did he already have a plan in mind, but he thought he'd found the passage leading to the school's basement. And the feat he'd pulled off at dinner was especially satisfying. While he was putting on his pajamas, he'd managed to slip the knife beneath his mattress without anyone seeing him. He wasn't sure what he was going to do with it yet, but having it made him feel more prepared for danger.

Closing his eyes, Valentyn thought about his family. His mother was probably home from the clinic by now. She and Lilya must be in the kitchen, worried to death about him. His mother had undoubtedly made herself a cup of tea, while Lilya did her homework. Then she'd go to bed. If she was thinking about him as hard as he was thinking about her, maybe their thoughts would meet in the sky. He squeezed his eyelids shut. Silently he wished her goodnight and told her he loved her more than anything in the world.

Danylo pulled the ambulance over onto the side of the road. He was hungry. And, being the foresighted fellow he was, he hadn't left the hospital in Kyiv without provisions. Sandwiches, bags of chips, a thermos of coffee, sugar. Enough for at least three meals. He'd also thought to buy two cartons of cigarettes: one for him, the other to smooth their way at the border crossings. The Russians would be suspicious, seeing them on the way back from the free zone. There was a good chance he'd be ordered to take off his shirt. That was what they did to verify the intentions of civilians in cars, checking to make sure their chests weren't tattooed with the Ukrainian crest, a trident framed by stalks of wheat, or their torsos with *Slava Ukraini*, the national motto, dating back to the 1917 War of Independence. These days, a simple tattoo could mean a death sentence. The Russians would cut it out of you with a knife after killing you, or sometimes before. They'd also check, at the border crossings, to make sure your upper body didn't bear the traces of having recently worn a machine gun in a shoulder holster.

It was too risky to pull off the road completely and park on the grassy shoulder, because of the mines the invaders had buried before retreating. Recently liberated zones were the most dangerous areas in which to stop.

Danylo opened his bag of provisions and offered the farmer a sandwich. He glanced at Veronika, who looked so peaceful he was reluctant to wake her.

"She's lucky," sighed the farmer. "I haven't been able to sleep a wink."

"And it's not my fault if the road's bumpy. Military vehicles dug those ruts, and driving at night without headlights isn't easy, even with the moonlight, believe me."

"I'll take your word for it. It's nothing to do with your driving, anyway; I think you're doing very well. It's just that I can't stop thinking about what you told us earlier."

"And what did I say, to keep you awake?"

"That shopping center the Russians bombed. How can they commit such atrocities? What was going through the mind of whoever pushed that button? They had to know exactly what they were doing, for God's sake! It's one thing to attack military infrastructure, destroy our roads and bridges. That I can understand. But to kill women and children—to wipe out whole families that were out running errands! And why? Why?" the farmer repeated, his voice quavering.

"Because he was following an order. Because if he'd refused to push that button, he'd have been killed himself."

The farmer, overwhelmed by sorrow, didn't say anything else, just shrugged and bit listlessly into his sandwich. Danylo's reasoning was impeccably logical, even if he was making excuses for a murdering bastard. Danylo shook a cigarette out of his pack and slipped it between his lips, then offered one to the farmer, who'd quit smoking years ago. He struck a match, the flame illuminating the lower half of his face, then extinguished it quickly.

"I was with two buddies the first time I smoked," he said. "My grandfather walked in on us. I thought he'd beat the hell out of us, but all he did was make us swear never to have three people use the same match."

"Why not?"

"Bad luck. And it's not some dumb superstition—it's a *historic* one!"

"A historic superstition?" repeated the farmer, laughing.

"Yeah. At night in the trenches, during the war, the 1914 one, I think, with the first man who lit his cigarette, the enemy soldiers saw the flame. The second one, they aimed, and the third one got shot."

"Well, look, it's nothing new that smoking can be deadly, right?" quipped the farmer, winking.

Danylo wondered if the man was making fun of him. He drew deeply on his cigarette, the smoke he exhaled covering the windshield with a grayish fog before escaping out the open window.

"And I didn't tell you everything earlier," he said after a moment.

He felt slightly guilty for having prevented his passenger from sleeping, but at least this way he had someone to keep him company. He hesitated, then decided to tell the man what had happened in Kremenchuk when rescuers found a woman beneath the debris, a dying little girl next to her. The firemen had managed to clear a way out for them, but the woman had refused to be extracted. She'd stayed there, holding the child's hand, until the child took her last breath. And then the woman herself died, asphyxiated by the fumes.

She hadn't even been the little girl's mother.

The story made the farmer retch with horror. He wondered what he would have done in similar circumstances. Veronika opened her eyes and sat up, glaring at Danylo.

"Can I ask how you learned about all these terrible things in such a short time?"

"And who spent half his day loitering around a hospital? And listening to stories he didn't want to hear?" he retorted.

Though she wasn't the slightest bit hungry, Veronika picked up the sandwich Danylo had put in her lap. She thought about the woman and child. And that reminded her of Valentyn.

Danylo pulled the ambulance back onto the road. If he'd estimated correctly, they'd enter the occupied zone just before sunrise.

Ilga had gone up to her room long ago. It was two o'clock in the morning. Vital, alone at his computer, was absorbed in his research. He'd done nothing else since Veronika left. The ventilation system keeping the basement air fresh let out a soft thud. Vital looked up. It was as if the rest of the chairs around the long table were occupied by ghosts. The coded messages sent by his friends in the Group of 9 had been more frequent when Kyiv was being subjected to regular bombardment. Now they were fewer and further between. Perhaps because he didn't always answer.

Mateo and Ekaterina had extended their honeymoon in Vietnam, with Ekaterina, a lecturer at the University of Oslo, taking a year's sabbatical. Mateo, who had sacrificed everything for a noble cause, was trying to rebuild and recover in the place where he'd been born. Vietnam was a beautiful country, and Ekaterina never grew tired of its wonders. Vital received the occasional message hidden in an email, always with a different signature. There, blending with the shadows in a photo of a landscape, he could always make out the silhouettes of the people who had taken it.

Janice, who had gone back to her life in Tel Aviv, swore that she hadn't touched a drop of alcohol since February 24. Out of solidarity for Vital. But she'd also written to him to say that the day the tyrant was deposed and peace restored, she would rush to join him at the manor for a drinking session that would be memorable.

Three months ago, Vital discovered a package on the porch steps containing anonymously delivered computer equipment and keys on a tiny Eiffel Tower keychain. Exactly how Maya had managed to get the equipment to him intact was a mystery he still hadn't figured out.

There'd been no word from Diego, whose restaurant in Madrid must be taking up all his time—unless Cordelia, Diego's sister, was the real reason for his silence.

Vital missed Cordelia every minute of every day, not to mention at night, when she was almost always in his dreams. Sometimes he wondered what was wrong with him. When you had happiness right there in your hands, you had to be a real idiot to let it slip through your fingers. And it was even worse in his case, because he'd chased her away. With her, he'd forgotten all about being in a wheelchair. The day he left London, she'd wanted to come back to Ukraine with him—and he'd refused, because loving her meant living with the fear of losing her, and he'd known war was coming. But when the moment came to say goodbye, he hadn't been able to find the words to tell her that, and she wouldn't have listened anyway. Long-distance relationships didn't work, and since he was abandoning her, he might as well not bother contacting her from now on, she'd shouted, before slamming the door of her apartment.

Months had gone by. Did she think about him sometimes, or had she already found someone else? The questions had haunted him. And then, suddenly, out of nowhere, a few words in Spanish, sent from a country at peace, had brought a semblance of an answer.

When his brother Malik left for the front, Vital joined the ranks of the so-called IT Army, invisible soldiers operating since the start of the conflict with keyboards as their weapons. He worked to weaken the enemy's IT infrastructures. Server attacks, hijacking television networks at prime time to broadcast reports showing the atrocities committed by occupying forces, footage of battlefields covered with the bodies of conscripts killed to serve the tyrant's madness, in the hope of discouraging anyone considering heeding the siren call of the propagandists that appeared one after the other on Russian television. The most labor-intensive missions consisted of tracking the assets hidden throughout Europe by those close to the Putin regime. It was painstaking work. Whenever Vital identified a yacht, opulent apartment, mansion, or luxury car in London, Brussels, Rome, or Madrid—or assets disguised as corporate stock—he relayed the information so that seizure operations could commence.

The kills he'd added to his tally included a yacht anchored at Málaga that had then been boarded by Spanish police, a chalet in Courchevel, a property in Switzerland, vineyards in Italy, and several securities portfolios. These results were the fruit of careful investigation, study, and cross-checking, usually carried out in solitude, or sometimes in conjunction with another member of the IT Army. Vital had refrained from getting his Group of 9 colleagues involved. The risk was too great, and after all, this wasn't their war.

He'd spent the hours since Veronika's visit on various dark web forums, hoping to pick up a trail that would lead him to Valentyn. Being a professional hacker had several advantages, and his affiliation with the IT Army offered others. Messages and regional maps were exchanged, enabling Vital to identify forty-three camps where Ukrainian children were being held. Twelve in the area around the Black Sea, seven in the occupied Crimea, ten in the suburbs of Moscow, Kazan, and Ekaterinburg. Plus eleven others located more than seven hundred kilometers from the Ukrainian-Russian border, two of which were in Siberia and one in the far east of Russia, in Magadan Oblast, which was three times closer to the United States than it was to Ukraine. At one o'clock in the morning, Vital was sent the coordinates of a psychiatric hospital and a family center involved with the deportation of orphans. Valentyn had parents—he had no reason to be there. Vital crossed these two places off the list, then took a closer look at the sites in Artek and Medvezhonok, holiday camps where parents had sent their children without imagining for a moment that they'd be held captive there. They'd been showing as full before the start of the war, so Vital thought it unlikely that they'd have taken in any new arrivals. The camps in Luchistyi and Orlyonok intrigued him. They'd cut off all communication. What was going on there? Under what conditions were the children being held in that far-flung corner of the world?

At three in the morning, Vital obtained a copy of a classified report marked *Do Not Disclose*. A reward in return for the services he'd performed since February 24. Hackers have their own code of honor.

The contents of the file both horrified him and confirmed what he'd learned earlier from sources he found even more trustworthy now. The deportation program was being controlled from the highest levels of the Russian government. Dozens of federal, regional, and local personnel were involved in its operation. Hundreds of bureaucrats had been mobilized: logistics specialists arranging transport of the children by car, train, and civil and military airplanes; and administrators responsible for fundraising and supplies. An entire department was devoted to the development of new facilities. Sixteen thousand children had been kidnapped since the start of the invasion, and Children's Rights Commissioner Maria Lvova-Belova didn't plan to stop there. Putin had asked her to take additional measures to identify all minors living in occupied territories. Children who, according to the dictator, were being deprived of adequate parental care. He'd ordered Maria Lvova-Belova to arrange the transport of two hundred thousand new subjects of the Russian Federation as soon as possible. Valentyn was one of them.

Vital pushed back his wheelchair. He'd read enough about this for one night. Too much. Keeping his promise to Veronika would mean reconsidering certain principles. The task was too enormous, the stakes too high, to go it alone. The decision of whether to call in his friends or not was difficult enough. The thought of telling Cordelia that he needed her was even harder to contemplate.

The farmer clung to the sides of his gurney. Danylo had just slammed on the brakes. Veronika woke with a start, thinking they'd struck an animal, but Danylo merely pointed at the reddish glow in the sky on the other side of the woods. It looked nothing like the rosy light of dawn.

"And there are snipers out there," he said. "It's too dangerous to go on."

Veronika looked at her watch. Five o'clock in the morning. They were already so late because of her, and if this forced delay stretched on too long, she wouldn't be home before her daughter got up. Lilya would surely call the clinic if that happened and be unable to reach her mother; Veronika hoped no one would make the mistake of telling Lilya that she'd been gone since yesterday morning.

"Is it much farther?" she asked anxiously.

"Five hours on the road, according to my calculations. Under normal circumstances, that is," Danylo replied.

They heard the sound of explosions. Ten kilometers away? Fifteen? Twenty? Impossible to tell how far away the fighting was. Sounds traveled differently at night.

"It's not smart to stay in a vehicle when there are bombs dropping," remarked the farmer.

"We can get blown up here or somewhere else; it won't make much of a difference," retorted Danylo, who had lost his verbal tic in the heat of the action. "And you're not very mobile, let me remind you."

Veronika reached into the glove compartment for the road map the surgeon had given her. Danylo indicated with a fingertip the area where he thought they were. Other than a village that appeared in the form of a tiny black dot, there was nothing but fields out here, nothing that would justify the Russians' wasting their ammunition.

"Well, I guess it might be our own men, attacking the Russian position to take back some ground."

The idea was a cheering one. Veronika found herself mesmerized by the rumbling sound of the explosions. Silence would descend for a few moments, and then fresh sparks would crack and explode before falling back to earth in a shower, lighting up the smoke-filled sky.

She covered her ears, thinking of a similar night, back when the Russians had first crossed the border. She remembered husbands and fathers strapping as many belongings as they could to the roofs of their cars, others siphoning every drop of gasoline from the tanks of their lawn mowers. She remembered those who had stayed because they didn't know where to go, or because they were convinced that no invading force could oust them from their land. She remembered the people who'd run toward the clinic on wobbly legs. She knew the darkness and chaos, the smell, the noises, the mass terror carried on the wind, the silence and the waiting, both equally terrifying. She'd been there with her children that night, keeping them safe, protecting them with her own arms as the Russian troops entered her town.

There were three of them there tonight, caught in the storm. A farmer, a temporary ambulance driver, and a nurse. Three souls lost in the midst of a decimated world.

8

Lilya stood at the window. With her mother gone, there was no one to keep her from raiding the coffee stash. It was the smell she liked, even more than the taste; it reminded her of peaceful mornings with the family chattering around the breakfast table. Back then all she'd longed for was silence or, better yet, to be allowed to go out with her friends. She looked around the empty room. Until now, her street and the schoolyard had been her territory, her friends, the center of her existence. If classes didn't start again soon, she'd lose her mind.

The coffee was scalding hot, but the heat reminded Lilya that she was alive. She was hungry, with a sudden craving for *paskas*, the delicious sweet buns her grandmother used to bake at Easter. It was probably better that Grandma had passed away before all this happened, Lilya thought, hoping she was watching over Valentyn from heaven.

There was an *X* marked in red felt-tip pen on the wall calendar. Today was the day to go and stand in line at the distribution center, and she'd better get there soon, or there wouldn't be anything left. Her mother detested taking charity, so it was always Lilya who went. She never knew what she'd end up getting; the goods the Russians hadn't confiscated changed every week. But she'd bring home as much as she could carry: canned food, cereal, flour, toiletries.

Lilya set her empty coffee cup on the counter. She'd wash it later—if her mother ever bothered to come home, she'd have *two* good reasons to be annoyed. She took the shopping bag down from its peg and put on her jacket.

Her father's bicycle was still cluttering up the front hallway. No one had the heart to take it down to the basement. What made it even worse was that she wasn't allowed to use it. Lilya had had enough of being forbidden to do things. It was a bike, not a precious relic! Why carry supplies home in your arms when you have a bike seat and a saddlebag available?

A few minutes later she was pedaling up the street, making excellent time. At this rate she'd be near the front of the line at the Red Cross distribution center. The bicycle's chain made a grinding noise when she changed gears, and the seat was slightly too high, but the wind in her hair felt wonderful. She slowed down as she passed Stefan's building, tempted to buzz the intercom and ask him to come with her. But he was probably asleep, and by the time he dressed and came down she'd lose her head start, and she really needed some toothpaste and a new toothbrush.

Nearing the town hall, she caught sight of the Russian commanding officer. He was pacing back and forth in front of the building, his mobile phone clamped to his ear and an unhappy expression on his face. She slowed down, still watching him, and thought for a moment. He'd promised to give her news of her brother, but not for "a few days"; if she approached him now, he'd tell her to get lost. She started pedaling again, glancing back at the commander as she passed him. Another thought occurred to her. The bike's front wheel veered sharply and she tumbled off, landing in the middle of the street.

It hurt more than she'd expected, and she felt a bit shaken. She was taking a risk, but how long can a person wait, crippled with sadness and worry, before taking matters into their own hands? At what point do you become complicit in your own unhappiness, if you don't do anything to fix it?

The commander was listening to his phone with one ear, distracted. The young cyclist hadn't gotten up. Several passersby were making their way toward the scene of the accident, but they were still relatively far away, while he was right nearby. It was a worrying situation; standing here and doing nothing would only encourage the people accusing him and his troops of every evil under the sun. He put his phone in his pocket, took three steps, and knelt beside Lilya, frowning.

Blood was trickling from her knee, where her jeans had torn. More people had arrived now, forming a large circle around the two of them. The commander grasped Lilya's arm and helped her to stand, then guided her, limping, to a bench. She didn't speak, just examined her injured knee, fighting back tears. The onlookers hesitated; the Russian officer seemed to have the situation in hand, and they were afraid that intervening might be seen as a challenge to his authority. And yet, playing paramedic wasn't in his job description. He held out a handkerchief to the girl. She looked at it warily. Growing impatient, he pressed it to the wound himself. Lilya let out a yelp and pushed his hands away. Her silence was becoming embarrassing, especially now that tears were running down her cheeks. He didn't like it that all these people were watching him; it felt like he was being put through some sort of test. What did they want from him? If the girl's leg was broken, she'd have screamed in pain when he helped her up. There was no need for so much drama over a mere scraped knee.

"Does it really hurt that much?"

Lilya didn't reply. The crowd watched attentively. The Russian commander had brutish features that looked like they'd been carved with an axe, but there was a helplessness in his eyes that delighted Lilya.

"Quit blubbering," he said, patting her shoulder awkwardly.

She lifted her head, making sure the crowd got a good look at her anguished expression. The murmuring grew louder. They were mocking his incompetence, the commander was sure of it. His ego recoiled at the blow.

"Okay," he said at last, heaving a sigh. "I'll give you a good reason to stop crying. Your brother is at a center for children around a hundred kilometers to the south. He's safe and doing well. See, I've kept my promise. Now be brave and go have someone take care of that knee."

He rose. "Nothing serious," he called to the watching crowd. "More scared than hurt. Now move along. Nothing much to see here."

The onlookers obeyed, dispersing, the street emptying out. The Russian commander moved off, satisfied. Lilya followed him with her eyes. The moment he'd vanished into the town hall, a malicious smile crept across her lips.

"Got you, asshole," she murmured, abandoning the handkerchief on the bench where the officer had sat.

A long line had already formed at the distribution center. Lilya was thrilled to spot Stefan, all the more so because he was near the front. She hurried over to him and took his arm.

"Sorry I made you wait," she said. "I fell off my bike."

"Are you only taking my arm so you can cut in line?" he whispered.

She rolled her eyes and showed him the bloody rip in her jeans. "Don't make that face," she said, when he winced. "It's only a little blood."

"Maybe, but you don't look very well."

"I'm not surprised. I haven't been sleeping much these past few days."

Stefan looked at her with regret for having added insult to injury. "I'm sorry about your brother."

"Who told you?" Lilya demanded.

"Not you, that's for sure."

"What should I have done, abandon my mother and come running to tell you my brother had been kidnapped?"

"Your mother's never there. You're always telling me that. Everyone around here's been talking about it. I thought you'd trust me enough to tell me what you're going through."

"*I'm* not going through anything; it's *Valentyn* something's happened to," she snapped.

Stefan nodded and didn't say anything further.

"That's not what I meant," Lilya said apologetically, after a moment. "At least, I didn't mean for it to come out that way. Quit making that face. I'll tell you a secret on the way back."

"What kind of secret?"

"On the way back, I said!"

The door opened. Stefan walked with Lilya from table to table while she filled her shopping bag to overflowing. Humanitarian aid had been generous this week—but no toothbrushes, unfortunately.

"You're still bleeding," said Stefan worriedly, taking the heavy shopping bag from her. "Let me take you to the clinic."

"No way. If my mother sees me, she'll kill me. I've got Papa's bicycle."

"You're going to get cleaned up, not killed. Don't argue. Come on."

The matron hadn't been standing by the dormitory door when the children filed out this morning. Nor was she present when they all gathered to sing the national anthem. The monitors were whispering to one another, their faces dismayed. Valentyn, who never missed a thing, wondered what had happened.

He learned the answer in math class. The matron's car had broken down. These things tend to happen with European cars, the teacher explained. To put a definitive end to any rumors, he reassured the students that the breakdown had occurred not far away from the school, and a member of staff had gone to pick her up. They'd be back soon, and she'd come to say hello to the children in the cafeteria at lunchtime.

An idea occurred to Valentyn. He wrote it down on a blank sheet torn from his workbook, folded it, and put it in his pocket.

The teacher was walking between the rows of desks, handing back marked work.

"Excellent," he said to Valentyn, handing him his paper.

Valentyn wished the teacher hadn't congratulated him. Some

of his classmates were staring at him now, and the envious looks on their faces weren't giving him a good feeling. He blushed and grimaced apologetically, hoping another pupil would come in for praise. His friend rolled his eyes, then turned his attention to the day's math problem written on the chalkboard.

His friend caught up with him in the hallway after class.

"It's not very smart to draw attention to yourself like that. I've been hearing things, and I think some people already have their sights set on you."

This was bad news. And yet, even if Valentyn had a way of justifying himself, what could he say to something like that, except that he didn't care what anyone thought of him? He was nine years old, with no desire to feel even more alone than he already did. At least the plan in his head was there to keep him company.

"Wait, don't walk away like that!" his friend called. "I'm on your side! We're in this together!"

We'll see, Valentyn thought, going into his history and geography class.

Lilya and Stefan had engaged in heated negotiations all the way back from the distribution center, with each having to make a few concessions. Stefan had retrieved the bicycle, which had a long scratch on the frame—but, fortunately for Lilya, it was on the side where the bike would be resting against the wall. Stefan hung their shopping bags from the handlebars and followed Lilya back to her house.

Now that the stolen object had been restored to its rightful place, she agreed to go to the clinic, but only under one condition: she would wait in the parking lot while Stefan went in to make sure her mother wasn't around.

He came back out shortly, with good news: the nurse's aide at reception had told him in no uncertain terms that the head nurse was in surgery and wouldn't be out for some time. Reassured, Lilya went into the clinic.

The nurse's aide hurried over as soon as she saw her. "What have you done to yourself? Well, come in, come in, what are you waiting for?"

"First you have to swear you won't tell my mom, otherwise I'm leaving."

"What, did you send him in on a scouting mission?" the woman asked, glaring at Stefan.

"Swear you won't tell!" Lilya repeated.

"Hop up on this table instead of talking nonsense. Your spy must already have told you I can't disturb her. You're lucky I was here! Now, how did this happen?"

"She fell off a bike," Stefan supplied.

"I'm talking to *her*. She hasn't injured her tongue, as far as I can tell." The nurse's aide paused. "I recognize you," she said to Stefan. "You're Mr. Vasylyk's son, aren't you?"

Stefan nodded. The woman's manner softened immediately. Mr. Vasylyk was a good carpenter, and an honest man. He'd sold his furniture at the Sunday market before the war, always at reasonable prices.

"Veronika's going to be furious with me."

"Not if you don't tell her."

"Bend and straighten your leg," the nurse's aide ordered.

Lilya obeyed, wincing. The knee was still bleeding a bit.

"Nothing broken, fortunately, but I can't simply bandage it; the cut is too deep. It'll have to be sewn up. Two stitches, at least."

The stitches were going to hurt, the aide warned. There wasn't enough anesthetic for them to use unless it was absolutely necessary. Lilya supposed she could have tried to get special treatment as the head nurse's daughter, but they'd never agree to give her an injection without her mother's consent. Suffering was preferable to coming clean by far, she decided. The needle hurt like hell when it pierced her flesh. Gritting her teeth, she gripped Stefan's hand as hard as she could. The second stitch hurt even more. Lilya let out a stream of curses.

"You're so much like your mother it's incredible," the nurse's aide remarked, putting a dressing over the stitches.

She went to the sink to clean her equipment. Lilya leaned in close to Stefan and whispered in his ear. He gave her a dirty look, but took the nurse's aide aside and used all his charm to persuade her not to report the incident. Lilya wouldn't get back on a bike for at least two weeks, he promised, nor would she do anything that might pop her stitches.

The nurse's aide turned back to Lilya, laid a hand on her forehead, looked her over carefully, and, reassured, dismissed them both.

"So, what about the secret?" Stefan asked, when they were outside his building.

Lilya looked at him with a strange intensity.

"We pretty much skipped the way back," he added.

She rose up on tiptoe and kissed him on the lips. "Don't say anything," she murmured. "You'll ruin it. Want to show me your room?"

"Uh . . . my mom's there . . ." he stammered.

"Don't be an idiot, I'm not going to jump on you. I just want to see what it looks like."

"My mom?"

"Your *room*. Are you mad because I kissed you?"

"No, of course not. If that was your secret, I've been keeping the same one for a long time."

"*That* wasn't a secret at all, silly."

The teacher's praise would have been all it took to make Valentyn persona non grata, if his mutism hadn't already made him a pariah from day one. No one spoke to him in the cafeteria; even his friend had distanced himself, sitting two places away from him at the table and keeping his head bent over his plate all through the meal, not even daring to look at him. Fear generally results in small acts of cowardice, which tend to grow larger and larger. Valentyn was hurt, but he'd never been too worried about filling silences. And he knew someone would be regretting his behavior soon enough.

The bell rang. The students lined up and filed toward the exit. Putting a hand into his pocket, Valentyn grasped the folded piece of paper between his fingers. He was on high alert; he'd have no more than a few seconds to put his plan into action.

The matron, though a bit less put together than usual, her bun slightly askew, was back at her post by the door. Fifteen yards. Five. Valentyn stepped to one side and slipped her the paper, then quickly rejoined the line.

Intrigued, the matron read what was written on the paper, then looked at the departing children.

"Wait a moment," she called to the monitor. The line stopped moving. Valentyn clenched his fists, trying not to grin. He was taking a big risk, and there was nothing to smile about, despite the fact that he found it a bit amusing finally to have put a face to the remote control that operated the robots.

The matron came over to where he was standing in the line. "So," she said quietly, "you're good with engines?"

Becoming the matron's special pet wasn't going to improve his popularity. But this was no time to chicken out, so he merely shrugged.

"I'd been wanting a word with you anyway," the matron continued. "Come with me and we'll see what you can do."

As tempted as the other students were to watch where she was taking Valentyn, they knew the slightest breach of discipline would result in punishment. Not a head turned as he was led away.

Followed by Valentyn, the matron crossed the main hall and unlocked the door to the outer courtyard. When the sedan had dropped Valentyn and his friend off at the school, it had been night. By day the courtyard looked even bigger, the fences higher, the gate more forbidding. The matron turned left, striding toward a covered enclosure where the gardeners kept their equipment. The monitor who had come to her rescue had done the job with zeal, towing her car all the way to the safety of the enclosure. Now the matron slid behind the wheel and turned the key in the ignition. The engine coughed and turned over a few times, but failed to start.

"It's not being very obedient today, as you can see," she said.

Valentyn spotted a toolbox on a workbench. He went over to it, then looked questioningly at the matron, who told him to do whatever he thought best. He had an inkling of what the problem might be already. The matron gave him a sly smile, as if she was testing him. Waiting for him to trip up. Valentyn leaned into the car and pulled on the handle to pop the hood. The matron stopped him just as he was about to open it.

"That's too heavy for you—you don't want your fingers to get smashed."

Her condescending attitude was infuriating, but Valentyn obeyed, stepping back. Once the hood's safety support was in place, she allowed him to approach. He reached for the toolbox, determined not to show how much effort it took, wanting to show that he was plenty strong enough to open a car's hood. Still, it took him two hands to lift the heavy box. He set it down in front of the car, then climbed up on the bumper, leaned over the engine, and studied it with the concentration of a doctor examining a patient.

The matron watched him, slightly unsettled by this child who was more articulate with gestures and facial expressions than many boys his age were with words. A nine-year-old shouldn't be able to repair a car engine, she thought, and yet she had a feeling he was about to prove her wrong.

Valentyn selected a wrench from the toolbox. Lesson One: disconnect the black cable from the battery so as not to be electrocuted. Clamping the wrench onto the nut, he pushed with all his might on the handle. It was out of the question for his scheme to fail because of an old piece of jammed metal. If he could get the matron's car working again, he'd score some major points with her, he was certain of it, and accomplish a major part of his plan at the same time. His father hadn't only taught him mechanics; he'd also showed him the importance of earning trust.

Seeing that Valentyn was struggling a bit, the matron offered to give him a hand. Fighting a recalcitrant nut together made him feel as if they were partners, in a way. When the nut finally came loose, she clapped.

Valentyn couldn't let himself be distracted. He reached for a screwdriver, removed the distributor from its base plate, and paused, thinking. The distributor cap of his father's Volkswagen Beetle had clogged frequently, and if his diagnosis was correct, he knew exactly what to do next—provided he could remember Lesson Two, of course.

Suddenly Valentyn felt a spreading warmth in his chest. His father was alive; he could feel his presence as if he were right there, leaning over his shoulder. He could hear his voice, murmuring instructions. *Take things one at a time. One spark plug at a time, so you don't put them back in the wrong order. If that happens, the engine will never start back up.*

The matron watched, fascinated. Valentyn was so calm, so sure of himself. He removed the first cap delicately, rummaged in the toolbox, chose the wrench he thought was best, and unscrewed the spark plug. Spotting a file in the box, he gently cleaned the buildup off the plug until it shone silver again, then he wiped the plug and screwed it back into its socket, replaced the hood, and moved on to the next one.

Fifteen minutes later, the matron slid behind the wheel again. She turned the key. The engine coughed. Valentyn held his breath. On the second try, the engine coughed again, spitting black smoke from the tailpipe . . . and then started to purr like a contented old cat.

"Bravo!" the matron exclaimed. "I'll be able to get home tonight, thanks to you. I owe you one for this."

Valentyn laughed. He was sweating and his hands were covered in grease, but the fact that the matron didn't spend her nights at the boarding school was a piece of information that might come in handy.

The real prize came when she invited him to wash up in her office. This was his chance to visit the tower that rose from one corner of the forbidden wing.

9

Two hours after it had begun to blaze red, the sky faded to black again. Two hours spent at the gates of hell, during which Danylo hadn't said a single word. A record. The farmer had tried to soothe Veronika with witty quips. Unsuccessfully.

At 5:00 a.m., with calm restored, the ambulance's three occupants found themselves unable to make a decision. A state that lasted until the first rays of the sun penetrated the gloom.

"And what do we do now?"

"We keep going. I don't see any other option," said the farmer.

"And if the Russians made it through the attack, they'll fire at anything that moves."

"No one could have survived that firestorm," sighed Veronika. "It must be a real bloodbath out there."

"From your lips to God's ears!" said the farmer, crossing himself.

Danylo pulled back onto the road, and soon they were driving through woodland. Everything seemed normal for the first few kilometers, though there was no birdsong. Then came fields, stretching away as far as the eye could see. No bodies on the side of the road, no burned-out vehicles, no trace of combat. Only the thick plume of black smoke rising from the end of a dirt road testified to the nature of the attack. Drones had struck a munitions depot installed by the Russians on the edge of the woods.

"There must have been a hell a lot of bombs in there to create that kind of fireworks display," commented the farmer.

"And artillery shells, and land mines, and maybe even some missiles," added Danylo, delighted that the enemy had lost so much firepower.

Veronika glanced at her watch and begged Danylo to drive as fast as he could. If they weren't hassled at the border crossing, they'd get back shortly before noon.

On the way, they passed two columns of military vehicles heading in the opposite direction, probably toward the site of the drone attack. The Russians paid no attention to the ambulance racing at top speed toward the occupied zone, perhaps assuming it carried one of their own, and the same was true at the border, where the guards simply waved them past the checkpoint.

As they entered the city, the farmer, who was heartily sick of hospital food, rubbed his hands together in anticipation of a home-cooked lunch. Veronika suggested that they drop him off first. "It's the least we can do, after all he's done for us." Danylo slowed, easing the ambulance down the rutted road leading to the farm.

"I really don't know how to thank you," Veronika said.

"I'm the one who should thank you for this little excursion. I got to see a bit of the countryside, and it was more fun than lying there bored to death in your clinic."

"You know exactly what I mean."

"All I know is that I'm going to eat twice as much as my wife thinks I should at lunch. Your surgeon must have taken off a big chunk of belly fat; my stomach's never been so flat," he joked, patting his middle. "And if the two of you would like to keep me company at the table, you're more than welcome."

"Not at the table! You're going straight to bed and staying there for at least a week, or I'm taking you right back to the clinic," Veronika said sternly.

Danylo pulled up in front of the house. The farmer's wife came out immediately along with their son, who was leaning on her shoulder for support. Veronika studied them while Danylo got down the stretcher. They knew what they had to do, but in Ukraine, the main thing is to keep smiling. Arms waved in farewell. Their humble courage forced restraint.

"Next stop, clinic!" Danylo exclaimed.

"No," Veronika objected. "I want to see Lilya. I've never missed her so much as in these past two days."

Danylo's fingers drummed the gearshift. Veronika covered his hand with her own. He looked at her and smiled for the first time. His toothless face was beautiful.

"And don't say a word. Tomorrow, when you go back to work, you'll be the head nurse again, stubborn and loudmouthed as ever. And I'll be the maintenance man again. This was no pleasure trip, that's for sure, but I'm glad we finally had a chance to get to know each other. And I hope you found what you were looking for. And . . . there's something I have to confess. While I was waiting for you at the hospital in Kyiv, I felt like life was almost back to normal there—though I know that's a big 'almost.' And did you feel that sense of freedom too? Because I did, and more than a little bit. And I thought . . ."

"But you came back because of me."

"No, I think I came back for myself," Danylo said, grudgingly. "And now here we are at your house. Go on, your daughter must be anxious to see you."

Veronika reached over and hugged Danylo, then again, and again. Each time, she thanked him. Once wouldn't have been nearly enough to show him how grateful she was. Then she got out of the ambulance.

Her house wasn't especially large. Two bedrooms, a kitchen, and a bathroom that was usually a mess. But how happy she was to be home. She called out for her daughter even before taking off her coat. There was no one downstairs, and no lights on. Lilya must be out running errands. No big deal, thought Veronika. It would give her time to shower and change, so she'd look as nice as possible when Lilya got home. She was eager to tell her daughter that she'd found someone to help them. A former patient who'd become someone very important. Thanks to him, they were going to get Valentyn back. Soon everything would be all right again.

Feeling the need for a coffee, she went into the kitchen to make one. There was a piece of paper on the table. She unfolded it and read the words:

Mom—

Since you're doing nothing, I've gone to find Valentyn myself.

Lilya

10

I was wondering when you'd show up!" exclaimed the surgeon. "How did the trip go?"

He seemed to have a knack for saying the wrong thing at the wrong time. Veronika handed him Lilya's note. The patient looked from one to the other, shocked that the surgeon had broken off in the middle of an examination. The surgeon pushed his glasses up his nose and read.

"I didn't tell her about it because I didn't want to worry her. She thought I was working extra shifts."

"The teen years are rough, so what else is new?" he grumbled.

That didn't make Veronika feel any better. Now the surgeon understood why his nurse had burst onto the ward without even putting on her medical smock. Deciding not to meet her eyes again, he turned back to his patient and pressed a stethoscope to the man's chest, his expression grave.

"Okay, everything seems fine," he said to the patient. "I'll come by again later."

"Why? Am I going to be worse later?" the man asked anxiously.

The surgeon waved away the question, then took Veronika's arm and steered her toward his office.

"When did she leave?" he asked.

"This morning, I think."

"You think? You're not sure?"

"The coffee pot was still slightly warm, and there was a full shopping bag on the table. I checked the calendar; it was her day to go to the distribution center."

"That means she ran away three hours ago at most," he said, looking at his watch.

"She didn't 'run away'; she's gone to look for her brother."

"She's an underage girl on the road, all alone—what else would you call it? Did she take her things with her?"

"I don't know . . . I didn't look in her room . . . I . . ."

Veronika couldn't finish the sentence. The surgeon's comment had been like a slap in the face. *An underage girl on the road, all alone . . .*

The trip to Kyiv had allowed her to stop thinking constantly of what might happen to Valentyn, though he'd been on her mind every minute, of course. Veronika had never given up on anything in her life; she was the type of woman who clung to hope even in the darkest moments. You don't choose to be a nurse if you're willing to accept defeat. Living without cynicism, even in times of war, takes a special kind of strength. Veronika's loneliness hit her in waves that came from far away, from the open sea. Enormous waves that knocked her flat on those evenings when, coming home much too late, she'd go upstairs to kiss her sleeping children and whisper in their ears that everything was going to be all right, then go down to eat dinner alone. Huge, crashing waves that submerged her, dragging her down, leaving her in the morning with just enough air to struggle back to the surface. But she'd mastered her loneliness, grown used to it. Conquering fear was something else altogether.

Veronika sagged limply into the chair opposite the surgeon's desk. They'd been through a hell of a lot together, but there was a grief in her eyes this time that cut him to the heart. He rose and came around his desk to put a hand on her shoulder.

"Go home. You need some rest, I can see it," he said. "I won't order you to sleep, because I know you won't be able to, and even if I gave you a sleeping pill you wouldn't take it. Look, thinking the worst isn't going to help anything. She's rebelling, that's all. It's just acting out. She'll walk around for a few hours, and when she gets tired she'll come back home. You'll see, she'll be knocking on the door by sunset—maybe a bit later, to punish you. Now, that doesn't mean there aren't a few things you can do, to be cautious. Check her room, see if she's taken any of her things with her, or any food, or if she left with nothing but the clothes on her back."

Veronika stood up without a word. The surgeon, unable to let her leave like that, walked her out of the clinic and through the parking lot. At the end of the street, he urged her not to give up, and then was quiet, saving his breath, because the hill was a steep one. A few minutes later Veronika stopped, taking his hand in hers, and told him gently to go back to the clinic. The patients needed his attention more than she did. She was feeling stronger already, and she was sure he was right; Lilya would be home soon. Really, she insisted. He didn't need to worry about leaving her alone. The surgeon scrutinized her face. He knew how people looked when they were pretending to be fine, for fear of being told they were ill. But what he saw in her eyes reassured him. He nodded once, then turned back toward the clinic.

Veronika quickened her pace.

Back in the house she hurried upstairs and, opening her daughter's closet, looked to see what clothes might be missing, then went through the contents of her small dresser. It quickly became apparent that Lilya had taken a pair of jeans, two sweaters, bras and underwear, her old toothbrush, and all her spending money. Clearly, she hadn't planned on coming back tonight.

Veronika went back downstairs. The sight of Lilya's abandoned coffee cup made a sob rise in her throat. She was still wearing her coat. She should hang it on the coat rack and then... what? Sit here in the kitchen, worrying herself to death? She reflected. Her boss might think he knew everything, but he didn't know her daughter.

Lilya's personality had changed in recent months, but she'd always had a good head on her shoulders. Becoming a teenager had done nothing to change that characteristic—which she'd inherited from her mother, who couldn't believe she'd run off on a whim like this. What had made her do it? Veronika couldn't imagine, and she was ashamed of herself for not having paid enough attention to her.

The prospect of waiting, of doing nothing, was more than she could bear. She needed to be useful, and there was only one place she could do that.

The matron had taken off her jacket and thrown it over the back of her chair.

"No, don't write anything. There's no need, and it's so relaxing to talk to someone who doesn't answer," she said, letting out a long breath.

She took a tissue from a box on her desk, dampened it with her tongue, and wiped a spot of grease from Valentyn's forehead.

"If you only knew how stressful my days are," she went on. "Today got off to a bad start, but it's looking up, thanks to you. And I don't mean your fixing my car. Your assessment report is remarkable. Despite your handicap, I definitely won't have any problems finding a family to adopt you. If you keep on going this way, there could be great things in store for you. Don't make that face! I'd imagine it was your father who made you into such a good little mechanic, but as you know, he's not around anymore."

The matron stroked Valentyn's hair, then tilted his chin up with a finger so he'd look at her.

"Don't be sad. You'll forget your parents very quickly. Children forget everything at your age, or almost. Believe me, placed with the right people, you'll be happier than you've ever been. If you don't disappoint me, that is."

This woman was a demon, every bit as bad as the ones in the stories Lilya read to him. But this wasn't just a creature confined to the pages of a book; she was right there in flesh and blood, terrifyingly real. He had to get out of this prison and back to his family before they sold him like a slave.

Valentyn couldn't bear her eyes on him. To keep her from seeing his fear and disgust, he went to the window.

Who would come to his rescue? None of his family or friends knew where he was. He had no one to rely on but himself. He considered deliberately failing his exams to thwart the matron's plans, but she was too clever to fall into such an obvious trap. And losing her trust would jeopardize his chances of escaping.

He pressed his face to the window, tuning out the monster's voice. He studied the garden in the inner courtyard, the classroom doors tucked into recesses in the corridors, focusing on a single objective: to memorize as many things as he could, just as he'd done during the bus, truck, and car journey here.

His gaze rested on the metal hatch set into the stone floor of the forbidden gallery. There was nothing to indicate what lay beneath it, but all it took was a little imagination to picture a staircase leading to ancient vaults and passageways. All he'd have to do at the bottom of those steps was pause for a moment to let his eyes adjust to the darkness, and then he'd be able to look for a way out, a tunnel beneath the school leading to the other side of the road, far away into the fields, where freedom awaited.

Imagination is a beautiful thing.

He could cut through the garden to get past the gates, even if it might be hard to do without being spotted. He should have made a break for it in the gardeners' enclosure—the courtyard gate was open—but the monster would have chased and caught him.

"It's high time you rejoined your classmates; you've missed two hours of class because of me," said the matron. "I'll speak to your teachers about making sure you catch up. Run along, now. All these stairs are too much for me. You'll be able to find your own way back."

Valentyn seized a piece of paper and wrote: *Who will open the gate at the end of the gallery for me?*

The matron thought for a moment, fingering the bunch of keys attached to her belt.

"All you have to do is climb over the low wall. If anyone sees you, tell them I've given you permission—ah, write it to them, I mean. You and I will be seeing plenty of each other. Now get yourself back to class, hurry up."

Valentyn went down the stairs. Three flights per floor, ten steps between landings, thirty in all. The wooden door to the passageway wasn't locked—not at this time of day, anyway. Sixty steps to the hatch. He slowed down to examine it, estimating its length by stepping along it heel-toe like a child playing hopscotch. He was sorely tempted to open it by pulling on the ring set into the metal, to see what was underneath, but it was too risky. The matron might be watching from her window.

Clambering over the low wall, he crossed the garden, went through the gate, and was back in the corridor.

The nurse's aide put down her book as Veronika entered the clinic.

"I know I overdid it a bit with the dressing, but I wanted to make sure it wouldn't get infected. It's nothing serious, I promise," she said, getting out of her chair.

Veronika stared at her uncomprehendingly.

"Don't give her too much of a hassle about it. I swore I wouldn't tell you, and I didn't tell her anything either, of course. Frankly, the two of you with your secrets are making my life far too complicated."

"You didn't tell who anything?" Veronika asked.

"Your daughter, obviously."

"You saw Lilya?"

"Yes, this morning, when I stitched her up."

"Stitched her up?"

The nurse's aide was now equally baffled. First of all, she'd done a beautiful job with Lilya's stitches. In a month you wouldn't even be able to see the scar. Neither did she understand why Veronika seemed more interested in when her daughter had been at the clinic than in what had happened to her. So she started over. Lilya had fallen from a bicycle, she explained. Nothing serious; no injuries to her head or face.

"I told her you were in surgery, the poor thing was so panicked at the thought of you seeing her. Are you wondering what time her boyfriend took her home? Is that it?"

"What boyfriend?" Veronika demanded, grasping her colleague's arm.

"Hey, don't get so worked up! I told you, she's fine."

"*What boyfriend?*" Veronika repeated, louder this time.

"The little Vasylyk boy, the carpenter's son—who's not little anymore at all, by the way; he's a big strapping fellow now. They grow up so fast. Your daughter, too—she's changed so much! Can you let go of my arm now?"

"Do you know where Mr. Vasylyk lives?"

The nurse's aide shook her head. "No idea. Wait—actually, I think I remember the father coming to the clinic. I don't remember why; it was quite a while ago, but if he did, we should still have a file for him. The 'V's are on the bottom shelf of the filing cabinet," she finished, now feeling that she'd done her duty that day and then some.

Veronika knelt and riffled through the folders, her hands shaking. The filing cabinet was always a mess. Mr. Lechsenko shouldn't be here, let alone Mrs. Gudzevich, who'd died a year ago. Realizing she'd gone too far, she backtracked. Veremchuk... Vashenko (who shouldn't be here either) ... Vasylyk ... bingo!

She opened the file. The carpenter's visit had been five years ago, a case of kidney stones she couldn't care less about; her only interest was the address written on the inside cover. Mr. Vasylyk lived around two hundred yards from the train station.

Veronika looked up at her colleague.

"Did it not occur to you to notify me that Lilya had been in an accident?"

"Notify you how? And where?"

"You could have messaged my pager, for a start. You seem to know perfectly well how to do that when you're overwhelmed and need a hand, don't you?"

"Maybe, but I don't know where I put the pager, and besides, things were very busy this morning."

"Yes, it certainly seems like it," Veronika said coldly.

"A 'thank you for taking care of my daughter while I was off on my little road trip' would have done nicely," sniffed the nurse's aide. She went back to her book, ignoring Veronika completely.

Veronika left the clinic, crossed the parking lot, and ran for the carpenter's house on Zelena Street.

From behind a closed garage door came the piercing whine of a circular saw. Veronika knocked as hard as she could on the metal shutter. The shrieking sound died away, succeeded by the grinding noise of the garage door being raised. The carpenter appeared with both hands up: he'd thought it was Russian soldiers pounding on his door. Instead he saw a woman whose face was familiar, though he couldn't put a name to it.

The workshop was an unbelievable mess. Sawdust covered the floor and hung in the sunlight streaming through the open door, filling the air with its scent. Furniture of all kinds was piled against the back wall, balancing precariously. Boards were stacked against the right-hand wall without regard to size, and the workbench was no more orderly.

Veronika introduced herself. Mr. Vasylyk exhaled. It was all coming back to him now; he'd been in agony from the kidney stones, and she'd administered painkillers. He should have recognized her immediately. An injection in the ass tends to be a bonding experience.

"I have every kind of table, chair, nightstand, and cabinet you could possibly need, at rock-bottom prices, of course. No one's buying anything at the moment, but I keep working to stay busy, otherwise I'd go off my rocker."

"I need to see your son."

"Is Stefan ill?"

"No, nothing like that. I need to talk to him."

"Can I ask what about?"

"My daughter. And it's urgent."

Vasylyk rubbed his temples. "Look, whatever she might have told you, Stefan hasn't done anything wrong. He's a good boy. Bit softer than I'd like, but his mother and I have raised him well."

"Mr. Vasylyk, my daughter has disappeared, and there's a good chance he was the last one to see her."

"What do you mean 'disappeared'?"

"She's run off in search of her brother. Where is Stefan?"

"Not in my workshop, that's for sure. Probably off somewhere with his nose in a book. He spends way too much time reading if you ask me, but my wife's delighted, so who cares what I think? That's how it is all the time, actually. I just bring in the money and keep my mouth shut."

The carpenter wasn't a complainer by nature, but he'd been caught on the back foot and was wary of anyone who might be getting his son tangled up in something unsavory, especially in these times. Now, having vented his frustration, he thought about how he would feel if he were in Veronika's shoes. He raised his head toward the ceiling and shouted:

"Stefan! Get down here, hurry up!"

The boy quickly made his appearance. Veronika was in a state of shock; when had she become so disconnected from her daughter that she didn't realize her little boy friends had turned into men?

"This is your friend's mother. She needs to ask you some questions, and you need to answer them," said the carpenter, his arms crossed to indicate that this was a serious conversation.

Stefan's cheeks flushed as red as if someone had turned on a light inside his mouth.

"She—she was the one who wanted to come up to my bedroom," he stammered. "But nothing happened, I swear! I even told her Mom was home, but she needed a kind of—of rear base. She only explained everything once we were here. She'd thought the whole thing out. It really surprised me, actually, because I hadn't realized a thing. I don't know how she did it—I mean, she mostly wanted me to give her the codes—she was so determined! And as far as the bike goes, she didn't do it on purpose. I mean—she *did*, but . . . she didn't expect to hurt herself . . ."

"Stefan," Veronika interrupted. "None of this is making any sense. Can you please put all those words in the right order, and into sentences I can understand?"

Stefan was quiet for a moment. He glanced at his father, who didn't look happy.

"It all started when she went to the distribution center this morning. She was passing the town hall and she saw that Russian officer, the one who's supposed to know where your son is."

"Your son's run away too?" asked the carpenter.

"My son's nine years old. He's been kidnapped by the Russians," Veronika answered shortly.

The carpenter was mortified. The one time he'd spoken up, and he'd have done better to keep his mouth shut.

"She fell off her bike on purpose, right in front of him, because she knew he'd come and help her up. She was laughing when she told me how confused he was. And her plan worked perfectly. The officer couldn't get her to stop crying and he didn't want to look bad in front of all the people who were watching, so he told her where Valentyn is. She didn't tell me any of that at the distribution center; she said she'd had a bad fall on her bike. She must have been afraid I'd try to stop her."

"Stop her from what?" asked Mr. Vasylyk, trying to redeem himself.

"Well... from what she was going to do at the clinic. I think she was planning to go there alone, right after she dropped the food off at home. But I insisted on going with her. And she agreed because it was good for her plan. Without knowing it, I created a diversion by talking to the nurse."

"Nurse's aide," corrected Veronika, who was going from surprise to surprise.

"What was she planning to do?" asked the carpenter again.

"Uh... steal her pager. The nurse's. Nurse's aide, I mean."

"What's a pager?" his father asked.

"It's a... thingy..."

"A 'thingy'?"

"It's a small electronic device we wear on our belts so we can be contacted at any time," explained Veronika. She turned to Stefan. "What was her reason for stealing it?"

"So we'd each have one. I'm the rear base."

"You stole a thing too?" demanded his father, gearing up for a tirade.

"No, I bought mine ages ago, secondhand. It's no big deal; a bunch of us in class have them. We use codes to communicate. The good thing about them is that they always work, even since the Russians cut off the networks. Come up to my room and I'll show you."

11

It hadn't taken Valentyn long to see, from the looks on his classmates' faces when he rejoined them, that he wasn't exactly welcome. His friend hadn't said a word to him in either the cafeteria or the hallway between classes, deliberately walking several paces behind him as they trooped to the gymnasium.

This was no ordinary day. At three o'clock there was a bicycle outing. That was the rule; twice a week, ever since the Children's Rights Commissioner had published a notice drawing educators' attention to the necessity of incorporating outdoor physical activities, which were essential for the good health and development of young future Russians. Naturally, the matron had implemented the directive immediately.

The outings lasted an hour for each class. The oldest students were exempt, as they were already being trained in combat sports, for which they dressed in uniforms with the Russian flag sewn to the shoulder.

This was the first time since his internment that Valentyn had gone out the main gate through which he'd first arrived. Lined up with his classmates, filing toward the bicycle shed, which was next to the gardeners' enclosure, Valentyn realized that he'd forgotten to formulate an important part of his plan. Until then, all he'd thought about was escaping. But if he did manage to get away, he'd have to hide somewhere. This bicycle trip was the perfect opportunity to do some scouting.

The first whistle-blow told the students to get on their bicycles; the second was the signal to start riding. Once past the gate, Valentyn was struck by the starkness of the landscape. A bleak plain, cut in half by the road they were on. The sun was setting on his right. In the car that had brought him here, it had appeared to be on his left. That meant he was riding north now, toward home, even if it was much too far to attempt an escape now. He wouldn't have a chance. The teacher was in the lead, and there was one monitor riding in the middle of the group of students and another bringing up the rear—just behind him, in fact, because his pace was deliberately slow.

His mother had taught him, one summer, how to find the cardinal points using the position of the sun. The names of the constellations too, and of the stars that glittered on clear nights. Cassiopeia was his favorite. He'd learned her name while lying in a hammock between his mother and sister, sharing a bag of sweets.

They were nearing a patch of woodland. The teacher slowed, then stopped, putting a foot down. The group turned around.

As they cycled back toward the school, Valentyn estimated the distance they'd traveled. The outing had lasted an hour in total, and the woods marked the halfway point. The bicycle trips to Petrivka with his father to buy tubes of paint and brushes used to take an hour too. The paint seller in Petrivka lived twenty kilometers from their house. The gym teacher cycled more slowly than his father, so Valentyn figured the distance between the woodland and the school was about eight kilometers, or around a two-hour walk. He could hide in the woods when he escaped, but he'd have to take provisions with him.

The bicycle trip had been time well spent. Valentyn should have been pleased. And yet, as the gate closed behind him, he felt a knot in his stomach, one that grew tighter as he stowed his bicycle in the shed. He thought of the night to come, when the matron would turn off the lights in the dormitory.

The lights of Novooleksiivka sparkled in the night. This small southern city was twice the size of Lilya's town. She'd traveled some twenty kilometers since leaving home; not as far as she'd have liked. The bike had slowed her down, her knee throbbing when she pedaled. She'd stopped several times to make sure her dressing wasn't spotted with blood, afraid she'd popped her stitches. So much bending of the knee had made the bandages come loose too; tomorrow she'd have to buy supplies to redo it. She probably would have covered more ground if she'd taken the main road, but the E105 was full of trucks traveling at high speed—and also, if her mother were trying to catch her before she reached the frontier, that was definitely the way she would go. That was why Lilya had chosen to take the road that ran alongside the railway line: a dirt road, rutted and rocky, on which it took a lot of effort to keep herself and the bike upright.

When the sun sank beneath the horizon, Lilya knew she needed to find shelter before it got dark. She headed for the cluster of railroad tracks on the outskirts of Novooleksiivka, where dozens of rusted freight cars sat sleeping on storage tracks, massive convoys without locomotives, forming a kind of iron rampart. Briefly she considered climbing into one of the cars and spending the night, but the barking of a dog dissuaded her—a big black mutt with a mangy coat and a long scar on its muzzle, weakened by hunger but still fierce enough to command respect. It was the dog's territory Lilya had just entered, after all, and she wasn't a welcome guest.

Lilya had never been afraid of dogs; on the contrary, she loved animals, and they could sense things like that. Kneeling as best she could with her injured knee, she held out a hand and softly called the first name that flashed into her head. Sobaka came closer, his teeth bared. Lilya stayed perfectly still, certain that as long as she didn't move and kept smiling, he wouldn't bite her. She spoke to the dog gently, promising not to hurt him. He backed up a few steps, then came closer again to sniff her. In the end he allowed her to the cross the tracks, but the train cars were clearly his domain. She ran and didn't turn around until she'd reached the paved road on the other side of the railyard. Then she waved at the dog in gratitude and continued on her way.

Lilya rode up the town's main street, past a grocery store whose metal shutter was closed. She would have to ditch the bike, she decided. Her knee really was too painful.

But first she looked around for a safe place to hide it, so she could pick it up again on the way back. And even if it got stolen, if she managed to save Valentyn, she knew her parents would forgive her. A bike for a brother wasn't such a bad swap, after all.

The dark street wasn't very promising but, in the light of the only streetlamp still working, Lilya spotted a small abandoned house. Its roof was gone, its rubble-strewn floor pocked with craters, the walls battered and no glass remaining in the windows. The stairs leading to the second floor had lost their railing. The place had probably been hit by a bomb, to end up in this condition. Neither was there any furniture; if the house's inhabitants had survived, they'd taken away everything they could save. Otherwise it was the neighbors, or maybe the Russians, who had pillaged the ruins. There was a smell of dust and ash in the air that bore no resemblance to the usual scent that rose from the fields at harvest time.

The bombed-out house would do the job. No one would take the risk of looking for her here. Lilya stepped through the ruined front door, which lay torn half off its hinges. Hoisting her bicycle onto her shoulder, she made her way up the stairs, being careful not to fall.

The stars were clearly visible from the roofless second floor, the moon almost full. Lilya peered outside through the remains of a wall. There were storm clouds being driven across the plain by a slight southerly wind, the wheat fields rippling in the breeze. It would rain soon. She hid the bicycle, picked up her backpack, and went back downstairs to find a niche to shelter in. She cleared the dirt from a patch of floor with her shoe as best she could, then sat down and rummaged in her bag. An apple and a bag of chips, with a granola bar for dessert. Just as she was about to bite into the apple, she stopped short. She'd heard footsteps in the street outside. Soft steps, as if someone were walking carefully. She regretted not having packed anything she could defend herself with, like a kitchen knife. Going back upstairs was too risky; the sound of her feet crunching on the rubble would give away her presence. The light of the streetlamp was blotted out by a shadowy figure in the doorway. She held her breath.

Then: "You followed me?" she whispered.

The black dog paused, sniffing the air.

"Don't be scared. I'm more afraid of you than you are of me."

Sobaka crept closer to Lilya, crouched low, his posture almost submissive.

"You hungry too? Come here."

The dog obeyed. Lilya broke her granola bar into equal halves and tossed one to him.

He swallowed it in one bite, so she shared her apple and chips with him too.

"Eat one chip at a time," she said. "There aren't any more."

It seemed as if he understood, because each time she handed him a chip, he took it carefully in his teeth before crunching it.

The meal finished, Lilya unscrewed the top of her water bottle, drank, then poured a little water into her cupped hand. The dog lapped it up happily, sniffed the dressing on her knee, looked at her with big eyes, then stretched and lay down at her feet.

His company was reassuring, especially as it was dawning on Lilya that she hadn't planned well enough for this journey. That it was going to take longer than she'd thought. That there would be more nights when she'd have to hide, more storms she'd have to face like the one now rumbling overhead and lashing the street outside with rain. That she had no idea where to look for her brother once she'd traveled the hundred kilometers south. And, worst of all, how very alone she felt.

Valentyn forced himself to eat, to show the others that their bullying hadn't had—wouldn't have—any effect on him. His ribs did hurt, though. He'd been subjected to a summary beating during shower time, four goons pouncing on him. There'd been no point in fighting back; he'd simply curled into a ball and clenched his fists as the blows rained down. They'd left his face alone, so the monitors wouldn't be able to tell anything had happened. When they were finished hitting him, they'd warned him that the same thing would happen tomorrow. It wasn't the beating that had made Valentyn so angry, though, but the fact that they'd called him a "dirty Ukrainian." Those morons were all Ukrainian too. He had to get out of here before the evil energy of this place turned him into a bully too.

It was time to go back to the dormitory. Before going to sleep, Valentyn looked over at his friend's bed. The other boy looked miserable. He'd been part of the crowd watching Valentyn get thrashed in the shower, standing slightly apart, silent and unmoving, a mixture of anxiety and pleasure on his face.

The matron turned out the lights. Valentyn waited for his eyes to adjust to the darkness. Lying on his side made his ribs hurt, but it was the only way to reach the knife hidden beneath his bed. He held it in his hand, and thought.

Vital listened as Veronika told him, her voice breaking, that her daughter had run away. It wasn't good news, but perhaps things weren't as bleak as they seemed. Knowing that Valentyn was a hundred kilometers south of Rykove was incredibly helpful. Even if it was only an estimation, the information would narrow the field of Vital's search considerably. He brought up a map of the region on his screen and saw only two possible routes to Crimea. One of these avoided the checkpoint at Chonhar but required a major detour, adding almost three hundred kilometers to the journey. Lilya must have chosen to travel straight toward her destination, which didn't explain how she was planning to get across the border. As soon as he hung up the phone, Vital would take a closer look at her itinerary, calculate the distance she could travel per day and, with a bit of luck, identify the places where she might choose to spend her nights. The pager Veronika mentioned was also of interest. Being able to communicate with Lilya would be a significant advantage, maybe even the key to rescuing her from the mess she'd gotten herself into before it was too late. As long as they didn't alarm her. She mustn't know that it was her mother on the other end of the line. Stefan would need to remain her only contact.

"I can't sleep even though I'm exhausted. And you told me to call you with even the smallest piece of information. I didn't even look at the time," Veronika apologized, embarrassed at having called Vital so late.

"No problem. Did this Stefan give you the list of codes?"

"Yes. It's so antiquated I don't even know how they can write like that."

"I'll need to have that list."

Veronika looked at the mobile phone Vital had given her, turning it over. She couldn't see any way to take a photo. And her own phone had no network coverage.

"There's a fax machine at the clinic," she said. "I can send it to you tomorrow."

"I need it right away."

"I'll go back there now, then. With my medical ID I don't need to worry about breaking curfew; it won't be the first time."

"No, we'll do this another way."

"How?"

"With patience," retorted Vital, wheeling his chair toward his computer.

And so Veronika read out the codes letter by letter, word by word, as Vital typed it out on his keyboard. Then he printed out the list.

"What's wrong?" Veronika asked anxiously, as silence fell on Vital's end of the line.

"Nothing, just feeling a bit nostalgic. Vintage pagers have become a collector's item, practically mythical. But who'd think to spy on pager messages?"

"I use mine every day," Veronika said primly. "And I don't consider myself old enough to be vintage, let alone mythical."

"Maybe, but the first telephone messaging services started way back in the early 1950s. They were designed for doctors and nurses even back then; they had a range of about forty kilometers, which was enough to reach medical staff day or night in case of emergency. It was in the '70s that they became widely popular. You'd even see them clipped to waitresses' aprons in American movies. My parents both had one—they'd send each other messages saying they'd be late for dinner, or setting a time for a phone call, or when one of them wanted to ask the other to pick something up at the store on the way home. There was a whole vocabulary coded in numbers. 'I love you' was 143. They used to send each other that one a lot."

"Why 143?"

"If you look at Stefan's code list, you'll see that it makes the letters I-L-Y, for *I Love You*. 123 meant 'I miss you.' There were coded words and expressions—you could type whole sentences with numbers, not perfectly, because certain letters were designated by the same number, but the meaning always came through in the end. The whole system fell into obscurity once cell phones hit the scene—except in rural areas, thanks to a new generation of pagers that functioned with satellite coverage. They're still widely used in places where cellular networks are unreliable or nonexistent. Haven't you noticed that your pager works even when there's no phone signal?"

"No, I guess I've never given it much thought."

"Neither have I, to be honest. If I'd thought of it, I would have taken one out of my desk drawer and given it to you so we could communicate that way. Lilya's boyfriend is making me feel old! Remember the London terrorist attacks in 2005? They made pagers trendy again. The authorities were afraid that more bombs would be set off by mobile phones, so they cut off the cellular networks, and emergency services went back to using pagers instead. After that people had learned their lesson, and it seems like pagers are here to stay now. It's not so easy to replace something that cheap and reliable after all. Please give your daughter's boyfriend my congratulations."

"For what?"

"Finding a means of communication that costs almost nothing and using it to exchange messages your parents will never understand—it's brilliant. I'm almost jealous, and when I tell certain friends of mine about it, I can guarantee they'll be even more upset than I am that they didn't think of it first."

"So what do we do now?"

"Nothing until tomorrow. Arrange to have Stefan there with you; you'd spend too much time typing the messages and I don't want you to even try. Stefan's the one Lilya chose as her contact, and we can't scare her away. She could put herself in even more danger than she is in already."

Vital regretted speaking so frankly about Lilya's precarious circumstances as soon as the words were out of his mouth. "Sorry," he apologized. "Tact isn't my strong suit. I've never known how to phrase things right."

"I know. I'd be more worried if you suddenly started now. I'll go and find Stefan as soon as it's a reasonable hour."

"We'll send a message to Lilya the minute he's with you. In the meantime, try to get some rest. I'm going to spend the rest of the night trying to find where they're keeping your son. If by some miracle Lilya manages to get into Crimea, that's where she'll go anyway. We'll try to catch them together and send them home to you safe and sound."

"Vital, do you honestly believe we can?"

"You just got a taste of my diplomatic talents—how can you even ask that question?"

Vital cut the call. Veronika stood still for a long moment, there in her kitchen. At around two o'clock in the morning, three numbers on a screen informed her that her daughter was about to go to sleep. The message might not have been intended for her, but it gave her the strength to go upstairs to bed.

12

It was early in London. There were still hours to go before sunrise. Cordelia paced her living room, hands cupped around a mug of tea. Pausing in front of the mirror above the fireplace, she studied her own puffy eyelids and dark-shadowed eyes. She'd tossed and turned in bed, unable to sleep, and she knew exactly why.

It wasn't a bouquet of roses, much less the letter of explanation she'd been expecting for months, but the unique signature attached to the message that popped up just as she was preparing for bed had made her heart leap in her chest all the same. Yet there was nothing personal about it, nothing personal from the man she once loved, and was still in love with, even if their relationship had come to an abrupt end. It wasn't even to her alone that Vital had written during the night, but the group of activist hackers they both belonged to.

As always when she was in turmoil about something, she felt an urge to talk to her brother. He was her anchor, the only person she felt able to complain to.

"I think I know why you're calling, but have you looked at the clock?" Diego grumbled.

"No. But what does it matter?"

Diego sat up in bed and gazed at the framed photo of Alba on his nightstand.

"I'm wasting my time, Diego. He isn't worth it."

"Everything you've done up to now—was it for him, or for you? I don't seem to remember him asking you for anything."

"No, but—"

"You have absolutely no sense of time. You think you're wasting it, but you're wrong; that's why you're always so rushed. You'll understand what time really means when you learn to think in terms of years. Right now you've got more than half your life ahead of you."

"I don't need your sermons, okay? I'm the big sister, remember?"

"It's getting harder and harder to tell. I'm always either at home or at the restaurant. Nothing but my memories to keep me company. The woman I love is dead. When your days are as long and lonely as mine are, then you can talk to me about wasted time."

"Alba, that was . . . different. Vital isn't the person I thought he was."

"And what about you? What kind of person are you? The man you love is alone and it would be a waste of your time to try to understand why? I don't know what's happened, but the last time I saw you two together, love was making you want to do the right thing. It's anger that's making you back away, and fear, which breeds cowardice, and *that's* a waste of time. You're welcome to come and stay with me in Madrid, if you want, or you can leave London and live your life anywhere you want. It's up to you."

"You drive me nuts, Diego."
"I usually do, when I'm right. And always when you're wrong."

Diego hung up. Cordelia sat down at her desk to read Vital's message again.
"One word, just to me, *one* sentence, to make me believe you miss me—is that too much to ask for, idiot?"

Cordelia took a quick shower, dabbed on a little concealer, and put on black trousers, a white T-shirt, and a blazer.
The sun wasn't yet up over Primrose Hill, but the dawn light was clear. She cycled to a bakery and bought a croissant to eat later, then rode down the hill, enjoying the sensation of speed, zigzagging between cars in the direction of her workplace, an IT security agency. Pausing at a red light, she wondered which of the Group of 9 would be the first to respond to Vital's call. Mateo and Ekaterina were too far away. Diego, maybe, just to annoy her, or maybe Maya; missing children were her specialty. Or why not Janice—unless Noa decided to emerge from the shadows at last?
She chained up her bike, crossed the lobby, showed her badge to the security guard, and settled down in her office to go over the day's agenda.
She had a meeting at ten o'clock with an important client. The thought of going over his file bored her to tears. Everything was boring this morning. She was in a terrible mood, so much so that she wondered what the hell she was even doing here, beyond "earning a good living." The last adrenaline rush she'd gotten was from riding a bike downhill. Unthinkable, for

the kind of woman she was. All of a sudden she couldn't bear the inaction anymore. She needed adventure. She needed to do something glorious. Something great. More than anything, she needed to be somewhere other than this soulless office.

Lilya woke with a start. The storm had kept her awake for much of the night, and now the silence jerked her from sleep.

She'd heard the trees on the plain cracking and snapping, buffeted by the wind. Leaving the dog asleep on the ground floor, she'd climbed upstairs to watch the mesmerizing spectacle. Wave after wave of rain like some menacing, unstoppable army; lightning splitting the sky, illuminating the fields for an instant before they were plunged into darkness again. The wind had blown harder and harder. With each flash of lightning the holes in the walls looked like the gaping mouths of monsters, ready to devour her. At around midnight, when the rain had become so heavy that even the stairs were running with water, Lilya had gone back downstairs to shelter from the weather, propping her rucksack against the house's rear wall. The storm had passed over the old house, the walls trembling with each crack of thunder. Sobaka had panted, letting out little whines and growls as if he were complaining about the commotion, the sight of his big, mournful eyes giving Lilya the courage to pull him into her arms and cuddle him close.

Everything was calm by morning. The dog was nowhere in sight. She called out his name a few times, then shrugged.

"You just smelled the storm and came to me for safety. So much for the loyalty of dogs! Well, you did the right thing, pulling a disappearing act, because if you thought I was going to get attached to an ugly mutt like you, you were wasting your time."

Her backpack felt damp, but the interior was dry. She dusted herself off, then found her brush and smoothed her hair back. She needed to find somewhere to buy fresh bandages for her knee, and maybe a change of clothes—it would be better not to look like a vagabond.

Leaving the house, she found the dog sitting outside the front door, as if guarding the entrance. He licked his chops, watching her.

"Soft touch too, aren't you?" Lilya said as she passed him.

On the corner she turned back, rolling her eyes, and sighed.

"Well, are you coming or not?"

Sobaka got up and trotted after her.

Valentyn walked slowly, wanting to be one of the last students to enter the cafeteria. He waited for his friend to sit down, then elbowed his way in to sit next to him. The other boy, looking chastened, eventually asked him how he'd slept.

Someone was crying last night, didn't you hear it? Valentyn wrote.

"Yeah, but it was too dark, I couldn't see who it was."

Guzenko, the big brown-haired one. The one who hit me first.

"I wanted to stop them, I swear, but I couldn't. It wasn't my fault."

I know, don't worry, Valentyn wrote, who didn't believe a word of it.

This truce was a calculated one. Valentyn scooted slightly closer to his friend so that no one could read what he was writing.

"You're out of your mind," the other boy said, reading the note. "It's much too risky. It'll never work."

And staying here isn't risky? It's them or me. You decide.

"How are you planning on accessing that trap door? Do you even know what's underneath it?"

I'll find out sooner or later.

"Well, talk to me again when you do. Now, tear up that piece of paper. You're going to get us in trouble."

Valentyn jabbed the tip of his pencil at where he had written *it's them or me* and added an exclamation point.

"Fine, I'll talk to them, tell them to leave you alone. For now, that's the best I can do."

Breakfast was over. They would be singing the national anthem in the cafeteria this morning, the matron announced. The sound of hammers could be heard over their heads; there was some kind of construction work going on in the auditorium.

When the music teacher picked up his guitar—they hadn't been able to bring the piano downstairs—and began strumming the chords of the Russian anthem, it was the Ukrainian one that Valentyn heard in his head. Silently he recited the words no one would ever make him forget:

The glory and freedom of Ukraine have not perished.
Destiny shall smile on us, fellow Ukrainians.
Our enemies shall vanish like dew in the sun.
And we shall soon reign over our land.

We shall lay down our bodies, our souls
For freedom.

Sleeping, even just for a few hours, had done Veronika good. She was no stranger to short nights; in her profession, you learned to get along without sleep. Closing your eyes and snatching ten minutes' rest in a chair, with your head on a table, or leaning against a wall, you were ready to go again. It was the only way to get through shifts that sometimes ran forty-eight hours or more.

She took a long, hot shower. It was still too early to knock on the carpenter's door. There was time to put away Lilya's shopping. What had she brought back from the distribution center this time?

Opening the bag, she felt a rush of emotion. Her daughter had remembered the tights and face cream she yearned for; maybe Lilya wasn't as angry as Veronika had feared she was. She hoped Lilya had been able to get the toothbrush she needed so badly.

A cracker, the last spoonful of strawberry jam in the jar, a cup of coffee. It was all Veronika could find in the kitchen cupboards. The hot coffee brought some comfort. She looked out the window; the sun wouldn't be up for a long time yet. To kill the time, she did the dishes and then set about straightening up the house, first the living room and then upstairs—but not the children's room, which would stay just as it was until they came home again. Everyone has their superstitions. Getting out the broom, she attacked the foyer, sweeping the dust out the front door. It was chilly outside; the sleeping town was blanketed in fog.

She took her wool jacket from its peg and went out. She needed to talk to someone.

※

"Just in time!" exclaimed the surgeon, as Veronika entered the staff room.

"Are we really that busy?"

"No, the opposite. It's dull as dishwater around here."

"Why are you here, then?" Veronika asked.

"Where else am I supposed to go? It's just as boring at home. Anyway, maybe you're the jinx."

"I beg your pardon?"

"The clinic's always rammed to the gills whenever you're here," said the surgeon.

"Are you suggesting that people get ill or injured because of me?"

"I'm not suggesting anything, merely observing, that's all. But if you came here looking for something to do, I'm afraid you're in for a disappointment."

"Is Danylo around?" Veronika asked.

"Do you know what time it is?"

Veronika sat down at the table and looked at the surgeon.

"I just felt the need for a bit of conversation."

"With the maintenance man," said the surgeon, folding his arms. "Well, I can offer you my services instead. As a second choice, naturally."

"They've taken Valentyn to Crimea," she said.

"Well, that's not too far away, at least. No fighting there either. Speaking of combat—have you heard anything from their father?"

"It's funny—your voice changes when you talk about my husband."

"I thought . . . well, it's none of my business."

"I wouldn't say that, necessarily."

"Sometimes I wonder if we haven't spent more time together than you and he ever did."

"Don't worry about that."

"It's because I dragged you out here to the middle of nowhere that the wheels came off your relationship."

"They'd come off long before you offered me the position here," Veronika assured him.

"Sorry. I have this ridiculous tendency to want to bear the world's problems on my shoulders. Forget I said anything."

The surgeon stared at his own hands for a minute, like a child who'd been caught doing something he shouldn't have and was trying to avoid the gaze directed at him.

"I get bored when I'm not operating."

"No, it isn't that," Veronika said. "You're feeling useless—and underestimating yourself. My husband calls when he can. They aren't permitted to use cell phones because the Russians track the signals to find out where our units are . . . sort of like using one match to light three cigarettes. Never mind—long story. Anyway, he usually finds a way to call me about once a month to let me know he's still alive, but it's been about five weeks since the last call, and I'm starting to worry."

"He'll call soon, I'm sure. What are you going to tell him about the children?"

"I have no idea," Veronika admitted.

"He'll want to talk to them."

"Oh, no—he only calls the clinic. Deliberately, I think. But he does always ask about them, which is something, at least."

The surgeon got up and went to the sideboard. The coffee in the pot was cold, from the previous day, but he poured himself a cup anyway.

"I understand him," he said over his shoulder.

"You do? What do you understand, exactly?"

"How many times have you told me he's a poet—and not always as a compliment, if I remember correctly. A poet who ended up in the trenches overnight. When you're looking a man you're supposed to kill right in the face, your humanity can keep you from pulling the trigger before he does. Talking to your children would be putting yourself in danger. It might crack the hard shell you've developed to keep yourself from thinking about the fact that the guy you're about to shoot might also have kids waiting for him at home. Survival is a complicated thing when you're at war. What? Why are you looking at me like that? What have I said now?"

"It's just . . . I never realized. My husband . . . he's a dreamer, living in a nightmare."

The surgeon and Veronika looked at one another sadly for a moment.

"Well," he said after a moment, rousing himself. "Let's go find ourselves something to do on the ward, shall we? There's probably a patient or two needing us by now, and if not, we can make it so there is."

Veronika responded to his small smile with one of her own and stood, wiping away the tears that had filled her eyes. He put an arm around her shoulders and they went out into the corridor together.

The sun was rising, and the light on the ward was beautiful, streaming amber-gold through the windows and over the beds.

The surgeon wished he could tell Veronika how important she was to him, even though he knew she would probably never love him the way he loved her.

Lilya made her way up Novooleksiivka's main street, the dressing on her knee getting looser with every step. A nearby café was turning on its lights. She looked over her shoulder at Sobaka, still trotting ten yards behind her.

"I'm not abandoning you, I'm just really cold," she said.

The dog lay down on the sidewalk and cocked his head to one side, watching her go into the café.

Sitting down at the counter, Lilya looked hungrily at the sticky buns piled on a plate. She was too proud to ask how much they cost, and she didn't have much money with her anyway. The woman who had served her a cup of coffee was now busily sweeping the floor and arranging chairs, paying no attention to her. It would be easy for Lilya to steal a bun, or two, so the dog could have breakfast too. All she had to do was reach out a hand. These things are tempting, when hunger is gnawing at your stomach.

Ten minutes later, leaving a twenty-hryvnia note on the counter to pay for her coffee, she thanked the waitress and left.

"Okay, you're not ugly, but you're very clingy, which is bad enough," she said to Sobaka, who'd been glued her side since she emerged from the café.

She took a bun out of her jacket pocket and gave it to the dog, who swallowed it in a single bite.

There was a pharmacy not far ahead. Lilya crossed the street and went inside.

"I need to redo a bandage. Whatever you have that's cheapest," she said to the pharmacist.

The cafeteria attendant at her brother's school looked like a delicate wisp compared to this woman. The eagle-eyed mother of a large family, she'd immediately noticed both Lilya's limp and the backpack slung over her shoulder.

"Go and sit down on that chair near the register and show me where you're hurt."

There was no point in arguing. Lilya obeyed, pulling her trousers down to just below the knee. The stitches had broken, but the wound hadn't reopened. The pharmacist applied disinfectant and a fresh bandage, then wrapped the knee securely.

"Haven't seen you around here before," she remarked as she worked. "Where are you coming from?"

"Rykove."

"By yourself?"

"Uh, no . . ." Lilya stammered. "My mother's visiting a friend up the street."

"Must be a very good friend, for your mother to be on the roads right now, especially with her daughter. Hop up and take a few steps for me, see if that's too tight."

The elastic bandage proved to be nicely supportive of Lilya's knee; she found she could walk almost normally—which didn't stop her from worrying about how much it might cost.

"What do I owe you?" she asked, timidly.

"Run along. Your mother can pay me when she's done visiting her friend."

At the door, Lilya turned. The pharmacist glanced up, pushing her glasses back up her nose. "You still here?" she asked.

"Thank you," Lilya said.

"Be very careful and look out for soldiers. The militia are very angry around here."

Lilya and Sobaka headed for the grocery store on the corner, a small, unprepossessing establishment. Lilya scanned the aisles and chose a packet of cookies, some discounted sliced ham that didn't look very appetizing, a wedge of hard cheese, and a small loaf of sliced bread. She briefly thought about buying herself a soda, but asked the cashier if she could refill her water bottle instead.

After she'd paid, she counted what money she had left. Enough for two more days, three if she tightened her belt.

The next stop was twenty kilometers away. If she didn't drag her heels, she'd be able to reach it in about four hours—that is, if she took the E105, which ran in a straight line. But at the crossroads she caught sight of a military convoy. Pickup trucks loaded with Wagner Group soldiers. The pharmacist had warned her. Making a move on the open road would be too risky, especially for a teenage girl roaming around on her own with a dog. Sobaka would be no match for predators of that caliber. Going through the fields would slow her down, but it was the only way she'd get to Nikolayevka.

Vital hadn't wanted any of the breakfast Ilga had made. Despite her protests, he'd gone straight down to his office in the mansion's basement. His work for the IT Army took up the whole morning. He was taking part in an interference operation this evening, a cyberattack on the computer systems relaying navigation information to a mobile enemy unit. These were missile launchers installed on trucks that had to be put out of commission before their cargo was launched at the targets: residential buildings. Civilian lives were depending on this mission. Putin had stated on television the previous evening that bombing population centers made no sense, his cynicism equaled only by his repeated lies.

From time to time, Vital took a few minutes away from his IT Army work to study a set of high-definition satellite images covering a radius of a hundred kilometers in the area south of Rykove. He'd done some calculations; if Lilya was traveling by bicycle like Veronika had said she was, she had probably reached Chonhar by now, but it would take time for her to find a way across the border. The Crimea checkpoint was a high-risk zone.

If Vital's continued freedom after so many years was due to any one thing, it was his obsession with planning for the unexpected, for the tiniest detail that could delay a mission or cause it to fail. Flat tires were a common occurrence when riding a bicycle on a dirt road, and he didn't think for a minute that Lilya would have ventured onto the main roads.

On foot, her average speed would drop to five kilometers an hour, making it a two- or three-day walk to the Crimean border. Where would she spend the night? Molenska? Nikolayevka?

He glanced at his watch. Veronika should be contacting him soon. In the meantime, he reread the message that had arrived an hour earlier. Just a few words, but they'd made him happy, even if he'd been slightly disappointed that they'd come from Paris and not London.

I'm with you.

It was not Cordelia but Maya who had been the first one to answer his call. Maya was a French luxury real estate agent whose profession supplied her with many contacts abroad and served as the perfect cover for her activist work. A courageous woman who had never obeyed the rules, she had more field experience than any of her Group of 9 colleagues

13

Veronika knocked on the door of the carpenter's workshop. But it was Mrs. Vasylyk who opened it. She stood with her hands on her hips, glaring.

"What do you want now?"

"To speak to your son."

"Stefan is busy."

"My daughter's life is at stake."

"You should have kept a closer eye on her. I'm sorry, but I don't want my son getting mixed up in your troubles."

"I only want to ask him to send a message," Veronika begged.

"Putting my son in danger is out of the question," Mrs. Vasylyk retorted, raising her voice now, as she usually did whenever anyone contradicted her. "None of this is any of my concern."

"It is mine, though," interrupted the carpenter, who had just appeared with his son. "Now, invite the lady inside properly, and make us some coffee while we do what needs to be done."

Mrs. Vasylyk's eyes widened with outrage.

"What did you say to me?" she sputtered.

"Is it all the nastiness that's making you deaf?"

Stefan couldn't believe his ears. His father standing up to his mother! This was the first time he could ever remember it happening, and it was *glorious*.

"I forbid you to speak to me in that tone!" Mrs. Vasylyk shouted.

"I really don't give a damn," the carpenter shrugged. "I'll make the coffee myself, and you can take my place in the workshop, since you know how to do everything."

Veronika edged past Mrs. Vasylyk, keeping her face carefully impassive. No point in adding fuel to the fire. Stefan sat down at the kitchen table. He'd thought to bring his pager downstairs with him.

"Okay, what are we writing to her?" he asked.

"Try to find out where she is. No—first ask if she's all right."

Veronika found she was too anxious to stay still, twisting her fingers together, biting her nails, standing up and then sitting down again.

"Try to convince her to come home," she said. "Tell her . . . you spoke to me . . . that I'd gone to find help . . . and the most important thing, that friends are working to get Valentyn back, and that—"

The carpenter patted her hand sympathetically.

"Probably better not to intrude on their conversation," he said gently.

Stefan certainly thought so. He wanted to go back upstairs to his room, to be alone with Lilya. It was awkward with these adults watching. He was afraid his messages wouldn't sound natural, that Lilya would notice.

"Okay," Veronika agreed. "But come back down as soon as you can. No—take all the time you need. The more you can find out, the better."

The carpenter busied himself making coffee, glancing out the window at his wife, who was hanging laundry on a clothesline in their small back garden. She was muttering to herself, occasionally flinging her arms in the air as if invoking all the gods to bear witness to the indignity she had just been subjected to. Mr. Vasylyk chuckled to himself. Since before the occupation of his city, he'd never been happier. In fact, he had to think back to well before the invasion to remember the last time he'd been quite so content.

Lilya's pager vibrated in her backpack. There were three numbers on the little screen: 390. They were all it took to make her feel less alone. She opened the little notebook Stefan had given her, in which he'd copied out the entire list of codes. She promised herself she'd memorize them all, even though just holding the little book in her hands made her happy.

390 meant *Where are you?*. It took a long time to type out the name of the town where she was, but she managed it. 17-0-11-0-0-4-3-15-51-11115-6.

She'd made a spelling error, but surely he'd figure out what she meant. To tell Stefan that she was all right, she settled for typing *Me OK*. Writing in code meant sacrificing vocabulary and syntax. The important thing was that they understood each other.

123. *I miss you*, he said. 001, she replied. *Yes*: me too. Stefan decided not to say anything about her mother. He knew Lilya wasn't going to abandon her mission, at least not right away. And besides, this was their first exchange. He wanted to keep it just between them.

372. He wanted to know what she was doing. 189, Lilya replied. Continuing on her route. She'd found a dog, she told him, that had stayed with her ever since.

312. She'd write to him again later.

393, Stefan typed. *When?*

5-0-1-12. She'd contact him this evening.

<hr />

"You've got a funny look on your face," Veronika said anxiously, as Stefan came downstairs. "Is something wrong?"

"Everything's fine, I promise. But . . . she's not going to come back without her brother."

"And exactly where is she expecting to find him?"

"Uh, south."

"Did she tell you where she was?" the carpenter put in.

"Not specifically."

"Stefan, I know when you're not telling the truth."

"She's in Novooleksiivka, but she was just about to leave, I swear."

"Did you tell her about our backup?" Veronika asked.

Stefan glanced at his father. He thought carefully before he spoke.

"No. It wasn't a good idea. She would have gotten suspicious. Trust me—I'll tell her tonight. She promised to get in touch again."

"What else did she say?" Veronika asked.

"That she was okay and she had a dog with her."

"A dog? That's all the two of you had to say to each other?"

"That's a lot, using pagers," Stefan said.

"Well, since she's going to be contacting you again, you'll

spend the evening at Mrs. Khodova's house," the carpenter told his son. "Can he stay the night?" he asked Veronika.

"You're sure you don't mind?" she asked.

"I'm not sure of anything anymore, except what's in store for me the minute you leave, and I'd rather spend tonight in my son's bed than on that damn uncomfortable old sofa in the living room."

Valentyn had paused in the doorway, surveying the classroom. The history and geography teacher was settling down at his desk.

"Well, what are you waiting for? Come in; you're going to be late!" he called.

Valentyn stood there, still hesitating. What he was about to do would take an enormous amount of courage, and he knew what it would likely cost him. Guzenko was sitting in the third row. Everything about him was arrogant and menacing, even down to his smile. He was the leader of the mob, a stupid brute who kept his eyes on Valentyn as he finally moved toward his seat. The day's classwork consisted of drawing the new borders of the Russian Federation on a map where Ukraine no longer existed. The professor had pinned an example on the blackboard for the students to copy. Copying was right up Guzenko's alley. He was unscrewing the cap on his bottle of red ink and dipping his pen in when Valentyn stopped next to his desk and stared at him. Guzenko couldn't believe it. He lifted his head slowly and looked back at Valentyn challengingly.

"What's the matter, stupid? Can't remember where your seat is?" he sneered.

His friends snickered. The teacher rapped for order and told

Valentyn to sit down. But Valentyn didn't move. He put a hand on Guzenko's desk and slid it toward the bottle of ink—slowly, deliberately, so the others would see that he wasn't afraid of the repercussions—then, casually, knocked over the bottle, spilling ink all over Guzenko's notebook, where it spread in a tiny crimson lake over the page, streaming down the desk and dripping onto the thug's trousers.

Guzenko leaped up, enraged, and grabbed Valentyn by the neck.

"You're going to pay for that!" he screamed.

Valentyn jerked out of the other boy's grip and hit him in the stomach with an uppercut. The two of them fell to the floor, punching each other furiously.

The teacher ran to separate them. He couldn't believe Valentyn had been the instigator of a fight. He seized him by the earlobe, ordering Guzenko to sit back down by jabbing a finger at his chair. Then he frog-marched Valentyn out the door, still holding his ear.

"I don't know what's gotten into you, but I'm really very disappointed. I'd never have expected behavior like this from you. And to think, I'd brought the book you asked me for! Now, you're going to spend the hour out here, and get ready for a serious punishment if the matron finds you. And I want you to see me after class and explain what led you to act so unacceptably."

The classroom door slammed behind him, leaving Valentyn alone in the deserted hallway. Which was exactly what he'd hoped would happen.

Since his arrival at the boarding school, Valentyn had been busily memorizing everything he could. Yesterday in the tower, he'd learned a lot. At this time of the morning, while the students and teachers were in class and the gardeners busy in the inner courtyard, the matron would be working in her office, and she didn't like to come downstairs. The housekeeping and maintenance staff would be attending to the dormitories, the monitors having their breakfast in the cafeteria, and the cooks at work in the kitchen.

The perfect time for an expedition.

He made his way along the passage with its arches, climbed the low wall, crossed the inner gardens, went through the gate, and found himself in the forbidden wing.

The trap door was much heavier than Valentyn had imagined. Even pulling on the metal ring with all his might, he could only lift it an inch or two. In this position it was impossible to see anything that might lie beneath it. And it took all his remaining strength to lower the door shut again without making any noise. His fingers hurt, his plan had failed, and it galled him to think about what might be in store for him now that he'd dared to humiliate Guzenko. Still, this was no time to stand around feeling sorry for himself. He had to retrace his steps; the monitors would be back on their rounds soon. Hurrying toward the inner garden, he went a bit too fast and tripped over a moss-covered stone, sprawling on the ground between two rosebushes. Thorns scratched his cheek. He put a hand to his stinging face. There was a trickle of blood. Getting back to his feet, he ran for the passage and stopped short. The cafeteria door was open, and two monitors were heading in his direction. He had barely enough time to hide behind a column, holding his breath as their footsteps came closer. He was too far away from his classroom; there was no reasonable explanation he could give.

One of the monitors patted his trouser pockets. He must have forgotten something at the table; his phone, probably. Frowning in annoyance, he and his colleague turned back toward the cafeteria.

"I'd figured on Oleksiivka. She's making faster progress than I expected, if she's already in Novooleksiivka," said Vital. "She must have walked all morning."

"She took her father's bicycle," Veronika reminded him.

"It would be much farther by bicycle. I've studied every possible route, trying to track her."

"In that case, why am I waiting around here doing nothing? Tell me where she is. I have plenty of gasoline, I'll go and get her."

"She's cutting across fields. You'll never find her. You could spend all day and night driving up and down the streets of Sal'Kove and Mykolaïvka and Novi—if she's hiding, you wouldn't have a chance. Not to mention that you might run into an enemy patrol and get yourself arrested. Let her stay out there one more night. I think she'll turn back tomorrow morning."

"You think, or you're sure?"

"I have good reasons for believing it."

"She's got a dog with her, apparently. That's what she told Stefan."

"Ah, well, then at least if anyone threatens her, she'll have some protection. I hope it's a big dog. What else did she tell Stefan?"

"Not very much, just that she was heading south and would give him an update this evening."

"If she keeps making good time, she'll have reached Chonhar by then, and that's where the problems are going to start."

"What problems?" asked Veronika, worriedly.

"She'll never get past the checkpoint. According to my sources, border crossings are almost at a standstill, they're letting very few people through, putting their papers under a magnifying glass. Lilya doesn't live in Crimea and she isn't old enough to be working there. They'll turn her away. So she'll have no choice but to go back home. Call me the minute she's made contact with Stefan, no matter what time it is. Tomorrow, once she's set off back toward home—that'll be the time to go pick her up. Unless you decide to let her find her own way. That's what my parents would have done."

"Your lips to God's ears!" said Veronika fervently.

"You believe in God now? You used to tell me the opposite, back in the day."

"I'm not in the mood to joke, Vital. Thank you again for trying."

"No problem. I'd better get back to work. Speak soon."

After Veronika had hung up, Vital enlarged the map on his screen to study the crossing zone at Chonhar. Walls topped with barbed wire had been erected on either side of the old bridge, and a watchtower built in the middle of the new bridge, the only one still navigable. The satellite photograph also revealed the presence of two checkpoints, one on the Ukrainian side, the other three kilometers farther along, in the occupied Crimea. Between the two was a stretch of saltwater marshland, cut through by the asphalt ribbon of the road running among the bogs and shifting sands.

"What were you thinking, going into a no-man's-land like this?" he murmured.

He checked his watch. It would take Lilya four or five more hours to reach Chonhar. However much he'd tried to reassure her mother, he was far from sanguine himself. The checkpoint was a dangerous place, full of predators: not just Russian soldiers and Wagner Group operatives, but also the muggers and human traffickers who were active day and night in such places. So many vultures for whom a young girl alone would be easy prey.

"Come on, we've got to keep going," Lilya told the dog.

Since they'd begun traveling along the main road again, she'd felt like she was being watched. She was almost positive she'd already seen the pickup truck that had slowed down as it passed them. One of the militiamen aboard had stuck his head out the window and ogled her. She was afraid to keep going; all they'd need to do was circle the block to be on her again. She should veer off in a different direction—but to go where? The deserted streets leading into the village didn't look very promising. If she hadn't stolen two sticky buns, she'd have returned to the shelter of the café. She thought of the pharmacist, but the woman would surely demand an explanation; she hadn't been fooled. She might keep Lilya there and call her mother.

"This isn't good," she said to Sobaka. "My brother needs me. So can you show me the right way, instead of staring at me with your tongue hanging out?"

She'd never know if Sobaka had understood her, or if he'd always intended to take the back lane she hadn't noticed. But now, for once, he took the lead.

She'd gone a hundred paces or so when the squealing of brakes made her turn around. The pickup had stopped at the end of the lane. Lilya's heart started hammering in her chest. No more doubt about it: the militiamen were after her.

The truck roared off down the main road and disappeared. Lilya took to her heels, running as fast as she could, then stopped short and shouted to Sobaka:

"Go back the other way! They're coming around from behind us!"

Bursting out onto the main road, Lilya ran back in the direction they'd come from, Sobaka, with his greater lung power, loping ahead. She could see the train station in the distance. There might be enough people there to dissuade the militiamen from doing anything to her. But there were still four intersections to go, plenty of time for them to catch up. The few pedestrians she met leaped aside to let her by. She passed the café, the pharmacy, the cultural center, gasping for breath, turning left onto Tsentral'na Street, then right on Narodiv Street, then right again on Zaliznychna Street. Just a hundred yards more and she'd reach the footbridge that crossed the railroad tracks.

But the militiamen had anticipated her every move. The pickup truck roared past her, then veered up onto the sidewalk and screeched to a halt, blocking her path. Three men jumped out and seized her by the collar of her jacket. Sobaka growled, baring his teeth. One of the men took out a gun.

"Call him off or I'll shoot," he warned, aiming his weapon at the dog.

"Down, Sobaka!"

The dog subsided, teeth still bared. A whistle-blow sounded and he bolted away.

14

The students were leaving the classroom. Valentyn stood just outside the door, waiting. Guzenko glared at him as he filed past, swearing under his breath that he'd get his revenge when the right moment came.

"Come in," instructed the teacher.

Valentyn obeyed, stepping onto the dais where the teacher's desk sat.

"Your friend told me what happened to you yesterday in the showers. I understand your actions better now, but I'm afraid you've only made the situation worse. And I'm sorry, but you'll have to be penalized for your behavior. You'll stay in study hall this afternoon instead of going out to play in the courtyard. I've given Guzenko the same punishment, which will give the two of you an opportunity to settle your differences amicably."

Valentyn nodded. The thought of Guzenko wanting to settle anything amicably—or even knowing what the word "amicably" meant—would have been almost funny, if he hadn't been the one on the receiving end of the other boy's temper. He was about to depart for his math class when the teacher told him to wait.

"I have something for you," he sighed, opening his satchel.

"Nothing to do with castles, but it's all I could find," he added, handing Valentyn a book about the Russian architect Semenov.

Valentyn couldn't resist flipping through the pages, which were filled with reproductions of plans and photos of Stalinist buildings.

"Haven't you had enough trouble today? Run along, before your math teacher sends you for a late slip!"

Valentyn obeyed, the book under his arm.

A police officer came over to where the four militiamen were holding Lilya.

"What's going on here?" he demanded.

"What business is it of yours?" retorted the group's leader, who had no intention of letting a uniformed cop intimidate him. "She was loitering in the streets, and she ran when she saw us, which probably means she's got something to hide. We're taking her back to HQ for questioning."

"No need. I know why she ran. We've been informed of a theft from a café very nearby, and she fits the description. She's a minor, and this is a police matter."

"That may be, but we're the ones who've arrested her!" protested the militiaman.

"And I thank you for it. A man of your stripe surely has more important things to do than interrogate a little girl."

"What did she steal?" asked another of the men, who was leaning against the pickup truck, nonchalantly chewing a plug of tobacco.

"A sticky bun, or so I'm told. No way to return that to the owner without opening her up."

The lead militiaman looked at his comrades. A sticky-bun thief wasn't much of a catch.

"Okay, she's yours," he said. "Don't forget, we did you a favor today. You owe us one."

"Of course," said the policeman, taking Lilya's arm.

The militiamen climbed back into their truck and roared off. The police officer waited until they were out of sight before releasing his grip.

"What's your name?" he asked.

"Lilya Khodova."

"Got your papers with you?"

She searched in her jacket pocket and handed them to him.

"Just what are you doing here, Lilya Khodova?"

"I came to get some medication for my mother."

"All the way from Rykove?"

"The pharmacist in our town is dead."

"You traveled forty kilometers in one day, to buy medication?"

"I was on my bike. It only took two hours."

"And where's this bike of yours?"

"Near the pharmacy. I got scared and ran when they came after me, there wasn't time to unchain it."

"Okay. Show me the prescription."

"The pharmacist kept it. I'm supposed to come back for the medication in two days."

"Sure you are. And if I take you to see her, she'll confirm everything you've just told me?"

"Yes, because it's the truth."

"The theft in the café, was that you?"

"I was hungry," Lilya explained.

"I'm hungry too, but it hasn't turned me into a thief. You're lucky I happened to be passing by, and even luckier that I have a daughter around your age. Go get your bike, and I don't want to see you hanging around here again, is that clear?"

Lilya, shaken by everything that had happened, thanked the policeman and walked off, head down, wondering where on earth to go next.

In the back of the pickup truck, one of the militiamen was staring at the screen of his phone.

"What are you looking at?" asked the leader.

"That girl. I took a picture of her while you were holding her."

"Yakov!" sighed the man next to him. "She can't be more than thirteen."

"Bit young, but damn cute with those little tits."

"I thought the same thing," agreed the man who was driving, laughing. "You believe that story about the sticky bun?"

"Maybe, maybe not," Yakov said, spitting tobacco juice out the window. "How long do you think that cop'll keep her?"

"Two hours," said the man sitting next to him. "But if we wait outside the jail someone'll spot us."

"Send her photo to HQ so they can circulate it. She'll run into one of our units sooner or later, or an informant. Spread the word that she's ours."

Yakov grinned toothlessly. Like his comrades, he was an ex-convict who'd joined the Wagner Group in exchange for early release and the erasure of his criminal record, an arrangement not to be turned down when you're looking at life in prison for violent crimes.

Ilga knocked on the office door and came in without waiting for a response.

"I'm not hungry, too much to do," Vital muttered, eyes glued to his screens. "Just put everything on the table, I'll eat later. Thanks, Ilga."

The housekeeper didn't answer. Vital looked up. Her hands were empty.

"You have a visitor," she said, then turned to leave.

"What kind of visitor?" he called after her.

"Come out of your lair and see for yourself," she replied, shouting in turn from the bottom of the stairs.

Heaving a sigh, Vital backed up his wheelchair. It took several minutes to secure the chair to the stair lift, and a few more to ascend to the ground floor. But the effort was worth it. He stared, open-mouthed, at the woman who stood in the lounge, an elbow propped casually on the fireplace mantel.

"A flight to Lviv, a train ride—second class, of course—*and* a crappy taxi to get here, you think you could cross the room to say hello to me, or are you just going to sit there staring at me like that?"

"What flight? All the airports are closed. And why are you wearing an aid worker's uniform?"

"Having a major NGO for a client was bound to come in handy one day. Especially when my services are free. They hired me last night, and by a stroke of good luck I was immediately assigned to a humanitarian convoy leaving for Lviv. You know how I got the rest of the way here, and I didn't have time to change my clothes in the crappy taxi. And that's the whole story. Now, are you going to kiss me, or do I need to show you my ID?"

Cordelia was visibly emotional, Vital nearly in tears. She had never left him; he'd felt her presence all over the mansion at every moment. She'd always been right there with him.

He wheeled his chair toward her. She took a step toward him.

They gazed at each other, Cordelia reaching out to touch his cheek. He kissed her, and she kissed him back, lips caressing, tongues tangling passionately.

"Don't make the mistake of thinking that kiss is going to be all it takes to make me forgive you for abandoning me in London," she murmured. She stepped away, turning to look out the window, letting the words hang ominously in the air.

"I didn't abandon you," Vital protested.

"If you say so. But you slipped away like a thief. I thought you had a mistress here or something."

"You're overestimating me. You didn't think that for long, did you?"

"I had to come up with a way of explaining to myself why you'd gone."

"And that was the only one you could think of?"

"No, but it was the one that made me angriest, and I needed to hate you, otherwise it would have been too painful."

"Do you know how many times I've come into this room hoping to hear your voice?"

"How could I possibly know? You told me not to follow you."

"The Russians were bombing Kyiv. I couldn't have borne it if anything happened to you."

"I figured that out in the end," Cordelia said, "but it took some time. Well, to be honest, it was Diego who made me see the truth; you know how persuasive my brother can be."

"What about you? Do you have someone else in London?"

"I fell in love with you because you're so intelligent. Make an effort, would you please?"

She kissed him again. All she wanted now was to take off her uniform, have a hot bath, and slip into something more seductive.

"I remember exactly how full my bottle of bath salts was at

the end of my last trip here. I'll know immediately if another woman's been using them," she murmured in his ear.

Vital grinned like a fool. He loved her ridiculous comments, her mouth, her skin. Her presence.

"I'll come up and join you in the dungeon a little later. You've probably got a ton of work to do," she said on her way out of the room.

"The computer room's in the basement now."

"Of course . . . the bombs . . ." she sighed. "Oh, and on that note—is it true that you've joined the IT Army?"

"How did you know that?"

"Instinct."

Lilya had walked for hours, unable to shake the thought of what might have happened to her that morning without the police officer's intervention. It was a comfort to think that his providential appearance had been due to her own lucky star smiling down on her, or maybe her grandmother watching over her from heaven, and yet she was still afraid. So afraid that she'd vomited, roaming the streets of Novooleksiivka in search of Sobaka. Her backpack slung over her shoulder, she'd gone back to the abandoned house, hoping he might be hiding there. In the end she'd found him behind a supermarket, muzzle buried in a garbage bag. He hadn't wanted to come to her until he'd finished his meal. She'd reproached him for being gross and willing to eat absolutely anything. Then they'd continued on their way together.

She was careful, as they cut through the fields, not to leave the rutted tracks dug by tractors. Wagner's men thought it was fun to plant mines in the fields. They'd double over laughing when they heard one exploding in the distance. Apparently, in the evenings, they drew an *X* on the walls of their headquarters for every Ukrainian they'd killed without even firing a single bullet.

Back bent low, she crept through the tall stalks of wheat that stretched endlessly in all directions, poking her head up from time to time to make sure she was still heading south.

The afternoon was drawing to a close by the time Lilya reached Sal'Kove, the fields ending at the village boundary. Out here, the railroad neared the E105 as both crossed the narrow strip of land skirting Lake Sokolos'ke. Two more kilometers before she and Sobaka could take refuge in the alfalfa fields. Four more hours to Chonhar.

A woman was hanging laundry on a clothesline stretched in front of her house. She waved a greeting to Lilya, beckoning her over. She was a very old lady, with braids that hung halfway down her back beneath her straw hat. Lilya hesitated. Her water bottle was empty and she was desperately thirsty. She looked up at the sky, hoping her lucky star was still with her.

Veronika couldn't stop checking her watch. Maybe the surgeon hadn't truly been joking. One man had fallen off a ladder and broken his leg; two men had been injured in a road accident, one slightly and one seriously; and at three o'clock, a child had been brought in suffering from appendicitis. He was about the same age as Valentyn, and Veronika had to step out of the room for a moment, to gain the composure necessary to treat him. Danylo had taken charge of triage, when he wasn't pushing a gurney or speed-cleaning the ward between cases. The surgeon was in his element, new emergency patients kept streaming through the door, and yet this seemed like the longest day of Veronika's life. In two hours she'd leave her post to pick up Stefan and take him back to her house, even if the sky over Rykove were filled with bombs.

Guzenko, at the back of the room, looked every bit as fierce as the monitor who had ordered Valentyn to sit down—right next to his adversary, so the man could keep them both in his field of vision without having to make an effort. Telling them both to stay quiet, the monitor sat down behind his desk.

Valentyn set his notebook and textbooks on the desk. Undoing the strap that held them together, he opened the architectural manual on Semenov the teacher had given him. Riffling through the pages, he pretended to admire the first skyscrapers of the Soviet era, lingering on the reproductions of building plans.

Guzenko turned his head slowly and watched Valentyn for a few minutes, then elbowed him to get his attention.

"What are you so interested in over there?" he whispered.

Valentyn scribbled that he hoped to be an architect someday.

"Shit, it's true, you're mute too. Nature really gave you a raw deal, eh?"

Guzenko quietly scooted his chair closer to Valentyn's, to get a closer look at his book. He studied the architectural plans in his turn, chewing his pencil, as if in deep thought.

"You're lying," he whispered after a moment. "If you wanted to do that job, you wouldn't be looking at such ugly old buildings."

Because you know so much about architecture? Valentyn wrote.

"My dad was a construction supervisor, so yeah, I know a little bit about that stuff."

Guzenko's use of the past tense hadn't escaped Valentyn. He decided not to ask any more questions.

"What the hell are you up to, Khodova? I've been watching you since you got here. You're different from everyone else, and not just because your beak's nailed shut."

You wouldn't understand.

"You think I'm stupid?"

No, but you think I am.

"You're wrong."

Why were you crying in the dormitory last night?

"You crazy? I've never cried. And if you tell that lie to anyone else, I'll rip you apart!"

Then it must have been someone else. Because there was definitely someone crying in the part of the room where your bed is.

"I bet it was Krivik, that wuss."

I cried too, but no one can hear me.

"You're such a weirdo, Khodova. Why would you admit that to me? Aren't you afraid I'll tell everyone you're a wuss too?"

"Quiet!" the monitor shouted.

They're the only ones I'm afraid of, wrote Valentyn, looking toward the blackboard.

Guzenko suddenly discovered the virtues of writing, when one wanted to talk in study hall without being noticed. He pointed his pencil at Valentyn's notebook, then scribbled below Valentyn's last remark:

Okay, it's true that I'm not happy. So what are you doing with that book? Tell the truth, otherwise I'll think you don't trust me.

After what happened yesterday, you mean?

Guzenko wrote, *Don't push me too far, Khodova. Just tell me what you have in mind.*

Valentyn sat, thinking. He needed a pair of strong arms to open that damn trap door, and his friend from home wasn't brave enough to put everything on the line in a bid for escape. He took his time writing the next sentence, just as a person would speak slowly when they wanted to give weight and importance to every word.

Don't you want to go home?

Guzenko narrowed his eyes, leaning closer to Valentyn, wanting to be sure the other boy wasn't making fun of him.

"Go on," he whispered.

I think I've found a way out.

"Are you sure? How?"

No, I'm not sure yet, that's why I'm studying these plans. I don't care about huge structures, even though they are impressive. It's these other ones I'm interested in.

Valentyn turned pages until he landed on a series of etchings showing buildings once occupied by the czar's armies, which Semenov had renovated.

Don't you think that looks like the boarding school? he wrote.

"It's not from the same period, but yeah, there is something about it. I still don't see where you're going with this," Guzenko whispered.

I found a trap door in the forbidden wing. I think there's a staircase beneath it, which might lead to a cellar and a tunnel that would come out on the other side of the embankment, near the road.

This sounded serious, so serious that Guzenko picked up his pencil again.

I don't know about a tunnel, but there's definitely a cellar, he wrote. *I've seen the gardeners going down through that trap door with big crates of supplies.*

The monitor was watching them. Valentyn hurriedly scratched out his conversation with Guzenko.

Stepping into the woman's house, Lilya wondered if maybe she hadn't come to the end of her adventure. The house was simple, the atmosphere peaceful, the water cool and fresh. And she was so tired.

"Goodness, my dear, you were dying of thirst!" the woman clucked, refilling the glass of water Lilya had drained at a gulp.

Even the dog seemed to appreciate the quiet tranquility of this place, lying down near the woodstove and closing his eyes.

The woman brought a tin of cookies to the table, opening it with difficulty. Lilya gazed at her gnarled, arthritic hands, which reminded her so much of her grandmother's.

"Aging is no picnic, you know. Enjoy your youth while you still have it. I'm curious, what's brought you to Sokolos'ke? We don't get many visitors around here. Whose house are you staying in?"

"I'm just passing through," Lilya said. "The Russians have kidnapped my brother. I'm looking for him."

The old woman patted Lilya's hand, her expression full of sympathy. "I'm sorry. I can imagine how much you must miss him. But surely it's not as terrible as you think. I often see school buses passing by, taking children to a holiday camp in the

Crimea, and they always look so healthy and happy when they come back. The salt marsh air does them a world of good. Sometimes they stop out there on the road near the house to stretch their legs. Although, now that I think of it, it's been quite a while since I saw a bus coming back. Still, my dear, I'm sure there's no reason for you to worry. He must be having a lot of fun there."

"Where is this holiday camp?" Lilya asked feverishly.

"The peninsula on the way to Prydorozhnje. Lovely area. It's a bit complicated to get there at the moment, though; it's not easy to cross the border, because of the terrorists. But that won't be a problem when we're at peace again."

"What terrorists?"

"The ones who are determined to remain Ukrainian at any price. What will it change for people like us to be Russian? Everyone who lives here speaks Russian anyway. People accuse them of the worst things, but they've always been very nice to me. I don't know who's supposed to benefit from all this drama. Becoming part of a powerful country again won't make us any poorer than we already are—in fact, the opposite will probably happen. Now, have another cookie. You're very pretty, but much too thin."

Lilya didn't answer; there was no point. The woman's words had dispelled both her doubts and her fatigue. All she could think about was her brother, alone and afraid in his Crimean prison. She'd already managed half the journey. Now that she knew where Valentyn was being held, all she had to do was figure out a way to rescue him. If she failed, she'd turn herself in to be locked up with him.

She got up from the table, explaining that she had to be on

her way before it got dark. Sobaka was sound asleep. He opened one eye, stretched lazily, and stood.

"Where do you think you're going? I told you—no one can get past Chonhar."

"I'll take my chances. I could use a holiday too," Lilya said from the doorway. "Thanks for the hospitality."

The old woman lifted the filmy curtains at her window to watch Lilya walk away, the dog by her side. It worried her to think of that girl going somewhere that wasn't safe. She wondered if perhaps she shouldn't inform the authorities, just to make sure nothing happened to the young lady, who'd been so polite, and so appreciative of her baking.

As soon as the house had vanished from sight behind a curve in the road, Lilya took a handful of cookies from her pocket and tossed them to Sobaka. She'd swiped them while the old lady was making tea.

Cordelia entered the computer room without knocking, took a seat in the chair next to Vital, and studied what was displayed on his screens.

"You're not supposed to be seeing this," he said calmly.

"Tiny question, just to be absolutely sure: when we stole 350 million dollars from insulin company executives and paid it back to their victims, were we supposed to do that? Or when we stole a bunch of billionaires' personal information and leaked proof of their corruption to the press—were we supposed to do that, or not? And blackmailing a dictator's entourage to free one of his political prisoners—was that something we were supposed to do? Everything we've done since we started acting outside the confines of international law—it's been justified, right? Now, tell me what all this is about."

"It's a military operation," Vital answered, without batting an eyelash at her recitation. "We're interfering with the guidance systems of enemy missile launchers. Sometimes we can redirect the missiles toward their own tanks."

"What a fabulous idea!" Cordelia exclaimed gleefully. "That's some pretty high-level madness . . . is it possible I'm sleeping with an IT Army bigwig without knowing it?"

"Can you be serious for *two* minutes, please?"

"With you? Not until it's absolutely necessary, my darling, otherwise we're going to get bored very quickly. Missile launchers! Let me help, Vital! *Please.*"

Cordelia put her bag down in front of Vital.

"Did you bring me any After Eights?"

She rolled her eyes and took out a thick file.

"History of the camp system for children, complete methodology, how and why they transport them to Russia or its occupied territories. Reeducation, academic instruction, and military training programs. You'll also find a list of the government officials involved in this child-trafficking scheme, and a list of occupying authority personnel aligned with Russia. Names and photos. And, last but not least, the locations of the reeducation centers."

"How did you get your hands on this?"

"High-level madness," she said, mysteriously.

Stefan set his overnight bag down at the foot of the stairs and looked at Lilya's mother.

"Do you know where the bedroom is?"

"No, ma'am. We've never spent time anywhere but the living room."

"Call me Veronika, it'll be easier. Upstairs, first door on the right. You can take Valentyn's bed."

"I'll be fine on the sofa, if that's okay with you."

"You're right—I haven't been able to set foot in their room since . . . anyway, go and sit down at the kitchen table. I'll make us some dinner."

"Can I help?"

"Can you cook?"

"I can make an omelet, if that sounds okay?"

"There are eggs in the fridge," she said wearily.

She showed him where the pots and pans were and set two places at the table while he busied himself at the stove. Lilya's absence felt more glaring to him, here at her house. He brought the eggs to the table, sat down across from Veronika, and waited for her to serve herself.

Neither of them spoke at first, their eyes glued to the pager sitting on the waxed tablecloth. Veronika had opened a bottle of wine. She filled her glass, then looked at Stefan.

"It isn't very good, but if you want a bit I won't say anything, I promise."

He agreed unhesitatingly. The liquor his father distilled was much stronger.

"Talk to me about her," Veronika entreated. "Tell me what her days at school are like. Does she have a lot of friends? She's so secretive with me."

"Yeah, she's really popular, to say the least."

"Really?"

"Yeah, really."

"Well, that's wonderful. I'm so glad to hear it."
The pager vibrated. They held their breath. Stefan seized it.
372. *What are you doing?* Lilya had asked.
"She's all right," murmured Veronika.
78 01173. *Having dinner,* Stefan replied.
7 61 7612. She was hungry.

They wrote as fast as they could punch in the codes. She told him about her trip. 440: she was tired. She described the people she'd met on her journey, without going into too much detail. Every time Veronika intervened to suggest a question, Stefan felt like he was betraying Lilya. Sometimes he didn't code them in. And when Lilya mentioned the mercenaries who had tried to capture her, he decided not to tell Veronika, but furiously typed 404. *Drop this whole thing.* 12317123. *Come back.* And was immediately angry at himself for saying it.

Quickly he changed tack, asking her what her next stop would be and when she hoped to get there, begging her not to take any unnecessary risks. His fingers froze at the news that she knew exactly where her brother was, and was now working on a plan to free him. She had to find shelter before nightfall. The world must be turning backward, she said; the farther south she traveled, the colder it got. She promised to contact him again tomorrow when she woke up, wished him good night, typed 143, and then erased it before pressing the "send" button. She'd tell him in person when she got home. If she still felt that way.

". . . and that's everything she said," Veronika finished.

Vital's fingers flew across his keyboard, bringing a satellite photo of the area around Prydorozhnje up on the screen.

"He's being held in former military barracks converted to a holiday camp. Even if I enlarge the image it's impossible to tell what's going on because of the way the complex is built; all I can see is the outer courtyard. Give me a few hours to find some older pictures, they should give us some information on the activities around the camp."

"And Lilya?"

"She'll probably reach Chonhar by dark. Two hours or so."

"I'm getting in my car and going to find her."

"At night, with all the patrols on the road? That's madness."

"She's my daughter."

"She's going to need her mother more than ever when she gets home. Don't take pointless risks, Veronika. I'm begging you to stay there and let me work."

Veronika hung up. Vital had taken the call right there in the dungeon; Cordelia had heard everything.

"Lilya will try absolutely anything to get into Crimea," Vital said.

"Of course she will; it's to save her brother! I'd do the same for Diego."

"I don't doubt it. And that's exactly what worries me."

"Unless her mother can get her back before it's too late," Cordelia added.

"What would you do, if you were in my place?" Vital asked.

"First of all, I'm pretty sure we *are* in the same place. And secondly, you already know my answer to that question."

Vital looked at Cordelia for a long moment. She smiled at him impishly.

"All right," he sighed at last. "We'll help her. But her mother can never know."

"Exactly how are you planning to help Lilya from a few thousand kilometers away?"

"I'll contact some Ukrainian resistance operatives in that part of Crimea. If Lilya does manage to get through, they'll pick her up."

"What if she doesn't get through?"

"We'll make sure that isn't the case."

It had been two hours since her exchange with Stefan. Sitting on a low wall, Lilya watched the crowd that stretched the whole three kilometers from the Chonhar exit to the border checkpoint. Men with a suitcase in each hand, women with a child in their arms and one or two more by the hand; elderly people leaning on canes. Grimy and exhausted, they'd been waiting for hours, sometimes whole days, at the checkpoint, where they were let through one by one. Whenever the crowd milled too close to the fence, a soldier fired shots into the air.

She could slip into the crowd, exchange complicit glances with a sympathetic mother and stick close to her, hoping she'd play along. She wouldn't be the first minor traveling with adults who weren't her parents. But she couldn't reconcile herself to the idea of joining the herd. These people were being treated like livestock. Even Sobaka seemed to have more pride.

The dog hopped up onto the wall beside Lilya, sniffing the air and looking toward the salt marsh.

"I wouldn't go that way if I were you."

Lilya jumped. The craggy-featured man who had made the remark wore an old sailor's overcoat, a linen shirt, canvas trousers, and battered, much-worn shoes. Beneath bushy eyebrows as white as his beard, his eyes were deeply melancholy. Sobaka didn't seem wary of him; maybe he'd come across him before as he roamed the streets. Maybe the dog had even ventured as far as Chonhar before.

"Pet him, otherwise he'll think you don't like him," Lilya told the man.

"My name's Dmitri," he said, patting Sobaka's head gently. "It's full of mines," he explained, motioning with his head toward the salt marsh. "We can't even dock our rowboats there anymore, there are so many. Your dog isn't heavy enough to set them off, but you are."

"He's much bigger than me," Lilya protested.

"Maybe, but his weight is distributed across four paws, and you only have two feet. Never seen a dog get blown up except by a trip wire, but men and women, yes—and I can assure you it's not pretty."

Dmitri's mouth twisted as he said this.

"Hell of a storm last night," he continued. "I hope you were somewhere dry."

Lilya nodded, not yet certain whether she wanted to engage in conversation with this man.

"If you're hoping to get into Crimea, it's too late for any more crossings today. You'll have to sleep on the bridge, but the wind off the water at night is damn cold."

Lilya didn't answer.

"You'll see a little blue house on the edge of the salt marsh. There's a rowboat lying on its side out in front. You can come and knock if you don't know where else to go. I won't tell anyone."

"Why?" Lilya asked.

"I haven't asked you any questions. Don't you ask me any

either. Because it's the done thing, I guess. Don't hang around here too long, and keep a discreet eye on the watchtower at the end of the bridge. The fellows posted up there are watching everything, and they've got good binoculars."

The old fisherman walked off along the causeway toward his house. Once inside, he took his cell phone from his jacket pocket.

"Yeah, I've seen her. She took the bait. An hour from now it'll be too cold to stay outside and she'll turn up here."

"Don't let her leave under any circumstances. You'll receive further instructions shortly. No one must lay a hand on her until everything's in place."

"Got it, don't worry. I can keep her here as long as I need to."

"Thank you for your assistance. You'll be rewarded for it," promised the voice on the other end of the line.

15

The whole band of them—Andriy, Romanyuk, Krivik, and Guzenko, in full tough-guy mode—had been waiting for him outside the shower room. Valentyn was under no illusions. Their hour in detention might have brought them closer, but Guzenko wasn't going to lose face in front of the others. The two of them had reached an agreement in study hall, and Guzenko had promised the blows wouldn't be as hard as the day before. This hadn't turned out to be entirely true in practice, however, and Valentyn's ribs were damn sore. Little though the bullying mattered to him, the memories of what he'd endured at the boarding school would remain buried forever among the secrets of his childhood.

His friend had looked miserable at dinner, and all the children in the cafeteria were feeling that vague sense of anxiety that creeps up on you as night approaches. Valentyn had left the room without finishing his meal.

The inner courtyard was cloaked in darkness, a few fireflies glowing among the begonias. Valentyn had made his way along the passage, determined that this would be the night he escaped.

He'd already been in bed when the rest of the students had

streamed into the dormitory. Guzenko, passing his bed surrounded by his entourage, hadn't even glanced at him.

"I'll keep talking to them, I swear," his friend had murmured from the next bed. "They'll get tired of bullying you, I promise."

Valentyn had smiled at him, then turned over to cry silently, his face buried in the pillow.

As it turned out, Valentyn wasn't the only one crying. Veronika stood next to her car in the clinic parking lot, in tears. After trying to start the engine a dozen times, she'd discovered that the gas cap was missing. Someone had siphoned every drop of fuel.

She slid into the driver's seat and slammed her fists on the steering wheel again and again, weeping with rage.

"And what's the matter with you?"

It was Danylo, sitting on a bench not far away, smoking a cigarette.

Veronika looked at him, then burst into fresh tears. Danylo left his bench and came to sit in the passenger seat.

"And what if I told you there's a big can of gasoline in the basement, would that make you feel better? And even if it's supposed to be reserved for the clinic's generator, I can spare a few liters."

"That's very generous, but it's too late now. By the time I get to Chonhar she'll have hidden somewhere for the night, I'll never find her."

"That's why you wanted to risk driving at night? To go and find your girl?"

"You and I have done worse together, haven't we?"

"That's true, but still, you shouldn't make a habit of it. And tomorrow morning, will she still be hiding?" Danylo asked.

Veronika dashed away her tears with the back of her hand, her face regaining some of its color.

"And here's my plan to put a spring back in your step: while you get some sleep, I'll put some fuel in the tank and put on a lockable gas gap, which you should have done ages ago, by the way; you know people are ready to beat each other to a pulp over a liter of gasoline these days. And if you leave at dawn, you'll get there just as your daughter is poking her head up. And Chonhar isn't very big, so you'll surely find her. And you'll both be home by lunchtime."

Veronika took Danylo's face in her hands and kissed him soundly on both cheeks. He was surprised, but not displeased.

"And I'll say again that my plan includes you getting some sleep, so go home, and I'll take care of the rest."

Lilya hovered uncertainly in the doorway. Dmitri held up his calloused hands.

"I can't even repair my fishing nets anymore, you see. Too old to be a threat. Come in and get warm, and close that door. The wind's freezing tonight."

The fisherman's cottage was modest, its wooden floor gleaming with age, and despite a slight scent of fish, its interior was much better-kept than the salt- and wind-lashed facade would suggest. The furniture was simple: a small table, two chairs, and a well-used armchair near the woodstove. In the back of the room, a sink and an old stove served as the kitchen, and a steep, ladder-like staircase led up to a loft where Lilya could see a mattress.

"Can I stay here for a little while?" she asked, eyeing the flames dancing behind the door of the woodstove.

"As long as you want. You hungry?"

She shrugged.

"I've got soup with a nice red mullet and some potatoes. You'll like it."

Lilya glanced at Sobaka, sitting at her feet.

"You can share it with him, I don't mind. I used to have a dog myself. Bit smaller than that one, but he was a very good fishing companion. Used to love to sit in the prow of my boat when I fished, nose in the wind. Blocked my view, of course. The other fellows used to tease me about it, they'd say all I had to do was set a course for his back to find the shore."

"Have you always lived here?"

"I don't want to talk about myself. My life hasn't been a very pretty story. But that doesn't mean you can't tell me why you're loitering around these parts with your dog."

Dmitri moved toward the stove, leaning over to smell the steam rising from a pot, then filled two shallow bowls with soup, then took a slightly rusted enamel dish from a cupboard and filled that with soup too, smiling. He served Sobaka first, then put the bowls down on the table.

"You aren't very chatty," he observed a few minutes later, watching Lilya devour her meal hungrily.

She looked at him for a moment, sizing him up.

"I need to get into Crimea," she said at last.

"Do you have family there?"

"My brother."

"And your parents?"

"We live in Rykove."

"Never been there," said the fisherman. "Never did much wandering on land, in fact, but at sea? Now *there* I've sailed far and wide."

"What do you mean, far? The Sea of Azov isn't much bigger than a lake," Lilya scoffed.

Her spoon scraped the bottom of her bowl. Dmitri took it from her, went to the stove, and refilled it.

"Nah, but I used to have a little trawler. We'd sail through the Kerch Strait to do some poaching in Turkish waters. Best not to get caught doing that, I can assure you. It's a journey of over three hundred nautical miles each way, hundred more if you sail along the coastline. We'd be at sea two full weeks. If you're from Rykove, what's your brother doing in Crimea?"

"That's the problem," Lilya said. "What side are you on?"

"I don't understand the question, kiddo."

"I'm not a kid, and you know exactly what I mean."

"In that case, start by lowering your voice," Dmitri admonished her quietly. "There aren't too many people around here who think the way I do."

"And just what 'way' do you think?"

"Who says I can trust you?"

"Do I look like a spy?" Lilya demanded. "Two seconds ago you were calling me 'kiddo.'"

The fisherman scratched his head. "You've got good timing, I'll say that. Let's say I'm not exactly fond of the people turning the marshes into minefields, how's that for an answer?"

The sound of their murmured conversation had lulled Sobaka into sleepiness. He yawned and stretched out at Lilya's feet. His tranquility made her feel more confident.

"Valentyn's there because they kidnapped him."

"The militiamen?"

"No. The Russians."

"And you want to bring him home?"

"Yes."

"You're lucky."

"Lucky? That the Russians took my brother?"

"That you have someone in your life to give you courage."

Dmitri rose to clear the table. Lilya brought their plates to the sink. There was only a bar of soap on the ledge. She scraped off a few shavings with her fingernails and swished them in the water to make suds. The fisherman sat down in his armchair by the stove. He'd lived alone for a long time, and the sight of Lilya washing dishes was soothing.

After a while he stood and fetched a towel from the cupboard, then pointed Lilya toward the bathroom door.

"You look even more tired than your dog. I usually spend the night in my chair, so why don't you sleep in the loft? You can rest easy; if I were going to hurt you, I'd have done it long before now."

Cordelia had printed out some thirty photos and arranged them on the big table in the dungeon. All were marked with the date and time when they'd been taken.

"Look," she said, having separated out six of them. "Tuesdays and Thursdays between two o'clock and five o'clock, they have a group outing."

Vital brought the photos up on his screen and zoomed in as close as possible.

"Are they on bicycles?"

"Looks like it," Cordelia said. "Thirty kids, and I only see three adults with them. One in front, one in the middle, and one bringing up the rear."

"Three successive outings. Ninety kids. The resistance could get involved, if they could be sure of knowing which one is Valentyn."

"I know one person who wouldn't have a problem with that."

"When do they have these trips?"

"The next one's tomorrow."

"Too soon to do anything. Lilya's not in position yet."

"But you've got a plan to help her get across the border tomorrow morning, right?"

"I have a military occupation to deal with first."

"You could let me help you. Things would go more quickly with the two of us working together."

"Do you still not understand the meaning of 'military operation'?"

"Of course I do. Now, are you going to give me the codes?"

Vital sighed. He was out of arguments. She'd never leave him to work alone, and he had neither the courage nor the desire to ask her to leave the dungeon.

Cordelia went to work the moment Vital had authorized access to his console. Outsmarting firewalls and breaking into enemy servers without triggering their defenses was unspeakably exciting. She'd been dreaming of a big job like this for months. The attacks she initiated for the security agency that employed her were only inconsequential simulations, but that wasn't the case tonight, and she couldn't imagine anything more romantic than hacking with Vital, just the two of them.

Like a four-handed piano concerto played by two virtuosos, the lines of code scrolled across the screen, the tension mounting with each phase of the breach. Cordelia paused from time to time to crack her knuckles, then typed even faster than before.

An hour of playing cat and mouse later, they'd reached the heart of the system and reprogrammed the coordinates of its targets. The job done, Vital sat back and gazed at his screen in silence.

"What now?" Cordelia asked.

"Nothing. We'll see if it worked once they launch the missiles." She stared at him. "Seriously? That's all?"

"What were you expecting? That we'd make them blow themselves up?"

"I wouldn't have minded something like that at all, actually. And don't tell me it's impossible."

"That would be against our code of conduct, and they'd suspect something right away. The beauty of what we've accomplished tonight is that every time their missiles miss their targets, they'll think their equipment is defective. That'll demoralize them *and* make them second-guess their chain of command. Two birds with one stone, see?"

"Want to come up and have a smoke with me in the garden? A breath of fresh air would do us both good."

"Oh, because smoking a cigarette means getting fresh air?"

Vital promised Cordelia he'd follow her as soon as he could attach his wheelchair to the stair lift.

The dormitory had been shrouded in darkness for hours. Valentyn listened to the other children breathing. Everything was quiet tonight; he couldn't hear anyone crying. His eyes had grown used to the lack of light. His friend was sleeping peacefully. Noiselessly, Valentyn got out of bed and slipped out of his pajamas, then put on the clothes he'd hidden under his pillow and tiptoed toward Guzenko. But the other boy turned over when Valentyn tapped him softly on the shoulder, whispering:

"Did you really think I was coming with you? You really are stupid. Go away and let me sleep."

Valentyn stood frozen for a moment, fists clenched, his hopes evaporating. He'd never be able to lift the trap door by himself. His eyes filled with tears.

He retrieved the pajamas he had stuffed beneath his bed, dark thoughts running through his mind when his fingers brushed the knife he'd stolen from the cafeteria.

A soft voice made him jump.

"Ready to go?" whispered his friend, fully dressed.

Lilya jumped when a hand touched her lower leg. Dmitri's head appeared at the top of the ladder. He gave her an odd look.

"Get up and join me downstairs."

She had no idea what time it was, much less what the fisherman's intentions might be. But she descended the ladder, because she had no choice. Dmitri had put on his overcoat and was waiting, leaning against the doorframe, lost in thought. Sobaka seemed thrilled by the idea of going outside. Lilya was slightly reassured by the sight of his wagging tail. He was her staunchest ally.

Dmitri tossed her an old cable-knit sweater and a scarf.

"Put those on. The wind's freezing out there."

"What are we going to do?"

"You still want to go to Crimea? Well, follow me and don't say anything."

He opened the door and paused, his eyes on Sobaka.

"You can't bring him. It's too dangerous."

"Forget it. I don't go anywhere without him. Otherwise, we're both out of here. Leave us alone."

Dmitri sighed. "Are you afraid of me? Is that it?"

"I'm afraid, period. I'm staying with my dog."

"There's no way. He'll bark."

"Sobaka, come here!" Lilya called. The dog got between them in a single bound, growling at Dmitri.

"Calm him down!" the fisherman ordered, gritting his teeth. "What do you think's going to happen? If I'd wanted to get rid of him, all I'd have had to do was put some rat poison in his bowl."

"I swear he's not going to hurt you."

"Fine, if it means that much to you. But you'll understand when we get out there." Dmitri stalked out the door.

Lilya pulled the sweater over her head, shoving up the sleeves, which were far too long. She knotted the scarf around her neck, grabbed her backpack, and followed Dmitri outside, holding Sobaka by the collar.

The salt marsh was cloaked in fog.

"Where are you taking me?" Lilya asked as they set off.

"We'll go along the bank. You need to walk in my footsteps because of the mines, and once we're out there, don't say another word, understood?"

Everything was dark and silent. Lilya was angry with herself for getting into this situation. She shouldn't have listened to the old fisherman when he approached her near the checkpoint, let alone given in to the temptation of getting warm in his cottage. He was right about the cold that settled over the marshes at night—she'd have had a hard time if she'd tried to sleep on the bridge—but nothing could be worse than finding herself at this man's mercy.

She considered simply running away with Sobaka as fast as

she could. Getting away from Dmitri would be easy, but how far would they get before she set off a land mine, and even if he'd been lying about the mines, where would she go? It was a long time yet to sunrise, and the countryside was deserted.

Heart pounding, she hopped over two tree trunks felled by lightning. The narrow path rose steeply upward. Dmitri turned to make sure she was still with him, then pointed in the direction they would take.

Eventually they neared a road. He gestured for her to crouch down as two trucks sped past.

"Now we'll cross and go down the other side of the bank. It's not much farther now," he said quietly.

"Where are you taking me?" Lilya asked again.

"Talk is for later. We've got to hurry now or you'll be too late."

Dmitri was off again, moving quickly. Halfway across the road, Lilya hesitated. If she were going to make a break for it, it was now or never. There were no mines buried beneath the asphalt. But Sobaka was already trotting down the opposite bank behind the fisherman.

Crossing a patch of wasteland, Lilya saw that they were approaching a stretch of railways, the tracks forking into multiple lines and merging together a bit farther on.

"This is the switchyard. The freight train parked on the middle track leaves in less than fifteen minutes. They've just finished loading it; the fellows are exhausted and they're more interested in their break than standing around in the cold keeping an eye on things. I'll help you climb into the last car. They're transporting fish in that one, so I'll warn you, it smells pretty strong in there, but it'll keep the dogs at the border from sniffing you out."

"Where is this train going?"

"You'll get off at Dzhankoi, forty kilometers away. It's on the other side of the border. You still want to go Crimea?"

Lilya looked at Sobaka, who seemed to be waiting for instructions.

"Listen carefully," Dmitri said. "The first stop's going to be at Solone Ozero. The Russians will check every car to make sure no one's hiding inside."

"With dogs?"

"Yes. Highly trained dogs. Stay hidden behind the crates of smoked fish, they smell the strongest, and the dogs won't be able to tell you're there. Now you understand why you can't take Sobaka with you. He'll bark and they'll arrest you."

"But I can't abandon him . . ."

"I'll keep him with me. I've got nothing against the thought of a new companion. And when you come back with your brother, you can always pick him up; you know where I live. Now, come on, and don't make any noise."

The trio picked their way carefully between two trains, one of which was set to leave another night. Gravel crunched beneath Lilya's feet, and Dmitri showed her how to walk along the sleepers. In the distance he could see the red dots of lit cigarettes glowing in the darkness: five railroad workers sitting on bumpers, smoking and talking.

"Good, they're occupied," he murmured, heading for the last car.

Carefully, Dmitri lifted the latch and eased open the sliding door just enough for Lilya to slip inside.

She climbed up and sat on the edge. Sobaka rose up on his hind legs, waiting for her to make room for him to jump up too.

"I can't take you with me, boy," she whispered. "Please, don't run off. Stay with him. I'll be back, I promise."

Sobaka didn't seem pleased by her words. He whined softly.

"Shh!" Dmitri hissed.

The fisherman gave Lilya a pointed look. This was her cue to retreat into the car.

"Hide in the back and remember to get off at the second stop. And make sure not to fall asleep; the cold will make you drowsy. The Dzhankoi freight yard is on the outskirts of the town. The Russians won't do an inspection, but they'll unload part of the cargo, so get off the tracks as fast as you can. As soon as you open that door, you jump out and *run*."

Lilya glanced one last time at her dog, then at Dmitri, who answered with a wink. Then the door slid shut, plunging her into darkness.

"Come on now, let's go," Dmitri said to Sobaka, who was still waiting next to the train car.

The dog gave itself a shake, then followed him.

At the top of the slope, the old fisherman paused to watch the train chugging away. He took his phone out of his coat pocket and dialed a number.

"In the last car. She's all yours; all you have to do is pick her up," he said, then hung up.

He looked down at Sobaka.

"Okay, mutt. Let's get home and go back to bed."

16

They shut the dormitory door behind them as soundlessly as they'd opened it. Valentyn's pockets were full of cookies he'd saved from the last few days' worth of afternoon snacks. The hall was dim, lit only by a single lamp, but it was enough light to show them which direction to take. Valentyn gestured to his friend that the coast was clear, and the two boys tiptoed down the stairs, opened another door, and emerged into the passage.

The wind was glacial. Valentyn's friend shivered and rubbed his arms, his teeth chattering. The trap door was on the other side of the garden. He hopped over the low wall first, then it was Valentyn's turn. They were creeping from hedge to hedge when Valentyn stopped abruptly and pointed at the illuminated window at the top of the tower. The light went out. Clearly the matron had worked late tonight. Valentyn recalled that it had taken him no more than a couple of minutes to descend the stairs when she had dismissed him from her office. He pushed his friend behind a shrub, then hunkered down next to him. Hardly had they done this when the beam of a flashlight swept the walls of the forbidden gallery, then crisscrossed the garden. The boys held their breath and, even in this freezing air, his friend felt sweat trickling down his back. The shadow holding the flashlight surely belonged to one of the monitors; what the man was doing in the matron's office at this time of night was a mystery Valentyn wouldn't need to solve, he told himself, because by tomorrow he'd be far away from here.

The monitor unlocked the gate, closing it behind him immediately, and continued on his rounds. Valentyn hoped he wasn't on his way to inspect the dormitories; the rolled-up pajamas he'd arranged beneath his covers wouldn't fool anyone, especially if Guzenko woke up and let the cat out of the bag. There wasn't a moment to lose. Once calm had been restored, Valentyn rose, crossed the garden, darted along the low wall, and jumped over it. His friend followed on his heels, scared to death.

Valentyn counted the columns, stopping at the fourth. There was the dark spot on the ground: the trap door. The boys grasped the ring and pulled on it together with all their strength. The door resisted, its hinges making a horrible squealing sound in the quiet night. But after two tries, the opening grew larger. Valentyn's friend smiled. "It's so rusted it'll stay open by itself," he murmured.

It was true. The hinges were so stiff that, though they made the trap door hard to manage, they also kept it from falling shut again under its own weight. Valentyn hadn't expected this. There was no ring on the underside of the door, no way to close it again once they'd slipped through. The monitor would find it open when he made his next circuit. Valentyn's friend watched him study the door, the enormity of the problem gradually dawning on him.

"Listen," he whispered. "Don't be mad at me, but I can't go down there, it's too dark. I already knew that when I came with you, and I also knew that wimp Guzenko would chicken out. He's a coward, even more scared than I was when the Russians trapped me in the bathroom. He's nothing without his three goons, and if you ask me, he's not much of a big deal even when they're around. I'll close the trap door behind you—we can manage it. Just give me a hand by pulling on the edge from below, and when you have to bring your fingers inside I'll push down on it as hard as I can. I'm strong enough. I know it."

Valentyn shook his head furiously, appalled at the thought of his friend sacrificing himself, but the other boy smiled with unexpected fondness.

"Come on, don't make that face. Consider us even. When you get home, tell my parents I'm fine, and that I'm thinking about them a lot, and please tell them it's not so bad here, so they won't worry too much. I'll find my own way out when the time is right. Well, I'm not positive about that part, but it'll be something for me to think about once you're gone. You have to make it out, okay? Then you'll be a hero, and I will too, for being your accomplice in the escape. Promise me, okay?"

Valentyn took his notebook and ballpoint pen out of his pocket and wrote, his hand trembling, that his friend had to come with him, that he'd guide him in the dark, that the tunnel couldn't be very long. That a few moments of fear were worth it to gain their freedom. That once they were on the other side of the road, they could cut through the fields and reach the woods in two hours. He'd done the calculations, he wrote. Two days' walk and they'd be home.

"You and your notebook . . . how am I supposed to read that in the dark? Go on, I need to get back to the dormitory soon. Don't forget the message for my parents."

His friend pushed down on the trap door with both hands.

The hinges shrieked. The line of light grew thinner and went out, leaving Valentyn alone in the darkness.

He made his way carefully down the stairs, hand flat against the wall for guidance, saltpeter rubbing off on his palm. It was less cold down here than it was outside, but the air was painfully damp, the ground so moist that it felt like he was walking in mud.

Valentyn had expected his eyes to adjust to the darkness, but he couldn't see anything at all. So he tried to picture what the place looked like, to keep his mind off the two rats that had just brushed his leg before skittering off.

In the book about the work of the architect Semenov, buildings always included cellars that, according to the plans, measured between twenty and one hundred yards long, and, since Semenov had no desire to complicate his life by drawing parts of his buildings hardly anyone ever visited, these cellars were always square or rectangular. Large structures would have several cellars in a row, separated by retaining vaults where the walls became narrower.

The boarding school wasn't exactly huge, and Valentyn had found only one access point, so he figured there was only a single cellar, fifty yards long—or the distance between the middle of the forbidden wing and the wall overlooking the outer courtyard. A calculation that would have left that jerk Guzenko speechless.

Still keeping to the wall, Valentyn decided to go in the same direction the rats had taken—they'd probably gone toward the tunnel's entrance, after all. To give himself courage, he pictured Lilya sitting on his bed, telling him her horror stories. None of them would ever be able to hold a candle to what he was going through right now.

When the wall rounded out before turning sharply right, Valentyn, caught off guard, felt a rush of icy terror.

He could hear rats again, but this time the sounds were different. Little splashes, like they were running through puddles. He strained his ears. The splashes grew closer together, as if the rodents were running through a stream of water. Maybe they weren't afraid of him—maybe they were even trying to show him the way out.

He had nothing left to lose, so he abandoned the wall, taking a step away from it—which produced the same splashing sound. He remembered another interesting detail from the Semenov book, about the drainage of wastewater. Runoff from the garden was now flowing beneath his feet, which explained the saltpeter on the walls and the dampness of the air. Wastewater always flows toward the outside. All he had to do was follow the stream.

Valentyn's fear had evaporated. He made his way forward, guiding himself by ear in the darkness. He was certain he'd passed beyond the enclosure perimeter a long time ago, certain the tunnel had been running alongside the road since it veered right.

All at once there was a faint gleam of light in the distance, a hint of illumination that grew brighter as he neared it. He could even make out the walls now. This wasn't a tunnel, as he'd thought; it was a sewer channel. And it occurred to him, as he caught a glimpse of starry sky, that he'd never pulled off a more impressive stunt in his life.

He broke into a sprint—and stopped short as he came up against a grate. The gaps between its bars were wide enough to let the stream of wastewater through, but not a little boy.

Valentyn pressed his face to the bars. The countryside beyond was washed in moonlight. He could see himself climbing the little hill, crossing the street, running through the fields. Within an hour he could have made it past the big farm he'd seen from the car. But there was nothing left to hope for now. The air was freezing again, and freedom seemed beyond reach.

He should turn around now. Cross the garden and get back to his bed before sunrise and the matron's arrival in the dormitory...

But how? He'd never be able to lift the trap door without his friend's help.

Valentyn sat down next to the grate. He watched the water flow past. After a moment he reached into his pocket for a cookie and took a bite.

The train had been moving at a snail's pace since leaving the switchyard, and Lilya was tossed around like a ragdoll every time it bumped past another set of track switches, the wheels letting out a metallic screech. The train car was old and rusty, moonlight streaming through holes in the walls and making faint circles of light on the crates. Her eyes had finally adjusted to the darkness, but the smell of fish was making her nauseous. The train kept speeding up and slowing down, as if the engineer couldn't settle on a cruising speed.

The train snaked along, the cars swayed, and Lilya held on as best she could. She put her eye to one of the holes in the wall and looked outside. She could see the salt marsh flashing past, followed abruptly by the framework of an old bridge. Then the train was on the bridge's decking, the steel posts going past one by one. Lilya counted eight of them, and when the last one had vanished, she clenched her fists in triumph. She was in Crimea.

Now the railroad track was running in a clean, straight line through open countryside, its speed slow and smooth. The swaying of the car lulled her. Despite the fisherman's warning, her eyelids grew heavy in the traitorous cold.

Abruptly, Lilya jerked awake, the sound of dogs barking jolting her from her torpor. The train had reached Solone Ozero station. She darted to the back of the wagon, crouched behind a pile of polystyrene foam crates, and held her breath. The lock clicked open ominously; the door slid open. A soldier gave a snort of disgust and immediately closed it again. His footsteps receded along the platform. A whistle blew, and the car swayed into motion again.

Lilya emerged from her hiding place and sat down on a crate, shivering. She propped herself against the wall, pillowing her head on the overlong sleeves of her sweater, her eyes drifting shut again. They'd reach Dzhankoi soon.

In her nightmare, Valentyn was stretched out on the sofa, reading a book. He kept glancing at her out of the corner of his eye, slyly, chewing a licorice candy with his mouth open to annoy her. Her mother was scouring a casserole dish; the scraping of the steel wool against the enameled cast iron sent shivers down her spine. How was she supposed to concentrate on her homework with all this racket? She'd had enough; no one respected her at all in this house. She was sure her mother was scrubbing so hard on purpose. And what the hell was Dmitri doing here, and why wasn't her mother paying any attention to him? The old sailor came toward her, his lips moving. His toothless mouth was a terrifying sight as he bent over her homework. Then he took the pen from her hands and wrote a zero in red ink on the paper. The house grew darker, the light fading. Valentyn had vanished from the sofa, and her mother was gone too. The fisherman was standing by the door.

I told you not to fall asleep, idiot. You really are stupid; you're going to ruin everything . . .

And he disappeared into the blizzard.

Lilya was numb with cold, her limbs heavy. She was suffocating. Dmitri had showed her the way; she had to get to the door, get outside, where there was oxygen and light. She cried out, taking in a huge gulp of air.

Noise. Voices. Something was going on at the front of the train. The car wasn't moving. With icy hands, she rubbed cheeks and shoulders she could hardly feel, her fingers stiff and swollen.

It took a superhuman effort to lift the metal latch. The door of the train car slid slowly aside. Lilya sat down on the edge, put the strap of her bag around her neck, and jumped. She stayed for a moment, crouched on the gravel, pulling herself together. Slowly, her head swiveled.

A lantern bobbing in the darkness. Four shadows moving toward her.

The minute you jump out onto the tracks, run.

She jumped to her feet and ran, swaying, toward the patch of wasteland bordering the freight station. Leaping over the barrier, she plunged into the wild grass.

"Stop!"

She was too petrified to look back. She could just make out

the shape of a barn in the darkness. If she could reach it, she could hide there. She leaped over a small stream. The overlarge sweater was slowing her down, the sleeves heavy as two anchors . . .

"Stop running!"

The shouts behind her were getting nearer. Lilya gave a kind of animal howl. Her knee hurt like the devil. She stepped in a rut and stumbled, righted herself and kept running, lurching slightly before she could regain her balance. She'd almost reached the barn when suddenly she remembered the fisherman's house; she couldn't let herself get cornered in an enclosed space. She passed the barn and kept running.

"Halt! Stop immediately!"

"Go right; cut her off!"

There were several men pursuing her, so close that she could hear the thud of their boots on the dried mud. She'd reached the foot of the hill Dmitri had told her about. If she could get to the summit, she'd be able to gain some distance by sliding down the other side.

She hurled herself forward, but a hand was closing on her shoulder, another shoving her to the ground. Lilya struggled and screamed, lashing out with her fists. Her journey couldn't end like this, not now, not when she was so close to finding her brother.

The man holding her down was at least a foot taller than she was. He lifted her up, her legs kicking in the air.

"Calm down, for God's sake! We're here to help you find Valentyn!"

Lilya froze. There was a taste of leather and blood in her mouth. Her face was covered in mud. She ached all over.

"And not a moment too soon," the resistance fighter continued. "They're coming to take your brother away tomorrow. But first you're going to have a bath and a change of clothes. You stink."

Vital had received a message from his fellow members of the resistance informing him of the mission's success. He immediately phoned Dmitri to thank him for the role he'd played in rescuing her. The old fisherman, who took the call while out walking with Sobaka, surprised himself by telling the dog that everything had gone as planned.

"You look very pleased with yourself," Cordelia observed, after Vital had hung up.

"The plan worked. She's in Crimea and in good hands. That's pretty good, don't you think?"

"Depends on who you're asking. Why haven't you called her mother yet?"

"It's too early."

The first rays of the rising sun were filtering through the window as Veronika opened her eyes. Her temples felt like they were being crushed in a vice. This was one hell of a hangover.

What was even worse was that she'd gotten Stefan drunk too. He'd sworn that it wasn't the first time, that his father had given him tastes of much stronger liquor, but he was only fifteen, despite insisting that he was "almost sixteen." Still, he'd only drunk so much because she kept refilling his glass, and maybe that was why she felt so guilty. They'd talked mostly about Lilya, and the conversation had only made clearer what Veronika had already known: that she'd failed to notice how much her daughter had changed, becoming a secret and solitary young woman, week by week. Between her failing marriage, the war, and her work at the clinic, Veronika had simply been too preoccupied. Stefan was a good boy, as country people say, with a poetic soul that reminded her of her husband. It was no surprise that Lilya had been drawn to him. He had the same dreamy way of looking at the world as her father.

Her eyes itched, and there was a bitter taste in her mouth. She took a shower, hoping it would clear her head. After that she'd go and wake up Stefan, make some coffee—a lot of coffee—and make him promise not to tell his mother about last night. And then she'd get in her car and drive to Chonhar to find Lilya. She'd be there by eight or so.

She blow-dried her hair and dabbed on a bit of makeup, wanting Lilya to think she looked pretty. She'd smile at her daughter with tenderness and love and say all kinds of comforting things to her.

Stefan was sprawled out on the sofa, his arms flung above his head. It amused Veronika that a young man of his age already snored so loudly. Whoever shared his bed as an adult wouldn't exactly have a restful time of it.

The noise from the kitchen woke him. He stretched, visibly trying to remember where he was. After a moment he jumped up, tucked his shirt back into his trousers, ran a hand through his messy hair, and asked Veronika if she needed any help.

"You can't possibly be this chipper," she protested.

"Oh sure, I feel great. I slept really well."

"You do realize that we drank two bottles of wine?"

"I think that second bottle was all you."

"Really? Well, that explains it. Any word from Lilya?"

"I think it's too early, but I'll check."

Stefan pulled the pager from his pocket and glanced at it, then looked up at Veronika, eyes wide. "She's in Crimea," he said. "She says she'll be bringing Valentyn home tonight."

The cup Veronika was about to fill with coffee slipped from her hands and shattered on the floor. She grasped the back of a chair for support. Stefan, seeing her sway, hurried to help her sit down.

"I'm all right," she murmured, pulling herself together. "What else does she say?"

"Nothing."

Stefan gathered up the broken pieces of ceramic. He retrieved two more mugs and filled them with coffee, then sat down across from Veronika.

"I left my phone upstairs on my nightstand. Would you mind getting it for me?" she asked.

"Do you have service here?"

"I'll explain when you bring it. Quickly, now."

Vital was sleeping the sleep of the righteous, lying on his side, one arm flung over Cordelia. In his dreams, his legs still worked. He walked, climbed stairs, ran in the parkland surrounding the mansion. Walked with Cordelia in the streets of a Kyiv at peace. Sometimes she watched him play soccer with his brother.

A sound woke him. He opened his eyes groggily and groped for his phone on the nightstand. It wasn't easy to feign surprise when Veronika told him that Lilya had made it into Crimea. He let out a little grunt, racking his brain for something to say that wouldn't make her suspicious.

"I had a feeling she might try her luck under cover of night," he said after a moment. "And since there were only two possible crossing points, I asked some friends in the resistance to go there and keep an eye on her, just in case. I didn't say anything to you yesterday because I didn't want to worry you for no reason. But it was better to watch our backs."

"But how did she manage it? You told me yourself that it was impossible to get through the checkpoint!"

"I guess I underestimated her."

"And you think your friends will find her?"

"I don't think so; I *know* so. They sent me a message at around four o'clock this morning, telling me they'd picked her up near the station at Dzhankoi."

"She got all the way to Dzhankoi?!"

"All that matters now is that she's safe. They're going to try to get Valentyn out this afternoon. I was waiting for a reasonable hour to tell you all this, and I stupidly fell asleep again."

Vital promised to contact Veronika as soon as he had anything new to tell her, then hung up before she could ask any more questions. He turned back to Cordelia, who was looking at him oddly, arms folded.

"What's the matter?" he asked.

"If you're ever late, or you stand me up, please don't give me one of those explanations."

"I'm always impeccably punctual," he retorted.

"Stop, you're doing it again!"

"Doing what?"

"Lying!"

"But I haven't lied to you," he protested.

"Not to me, not yet. To Lilya's mother, on the other hand... it was terrifying to watch you sweet-talking her so easily. You didn't even bat an eyelash."

"What *should* I have said to her, then?"

"If you'd called her last night instead of arranging things behind her back, you could have told her Lilya spent the night in an old fisherman's house in Chonhar, for a start. That Lilya was safe at that point, and she could either go and collect her daughter as soon as she woke up, or let her continue with her risky plan to save Valentyn. That should have been Veronika's decision, it seems to me. It's called parental authority."

"What about parental guilt? If Veronika had decided to go get Lilya, and her son never came home, she'd have felt guilty about it for the rest of her life. But it would have been just as bad if she'd decided to let Lilya keep going, and something bad happened to her. I took responsibility for the decision myself to spare a mother from having to make such a painful choice."

"But now that Lilya is so close to Valentyn—what if something happens to both of them?"

"Then I'll hate myself until the day I die."

Cordelia threw back the sheets and got out of bed, walking into the bathroom without another word. Vital could hear her furiously brushing her teeth.

"What have I said this time, to make you so mad?" he called.

"You are so unbearably sweet, you know that? How is any woman supposed to resist you?"

The first thing Lilya did on waking was to sniff herself all over. She'd scrubbed herself thoroughly in the shower, but she still stank. She promised herself never to go near another fish as long as she lived. The four resistance fighters, sitting around a table nearby, watched her with amusement.

"We decided we'd rather sleep outside," joked Artëm. "And look, even with the door open—there isn't a single mosquito in the house!"

"Very funny," Lilya grumbled.

"Come on over here, we'll explain what's going to happen today," Artëm said. He relit the stub of a cigarette, scratched at his thick beard, and unfolded a sheet of paper on the table. He was a plasterer by trade, his face lined and weather-beaten though he couldn't have been more than forty.

On his right sat Petro, a railwayman; it was thanks to him that they'd been able to recover Lilya without too much difficulty. Petro was a dyed-in-the-wool union man who reigned over the railways of northern Crimea, and whose authority the Russians had never been able to diminish.

Next to Petro sat Taras, a truck driver and master smuggler: liquor, cigarettes, cigars, and chocolates when the raids on Russian trains had been fruitful, but never drugs or medication—except when they were destined for Russian troops.

Finally, next to Artëm, there was Bodhan, or Big Bodhan, as he referred to himself, proud of his immense physique. Bodhan could knock an adversary flat with a single punch, and without even breaking a sweat. He could lift a hundred kilos without wincing and, to defy any stereotypes, was a passionate reader who adored the Russian romantics: Lermontov, Dostoyevsky, Chekhov. He'd never developed a taste for Gogol, but his love of Tolstoy and Solzhenitsyn was boundless.

Lilya abandoned her bedroll. She was stiff and achy, her knee swollen and her face covered with scratches from yesterday's wild grass. Sketching on a sheet of paper as he talked, Artëm went over the plan he and his comrades had come up with to rescue Valentyn.

"According to the information we've received from Kyiv, there are three groups of students going on bicycle outings, one after the other. You'll need to be part of this," he told Lilya, "so that you can tell us which group your brother's in. The children leave the boarding school by the main gate and take this road. It runs in a straight line for about six hundred yards, then veers sharply right, bordered by a ditch. That's where we'll intervene. Petro and Taras will hide in the ditch while Bodhan and I will be standing by our truck with the hood open, pretending we've had a breakdown. As for you, you'll be in the back of the truck, positioned so you can see the bikes approaching. The right turn will slow them down. As soon as you spot your brother, whistle. Can you whistle?"

Lilya could. She demonstrated with a two-finger whistle.

"Perfect. That'll be our signal to act. While we deal with the monitors, you head straight for your brother as fast as you can. He has to see you right away, otherwise he might think he's being kidnapped again. He must still be traumatized and I'd rather not have to chase him through the fields like we did with you yesterday."

"What then?" Lilya asked.

"You get him into the back of the truck and off we go. The border's forty kilometers away; we can reach it in thirty minutes if we speed."

"And the Russians will let us through?"

"The back of the truck has a false bottom with a compartment underneath, and the two of you will be hidden in there when we get to the checkpoint. Petro and Taras will deal with the guards;

they're used to greasing their palms. Two cartons of cigarettes and the barrier goes away. After that we drop you in Rykove and come back home. Is that all clear?"

"How much room is there under the floor of your truck?" Lilya asked.

"Just enough for you and your brother. Why?"

"It's just that Valentyn was kidnapped along with a classmate," she explained.

Artëm raked a hand through his hair and glanced at his comrades, who nodded.

"Okay. We'll see how things go. But it'll be a tight squeeze for the three of you. In the meantime, let's have some chow, and then we'll take Bodhan's car out to the boarding school for a little route reconnaissance."

17

There were field mice scurrying in and out of the sewer grate. Valentyn preferred their company to that of the rats. He watched them thoughtfully. He'd eaten his last cookie around noon, when the sun was high in the sky, then dozed off. When he woke, he was hungrier than ever, not to mention desperately thirsty. He looked at the water streaming out of the drain through the bars. It was torture not to be able to drink it. He didn't know how much longer he'd be able to hold on. It had been bad enough creeping through that pitch-black dungeon when he'd thought he was escaping, but now, with his prison waiting for him at the other end, he wasn't sure he had the courage to do it again. He would have to go back and bang on the trap door until someone heard him, but more than the fear of getting lost in the subterranean maze, or the punishment in store, it was the idea of Guzenko's ridicule keeping him out here. Even behind these bars, he felt freer than he did between the walls of the school.

He was so exhausted that it was hard to stand up. When he finally managed it, his legs wobbled beneath him, and he sat back down.

Just then he caught sight of the gym teacher passing on a bicycle outside. The students following him weren't the ones from Valentyn's class. At least he'd gotten out of that stupid bike ride, Valentyn thought. Half an hour later he saw them again, pedaling back the other way. And then he had the pleasure of seeing Guzenko huffing and puffing on his bike in the next group, his cheeks flushed scarlet with the effort. His friend was in that bunch too. Valentyn ducked down to make sure he wouldn't see him. The other boy would be so disappointed when he found out the escape attempt had failed. *Some hero*, Valentyn grumbled silently to himself. But after a moment his naturally optimistic nature asserted itself, and he thought that maybe having attempted to pull off an escape would make the other students consider him less of a pariah.

These musings made him think of his father. Maybe the Russians had taken him prisoner too. One day, when the Ukrainians had won the war, they'd both tell the stories of their adventures around the dinner table. Lilya would be slightly jealous, but proud of them. He missed her and Mama just as much as he missed his father.

Before plunging back into the darkness, Valentyn went to the grate again. He needed one last breath of fresh air to summon the courage to face what came next: the sewer pipe, the cellar with the rats, and the matron, who would make him pay dearly for his act of daring.

Face pressed to the bars, Valentyn spotted a truck parked at the side of the road. It must have broken down; there were two men bent over the engine. If only he could go and join them. He'd give them a hand with the car, and in return they'd take him home.

Then he sprang to his feet, his legs suddenly regaining their strength. He clung to the bars of the sewer grate, his eyes wide. The girl leaning against the back of the truck—it was Lilya!

She was some twenty meters away from him, looking off down the road. All she had to do was turn her head and she'd see him. He filled his lungs with air and tried to shout. Tried again, drawing in such a deep breath that his chest burned. But no sound came from his throat. He jumped up and down and waved his arms, hammered on the grate with his fists until they bled. Still Lilya didn't take her eyes off the road.

He rummaged in his pocket for the knife he'd stolen from the cafeteria and tapped the blade hard against the bars of the grate. Right then the second group came around the turn, a blur of bicycles blocking his sister from sight.

Lilya could hardly contain her excitement as the group of cyclists approached. Her eyes lit up—there was Valentyn's friend! Things were happening fast; there wasn't much time to think. He and her brother were the same age and in the same class; Valentyn *must* be part of this group. She whistled as loudly as she could. Artëm and Bodhan leaped on the gym teacher, Bodhan knocking him off his bicycle and pinning him to the ground. Petro and Taras did the same with the monitors, while Artëm ran to stand in the middle of the street, holding his arms out wide to stop the group of students. He glanced over his shoulder at Lilya.

"Where's your brother!" he shouted.

"I don't see him!"

"Then why'd you give the signal?" Artëm bellowed.

Lilya pointed at a boy. "Because that's his friend!"

Artëm dashed over to the boy. "Where's Valentyn? Isn't he with you?"

"N–no," Valentyn's friend stammered fearfully. "He escaped."

Artëm glanced at his comrades, stunned. Then: "Take him and let's go!"

Lilya grabbed Valentyn's friend by the hand and ran with him toward the truck. Petro and Taras checked the knots on the rope they'd used to tie up the adults. The children stood, riveted by the spectacle unfolding in front of them. Some of them were clearly terrified, but others were laughing and jumping up and down with glee.

"We're good, let's go!" Petro shouted.

Bodhan jumped behind the wheel. Artëm boosted the two children into the back of the truck, then climbed in himself. Petro slid into the middle of the truck's bench seat, leaving room for Taras, who leaped in and slammed the door behind him, and they screeched off in a cloud of dust.

Behind the sewer grate, Valentyn smiled through tears. Thanks to his friend, he'd be a hero after all. Lilya and his mother would be proud of him, as proud as he was of his sister.

Retracing his steps toward the boarding school would mean squandering all his hard work. His friend's escape was more than worth spending a night out here, and he knew that even when it got dark, he wouldn't feel alone anymore.

His family hadn't abandoned him. Lilya would be back to save him.

In the truck, no one spoke. Artëm and his comrades had no idea what to say to Lilya. In the end it was Valentyn's friend, still buzzing with excitement from his escape, who broke the silence.

"He'd figured everything out, but Guzenko chickened out on him. The trap door was too heavy, it took two people to open it. So I went to help him. But I—I wasn't brave enough to go any further. I'm claustrophobic. I just couldn't go down into that cellar. But he could. Even when Guzenko and his goons beat him up, he wasn't afraid. He even smiled, to show them he didn't care."

At that, Lilya could no longer hold back her emotion.

"Don't cry. He's a hero, I swear."

"Did he tell you where he was planning to go?" asked Artëm.

"No, that was his secret, but I know he kept track of the route when they first brought us here."

"Let me out of the truck!" Lilya begged. "You can take him back to Rykove, but I'm staying here. I'll catch up with you when I have my brother with me."

Artëm looked at her sternly. "Listen to me. I don't know how long it'll take those kids to untie the teachers, or if they'll sound the alarm, but very soon the people in charge are going to find out what happened. They'll blow the whistle, and I doubt it'll be an hour before the borders are closed. We have to get across now. I have my orders and I'm planning to follow them. This is the end of your adventure—be proud of yourself. Think of this boy's parents. And as for your brother, we have his photo. We'll search the countryside and every village; we've got a lot of friends around here. Everyone will be on the lookout for him. We'll find him in no time and bring him home to you. And if he gets caught again, even though I don't think there'll be many more bike outings for the foreseeable future, sooner or later things will calm down, and we'll grab him at the first opportunity. Be patient.

You've seen what we're capable of. Trust me—we're not going to abandon him, you have my word. Now, I'm taking you both home. End of discussion."

Artëm was deadly serious, and though the idea of jumping out of the moving vehicle briefly crossed Lilya's mind, betraying the trust of these men would jeopardize the chances of saving Valentyn. She also knew she was at the limits of her strength. So when the little boy looked at her with big eyes and asked if he was really going home, she hugged him tightly and said yes.

Artëm lifted the two panels set into the floor in the back of the truck. The boy looked at the space beneath them and turned pale.

"I'm claustrophobic too," Lilya told him. "And I really need you to hold my hand. We'll be brave together, and it won't be for very long, I promise. Close your eyes and remember that you'll be with your family again soon."

They folded themselves into the small space. Lilya gripped the boy's hand. Artëm gave them a last smile, then replaced the panels. They were nearing the border.

"I've forgotten your first name," Lilya whispered.

"I'm Mykolai," Valentyn's friend whispered back.

18

Valentyn wanted to stay awake until night fell, to watch the sun sink behind the fields, and then he'd close his eyes. Not before. The truck had driven off long ago. The students had untied the teacher and the monitors in a babble of shouts, laughter, and reprimands. Then they'd gotten back on their bikes, and since then there had been only silence.

He sat and brooded. His imagination and his courage had cost him his freedom, but he refused to feel sorry for himself. He took out his notebook and wrote, more resolved than ever:

My name is Valentyn Khodova. I'm going to escape one day soon, and when I'm free, I'm going home.

To fight his tiredness, he flapped his arms as if they were wings, once again picturing himself flying high above the road, the villages. Making his getaway before it grew dark.

Splish-splash. There it was again, the splashing noise. Too loud to be rats this time, though. Valentyn squinted into the darkness. Footsteps sounded, grew closer. A figure appeared at the end of the pipe. The beam of a flashlight shone in his face. Then a monitor seized his arm and yanked him to his feet.

The way back through the sewer seemed shorter this time, the cellar smaller in the flashlight's glow. The trap door was open. The monitor, who hadn't said a word, pushed Valentyn toward the steps.

Children's faces were pressed against the cafeteria windows overlooking the arched passageway. They were all staring at him, some with admiration, others with disdain. Some of the faces were merely blank. The monitor steered him toward the hall, still gripping him by the arm. Valentyn steeled himself to face the matron, but they kept on going, ending at the showers.

The monitor waited, arms folded, while his prisoner bathed. Then he tossed him a towel and pointed, face impassive, at a bench where a folded uniform had been left for him.

Blue trousers, a striped undershirt, a blazer, and a pair of loafers. Valentyn dressed and glanced at himself in the mirror. He looked like a junior officer in the Russian navy.

The monitor looked him over and then, satisfied, gestured for him to follow.

The gate to the forbidden wing closed behind them. As they climbed the staircase in the tower, Valentyn tried to imagine the punishment in store for him. Maybe they'd whip him with a belt on a podium in front of all the other students, in the room where they sang the national anthem. They'd probably given him these special clothes for that exact purpose. And then they'd make him stand in the courtyard all night until he collapsed, just like in *The Great Escape*. Well, a few more steps and he'd know for sure.

The matron, seated behind her desk, dismissed the monitor with a flick of her hand. The silence that reigned once he'd gone was thick enough to cut with a knife. Valentyn wanted to hold on to his pride, but like any terrified little boy, he couldn't keep from shaking.

"You've disappointed me deeply," sighed the monster.

She rose and went to the window, refusing to look at Valentyn.

"I'd taken you under my wing, and this is how you repay me. You can thank your classmate Guzenko; if he hadn't said anything, you would have died of hunger and thirst before anyone found you. What were you thinking?"

She knew he couldn't answer. And clearly she didn't want him to, because she'd taken care to remove all the pens from her desk.

"I can't believe you wanted to go back to the people who abandoned you. So ungrateful!"

She emphasized her displeasure by stamping a foot hard on the floor. Her face was terrifying enough as she loomed over him, but somehow it got even worse when her expression suddenly lit up.

"You're very intelligent," she mused. "Too much so for your age, in fact, but a proper education will take care of that. And your intelligence, combined with that unique silence of yours, is going to serve us both well. Isn't it nice that we can have a project together? Since I can see that you agree, we'll consider this silly little stunt of yours a youthful error. Boys will be boys, after all. But I want you to swear to me that you won't tell anyone about your escapade. It'll be our secret. Do you promise?"

She didn't wait for him to respond, just kept talking, a faraway look in her eyes, her gaze fixed so ardently on something in the distance that Valentyn wondered, terrified, if she was talking to him or to a group of invisible monsters.

"Very good," she went on. "Then you're forgiven. I'll admit, I'm relieved. I dislike having to be severe, you know, even though sometimes I don't have a choice."

Seeing the fear on Valentyn's face, she hurried to reassure him.

"Now, sit down in this chair. You're forgiven, I told you, so calm down."

When he'd obeyed, she took a handkerchief out of her pocket and dabbed the cold sweat from his forehead.

"When I think about how you almost ruined everything—how would it have looked? What a day, honestly. But it's ending well, and just in time, that's the important thing."

Valentyn had no idea what she was talking about, but it was clear that the matron was even more insane than he'd thought. At least he hadn't been whipped with a belt; that was something, even if the thought of thanking Guzenko for ratting him out made him sick to his stomach.

"Surely you're wondering why you're wearing those smart clothes?" the matron continued, glancing at her watch. "I promised you that great things were in store for you, didn't I? And you see, I always keep my promises."

She went back to the window and looked out. Two black sedans had driven through the front gate and were parking in the courtyard.

"You're about to understand how lucky you are to have met me," she said.

She came back to Valentyn, adjusted his blazer, and told him to stand up straight. Then she stood back, looking him over with satisfaction.

There was a knock on the door. The monitor ushered in a woman accompanied by her secretary. There was a brief instant of silence, the matron admiring the new arrival's effortless air of authority. She wore a silk scarf draped artfully around her neck, and silver earrings peeked from beneath her blond coiffure.

The matron took Valentyn's hand and said softly:

"Allow me to introduce a very great lady and close friend of our president, Maria Alexeyevna Lvova-Belova. Your new Mama."

Unbuttoning her white wool coat in a single smooth motion, Maria Lvova-Belova bent to brush her lips against Valentyn's cheek while her assistant snapped a photo.

"I'm so pleased to meet you," she said. "The matron's report to us was outstanding. I'm taking you to Moscow tonight, where you'll live in a magnificent house. You're no longer an orphan, and you're about to have your first plane ride—isn't this a wonderful night?"

19

Vital had done his clumsy best to reassure Veronika, but the truth is cruel when you have to explain to a mother that, while her daughter is on the way home, her son is lost in the countryside somewhere.

The mixture of gentleness and guilt in his voice touched Cordelia's heart. She relieved him of his phone and took charge of the situation.

"The fact that Lilya and the little boy are home will have to be kept quiet," she explained to Veronika. "The people who run the boarding school will be out for revenge. They'll find out where Mykolai lives from their files, and they might try to make an example out of him by sending militiamen to get him back."

"How much time do we have to find a drop-off point for them?" asked Veronika, her voice calm.

"Not much. Artëm and his friends were past Chonhar when they called us, so they should be in Rykove within the hour."

"I could go to Mykolai's parents and offer to host them at my house," Veronika suggested.

"No, that's not a good idea. Given Valentyn's escape, it's

not impossible that the Russians will be paying you a visit too. Moreover, when the resistance men find Valentyn and bring him home, you'll all have to hide."

"When will they find him?"

"Artëm has circulated his description among the resistance, and they've arranged for searches in the countryside and the villages between Dzhankoi and the border. Everyone sympathetic to the cause is on the lookout for him. The Russians don't have as many men available. It's only a matter of hours, I'm sure of it."

"But what if they don't find him? Where will he spend the night?"

"They'll find him."

The certainty in Cordelia's voice seemed to reassure Veronika.

"Okay," she said. "I'll ask Stefan's father if we can meet at his house today. We'll be in touch."

Veronika gave Cordelia the Vasylyks' address and hung up. She was preparing to leave the clinic when the surgeon, who hadn't said anything up to that point, caught her hand to hold her back, then handed her a bunch of keys.

"My house is big and very empty. The little boy and his family can stay there; they'd be welcome. And you too, if you like," he added.

Veronika was touched by this sudden display of sensitivity.

"That is really generous of you," she said. "But I'm sure Lilya will want to sleep in her own bed tonight, and I need to be alone with her."

"Of course," the surgeon murmured. "Give her my congratulations. What she's accomplished is remarkable."

"Thank you," Veronika said, softly.

"For what?"

"Giving me the words I wouldn't have been able to find."

She ran across the parking lot, the wind whipping her face, and headed for Mykolai's parents' house.

They'd crossed paths a hundred times, in front of the school at pickup time, at parent-teacher meetings and end-of-year celebrations, but they'd never really gotten to know each other. Despite being bound by the same tragedy since the Russian raid, they'd found it too painful to see each other, and the long, difficult days had passed in silence. Mykolai's mother Hanna, a pretty woman of thirty, turned white as a sheet when she opened the door to Veronika's knock, like the mother of a soldier seeing men in uniform coming up the walk. Veronika, a fragile smile on her lips, wasted no time in telling her that her boy was coming home. The news affected Hanna so strongly that she almost collapsed, her husband catching her before she fell. They didn't dare ask if Valentyn had also been rescued, but the look on Veronika's face was enough to tell them that she didn't share their joy.

"We have to hurry," Veronika explained. "Pack enough clothes for a few days; you can't stay here."

Hanna and Marko rushed to do what needed to be done, Hanna tucking a few toys into her bag: three little cars, two planes, and Mykolai's security blanket. He didn't drag it everywhere with him anymore, not since starting elementary school, but he always needed to have it on the pillow beside him in order to fall asleep. Soon everything would be back to normal, she thought, as they locked up the house and left.

The trio hurried through the streets of Rykove toward Zelena

Street, Hanna walking so quickly that Marko had trouble keeping up. As they approached the Vasylyks' house, Veronika advised them to deal with the carpenter, rather than his wife, if possible:

"She's a real piece of work, that one."

The Vasylyk residence was brightly lit. Mrs. Vasylyk opened the door and eyed Veronika and the two strangers she'd brought with her. Marko took the situation in hand, explaining the circumstances and calling on local solidarity, the deep necessity of their helping one another, and, of course, their eternal gratitude if she would agree to the use of her house as the drop-off point for the resistance fighters who were bringing his son back home.

Mrs. Vasylyk's demeanor underwent a rapid change as she listened to Mykolai's father. If her son's girlfriend had managed to bring a kidnapped boy home, then surely the glow of her triumph would be reflected onto the family that had taken great risks to help her. All their friends and acquaintances would be impressed, which would also be good for her husband's business. And when Ukraine was liberated, she'd even be able to brag about having been in the resistance.

She ushered them into the living room and then hurried into the kitchen to prepare a bite to eat, something worthy of the gallant heroes who'd saved the little boy—they'd surely be starving after such daring exploits. She told her husband to fetch two bottles of the liquor he distilled himself: one to celebrate the rescuers' arrival, and another they could take away as a souvenir.

She spread out her prettiest tablecloth, got her best glasses out of the sideboard, put out several trays of canapés, plumped up the sofa cushions—and made sure the curtains were open just enough to let the neighbors see what interesting people she was entertaining. Tomorrow they'd ask questions, and since discretion was of the utmost importance, she'd have the extra satisfaction of leaving them hanging.

She took off her apron and glanced in the mirror, smoothing her blouse. The sound of a knock on the door made her blush almost as deeply as her son.

Mykolai threw himself into his mother's arms; his father embraced both of them at once.

Veronika gazed at their faces, contemplating with love and envy the deep emotion that bound them. Unconsciously, her hand made the same movements as Hanna's, as if she were caressing Valentyn's face and holding him tightly to her in order to prove to herself that he was really there.

Now Artëm, Bodhan, Taras, and Petro made their entrance.

"She's waiting for you outside," Artëm told Veronika, having picked her out of the group at a single glance.

And while Mrs. Vasylyk poured a round of shots, Veronika slipped out the door.

Lilya was standing beneath the porch light, scuffing the toe of one shoe against the ground.

"I'm sorry, Mama," she muttered.

And then she flung herself into her mother's arms. Veronika

held her close, surrounding her with love, burying her face in her hair, kissing her and squeezing her and kissing her again. Her daughter looked so fragile. Lilya dissolved in tears, the terrors of her journey banished now by the motherly tenderness she'd pushed away so often in the past.

"I always used to brag to your father about how brave I'd taught you to be. There's nothing to be sorry for."

"I'm so tired, Mama."

"You don't look too good," Veronika admitted.

"Neither do you. I have so much to tell you."

"I know. I have a lot to tell you too. I don't mean to rush this moment—I've waited for it so desperately—but I have to go and thank them. Would you like to come with me, or do you want to see Stefan first?"

"Can you ask him to join me out here? I don't want to talk to him in front of everyone."

Veronika kissed her daughter's forehead, stroked her cheek, and went back into the house.

The glasses were being emptied as fast as Mrs. Vasylyk could fill them. The carpenter's wife didn't know which way to turn. Her husband had taken an immediate liking to Taras, and the feeling was mutual. The smuggler couldn't praise his host's home-distilled liquor highly enough and thought it should be enjoyed on the other side of the border. Already he was asking how much Mr. Vasylyk could produce per month and offering to handle the transport. Even dividing the profits into three equal shares—because he and Petro were business partners—the carpenter could earn a lot more than he did by making furniture. They concluded the conversation, which was conducted well out of Mrs. Vasylyk's earshot, with a firm handshake.

Bodhan and Petro had nothing against the idea of toasting

the resistance one more time, but Artëm wanted to get back across the border before the shift change, when the guards he'd bribed earlier would go off duty. Mrs. Vasylyk, though, insisted on refilling the glasses yet again.

Outside, well away from the noisy living room, Stefan came toward Lilya. She held up a hand to stop him.

"Don't come any closer, please."

"What's wrong?"

"Nothing—it's just that . . ."

She hesitated, then decided an embarrassing confession was better than a misunderstanding.

"Even I can't stand the way I smell. I'm never going to forgive myself for telling you that. I was in a train car with a lot of stinky fish, and I can't get the smell off my skin. And anyway, I've never looked so ugly!"

Stefan had that quirky expression on his face that she found so irresistible. He stepped closer to her and took her hand.

"It's not that bad," he said softly.

He leaned closer, looking into her eyes, searching for permission to kiss her. Her face didn't look like a teenage girl's anymore; she'd become a young woman. She put her arms around his neck and gazed back at him.

"Children! What are you doing out there?" Mrs. Vasylyk called from the doorway. "Our friends are leaving, come and say goodbye. It's the least you can do, really!"

Stefan's cheeks were scarlet. Smiling, Lilya kissed him, right in front of his scandalized mother, who turned on her heel and stalked back inside.

In the living room, everyone was saying their farewells, Petro and Taras exchanging winks with Mr. Vasylyk. Bodhan wasn't in the best shape to get behind the wheel, but he'd driven in worse condition before.

Everyone walked the four men out to their truck. Artëm shook Stefan's hand, then took Lilya aside.

"I know you aren't happy about the way things turned out today, but you made the right decision. Did you see the joy in that room? That's thanks to you. I want you to focus on that when you're falling asleep tonight. We'll get your brother back, I give you my word. I'm glad to have met you, Lilya Khodova. When our country is fully free, you'll have to come and visit, and I'll show you how beautiful Crimea is."

Stefan and his parents had gone back inside, Mykolai's parents following them to retrieve their belongings before going to the surgeon's house. The idea of following their lead was actually rather appealing to Veronika; she was curious to see where the surgeon lived.

Lilya stood on the sidewalk, following the truck with her eyes until it disappeared from view.

"Who sent them?" she asked her mother.

"A friend from Kyiv."

"And you asked him to do it?"

"He acted on his own initiative. He did well, wouldn't you say?"

"Maybe. I mean—yeah. The truth is, I was just about at the end of my rope when they found me."

"Will you tell me about the journey?"

"Yeah. But not right now."

"Well, what do you want to do right now, then?"

"Go back there and kick Guzenko's ass."

"Is he a Russian? Someone who hurt you?"

"No. Just a kid who went after my brother—and don't start worrying for no reason; Valentyn didn't stand for it."

"I see. And other than kicking the ass of an eleven-year-old boy, what are your plans?"

"Just to spend a little time with Stefan this evening."

"Okay. Then we'll talk tomorrow."

"When you get home from work?"

"First thing in the morning. And I'll stay with you as long as you want me to."

"All day?"

"And the next day too, if that sounds good."

"I need you to drive me somewhere tomorrow, then. We won't stay long, I promise."

"Where?"

"You'll see when we get there."

Lilya came home at midnight. Veronika, who had dozed off on the sofa, woke up immediately.

"Are you hungry?" she asked.

"I couldn't eat another bite. We finished all the leftover canapés. What was your surgeon's house like?"

"Very different from how I thought it would be."

"Like how?"

"Elegant. Minimalist, but incredibly refined. He's got fantastic taste. I wasn't expecting the bouquet of flowers on his nightstand."

"Wait, you were in his bedroom?"

"Yes—I mean, no, I was looking for the room he told me to put Mykolai's parents in, and I got the wrong door," Veronika explained, amused.

"It's funny, I haven't seen you look this happy since . . . I mean, it's been a long time since Papa made you smile like that."

"I wasn't smiling! What are you talking about?"

"Yes you were, but I'm not complaining. It's nice to see you smile. When Valentyn comes back, will we have to leave our house too?"

"Probably."

"Where will we go?"

"Kyiv, I think. But only for a while."

20

Valentyn hadn't been afraid, just disappointed that there hadn't been much to see once the plane took off. When the runway was out of site, everything was dark. And it hadn't been any better when they were in the air. He'd hoped the stars would seem closer, but it turned out they were as small when seen from the sky as when he'd looked up at them with Mama in the back garden.

The landing, though, had been a different story. Face pressed to the window, he'd been dazzled by the most magnificent sight he'd ever seen in his life: Moscow, immense and minuscule at the same time, with its millions of lights, everything glittering as if the sky had been turned upside down. He'd found the turbulence exciting too, and when the wheels had touched the ground, he'd been thrilled by the sudden roar of the engines.

And on the tarmac, at the foot of the gangway, Valentyn had found his calling. Pilot. The thing that made him different wouldn't be a problem if he were an airline captain; the cockpit door had remained open all during the flight, and he'd seen that the copilot could easily handle speaking to air traffic control.

Now, the assistant ushered them into a luxury car waiting near the plane. In the back of the car, two pairs of comfortable seats faced each other, upholstered in creamy white leather that matched Ms. Belova's coat. This would be Valentyn's first time riding backward in a car.

Ms. Belova hadn't said a word since they left the boarding school. All she'd done was glance up from her reading from time to time, as if to make sure Valentyn was still there. The assistant was more talkative.

"Madame's driver will take you to school and bring you back as soon as classes are over," he told Valentyn, whispering so as not to disturb his boss.

Valentyn looked out the car window. The suburbs of Moscow looked grim to him, even sinister, but once they'd passed the ring road everything changed. The buildings were painted in brilliant shades of red, yellow, green, and blue, and the wide avenues were lit up as bright as day, immense golden domes gleaming in the night. When the car reached the banks of the Moskva River, the presidential palace looked like something out of a fairy tale.

"Magnificent, isn't it?" the assistant said.

Valentyn nodded. The smell of leather was making him nauseous. The sedan entered the Golden Mile, the most expensive neighborhood in the city, turned up Ostozhenka Street, and stopped in front of the wrought-iron gate of a sumptuous residence.

"Your new home. I'm sure you'll find it nicer than your old one," said the assistant happily.

Ms. Belova gave the man a pointed glare. References to the past were strictly prohibited. Only the future existed for Valentyn now.

It wasn't just the Kremlin that looked like it belonged in *One Thousand and One Nights*. The vast lobby had a white marble floor and a golden ceiling. Valentyn was soon experiencing another first—he'd never ridden in an elevator before, and this one had mirrored walls.

To get into the apartment, you had to punch a code into a keypad, and there were still more surprises in store. Three doors opened off the foyer, which alone was larger than his entire house in Rykove. Ms. Belova put her bag down on a sideboard and disappeared behind the left-hand door without so much as a goodnight.

"That's her private suite," explained the assistant. "You must never go inside without being invited. The reception rooms are behind the middle door: the blue salon and the small salon."

Valentyn wondered what a blue salon was, and he ventured to ask the question by writing on the notepad he'd pilfered on the plane. The assistant looked at him condescendingly.

"The floors of the grand salon are made of lapis lazuli, a semiprecious stone whose color gives the room its name. The small salon features exquisite woodwork—I shouldn't have to tell you what woodwork is; I've been told you're very intelligent."

The man could patronize Valentyn all he wanted; his house in Rykove had much more character than this soulless ice palace, semiprecious stone or no.

"And at the very back is the kitchen, where you'll have your meals," the assistant continued imperturbably.

Opening the third door, he led Valentyn down a long corridor.

"This is the children's area," he explained as they went. "Each room has its own bathroom. Yours is at the very end of the hall, as you're the last to join the family. Tomorrow I'll introduce you to the staff, the cooks, the valet, the maids, and Anatoly, the butler, who runs this whole place. Your brothers and sisters are all older than you . . . anyway, you'll meet them sooner or later."

Valentyn counted six rooms. Far fewer than at the boarding

school, which wasn't displeasing, but of course, Valentyn thought, he would only ever have one sister, and that was Lilya.

"And here is your new room," said the assistant, pushing open a door. "Wakeup is at eight. You'll find clothes in your size in the wardrobe. Tomorrow, put on the outfit laid out on the armchair over there. I'll come for you after breakfast. We'll be leaving with Ms. Belova for a press conference. Don't worry, though; I'm the one they'll be asking questions. All you have to do is smile and be quiet. Easy, right? Oh—one last thing. Ms. Belova is very busy. Don't disturb her for any reason. If you need anything, go to Anatoly, the butler I told you about. And now I'll bid you goodnight. Don't stay up too late; tomorrow will be a long day."

With that, the assistant departed, shutting the door behind him.

The large room had everything: a desk at which to do his homework and a cozy armchair to relax in. The carpet was whimsically patterned with streets and crosswalks. And yet, between these white walls hung with prints of birds and rabbits, Valentyn felt as if he'd been transported to a world much smaller and narrower than his own.

There were no bars on the windows here on the sixth floor; it would have been pointless. Valentyn sat down on his bed, took off his loafers, and looked at the clothes he'd been ordered to wear the next day. They were even more austere than the uniform. He didn't mind wearing a necktie, but he had no idea how to tie one. Oh, well. He'd put it on like a scarf.

He undressed, showered, put on the pajamas that had been left for him, neatly folded, at the foot of the bed. Then he slipped beneath the covers and turned out the light.

But sleep didn't come. The night seemed especially dark, and he missed the presence of the other children in the dormitory. He thought of Mykolai, who must be home by now, and Lilya too. He missed her terribly, almost as much as his mother. He clenched his fists, turned over, buried his face in the pillow, and sobbed.

The door opened a crack, a thin slice of light falling across the bed. Valentyn sat up. A man was standing there.

"Is something wrong?" the man asked. He had a strong accent of some kind. "Oh dear, I can see that something is very wrong indeed. Hungry? Thirsty? Wet the bed? Afraid of the dark? All of them at once, perhaps? Well, let's start from the beginning. What is bothering you the most?"

Anyone who could reel off a list of problems so cheerfully could only be an ally, Valentyn thought. He wiped the tears from his cheeks.

"Let's not stay in here," the man said. "Get up and come with me."

A lamp glowed on the butler's desk. Valentyn was expecting to see someone slender and refined, immaculately dressed. But instead, here was the complete opposite: Anatoly was a plump, elderly Turkish man sporting baggy purple trousers, a brightly colored shirt, and two gold teeth. His wrinkled face was ageless, and his large eyes looked warm and kindly.

The butler sank into his chair. With a look, Valentyn asked to use the pen on his desk, a black lacquer affair with a silver tip, and Anatoly nodded: *of course*. Then he handed over a thick sheet of fine writing paper, which Valentyn couldn't resist caressing appreciatively.

What is a press conference? he wrote.

Anatoly put his hands on his chubby hips. "So it's true—you don't speak!" he exclaimed. "Madame did tell me that yesterday, but I must have forgotten. Before I answer your question, I'm going to confess a secret. But if I do, you have to promise not to say anything to anyone. *Write* anything, I mean. Everyone who lives here thinks I'm hard of hearing. Deaf as a post. But that isn't quite true; it's just that I only hear what interests me. Very practical in my profession, you know. You can't imagine how many answers it turns out that the cooks, the valet, the children, and Madame's assistant are able to find out all by themselves, once I've asked them to repeat their questions three times. But I'm not going to ask you to write pages and pages every time you need something—that's why I've taken you into my confidence like this."

Anatoly inclined his head and frowned, seeming deep in thought all of a sudden.

"But that doesn't make any sense, does it? I've never claimed to be short-sighted. Well, at any rate—why do you want to know what a press conference is?"

Valentyn wrote that he'd missed the last two days of school. Was he supposed to study anything, to prepare for the conference?

Anatoly's laugh was deafening.

Because they're taking me to this conference tomorrow morning, Valentyn added.

"I see," Anatoly said. "Well, a press conference is something very dull. Duller than dull, in fact. They're attended by a bunch of journalists, who come mostly for the caviar sandwiches and champagne. Once they've stuffed themselves, they'll listen religiously to whatever Madame or her assistant want to tell them. Watch out for that assistant, by the way. He's a filthy hypocrite. Er, where was I?"

Journalists, Valentyn wrote.

"Which journalists?" asked the butler, gazing at the ceiling. "Oh yes, of course. Anyway, they'll take notes, and the teacher's pets will even raise their hands—you'll see them quiver with excitement when the assistant calls on them to ask their questions. Then it'll be time for photos, and they'll shout at you to smile, and *voilà*. Not *bad*, exactly, but dull. Deadly dull."

Valentyn nodded. Anatoly must never have gone to boarding school, he thought. If he had, his definition of dullness would have been very different.

"Now, it's high time you were in bed! If you yawn in public tomorrow, Madame will be very angry. Did you have any other questions?"

Valentyn shook his head. The butler rose stiffly from his chair and ushered him back to his room.

"Madame's assistant is a snake, and not the harmless kind, if you take my meaning," he said quietly, as they walked. He paused, there in the hallways, to imitate a swaying cobra, flicking his tongue out between his gold teeth, which made Valentyn burst into silent laughter.

"At least when you laugh, you don't wake up the whole house!" Anatoly chuckled.

He boosted Valentyn into bed, smiled at him one last time, and departed.

All at once, Valentyn felt less alone. He fell asleep thinking of the day that awaited him tomorrow. He'd start checking out his surroundings first thing in the morning, and this time, he'd find a way out that wasn't a sewer line.

21

Valentyn's bedroom looked even larger by daylight. There had been a knock on his door at 8:00 a.m., and he'd put on the clothes from the armchair. Stepping into the hallway, he'd bumped into a chambermaid, who had stopped to tie his necktie correctly and taken him to the kitchen.

He'd never seen anything like that kitchen. There were two of everything: two ovens, two refrigerators, two dishwashers, two sinks. Light streamed in through a tall window. The tile floor shone. The cook showed him where to sit at the table, which was loaded with delectable things: crusty bread, butter and jam, yogurts, fruit salad, and his favorite, chocolate croissants. He wished he could slip one into his pocket for Lilya; she loved them, and it had been so long since they'd been available at home. He couldn't tear his eyes away from those croissants—until Evgenia came into the kitchen and sat down across the table from him.

She was maybe three or four years older than Lilya, and so beautiful that Valentyn thought nature must have created her to make up for all the Russians' mistakes. Her golden hair shone, and the high forehead, blue eyes, and soft lips were so gracefully perfect that it was as if some master painter had dreamed up her face. Equally impressive, to Valentyn at least, was her attitude.

Evgenia seemed unhappy to be there. When the cook spoke to her, her already white skin turned even paler. She must have no idea of her own loveliness, to look so sad.

Valentyn wondered if it was possible to fall in love with your fake sister. He'd certainly never felt his heart pound this way when having breakfast with his *real* sister.

Impulsively, he offered her half of his chocolate croissant. Evgenia accepted it with a smile. She selected a yogurt, and so did Valentyn. Then she poured herself a glass of orange juice, which Valentyn didn't normally like but would drink this morning. He had some fruit salad, even though pineapple made him shudder. Taking a piece of paper and a pen out of his pocket, he summoned up the courage to ask Evgenia if she thought airline pilot was a good job, especially if you were a captain.

"Sometimes, I wish I were a bird," she answered, in a voice so sweet it made him shiver even more than the pineapple.

And Valentyn started to think that life in Moscow might not be so bad after all.

Ms. Belova had exchanged her white wool coat for a flowered dress and pinned her hair into a low chignon. In the car, she paid more attention to Valentyn than she had the night before, even smoothing his hair with her hand. She tightened the knot of his necktie, looked him over carefully, then went back to her reading. She must have an insatiable hunger for knowledge, to love reading so much, Valentyn thought. The assistant's cheerful face quickly dimmed when she mentioned how "charming" Anatoly had found the boy.

The sedan pulled up in front of a school for children with

disabilities, its principal waiting on the sidewalk to receive his esteemed guests. Ms. Belova got out of the car first, taking Valentyn's hand. He didn't like the physical contact, but her grip was so tight that he couldn't free himself. Photographers trailed behind them as they visited the classrooms. In each one, the Russian Children's Rights Commissioner knelt to stroke the hair of a little boy or girl. Her assistant carried a large bag full of stuffed animals that Ms. Belova handed out, smiling widely, as the flashbulbs popped. When the toys were all received, they were escorted to the cafeteria, where the starstruck staff would have loved to have their photos taken, but Valentyn, the principal, and Ms. Belova were the sole focus of the cameras' attention.

A podium had been set up in the middle of the cafeteria. Stepping behind it, the commissioner delivered the speech she'd been reviewing in the car.

"Eight years ago, I created Louis Quarter, a center for children with disabilities. So much has happened since then. I have never stopped fighting for the rights of children, *all* children, even those in difficult situations. When I joined the United Russia party a few years later, at around the same time as my husband became a priest, I could never have hoped to receive such support from our government—and yet, our beloved president has extended a helping hand to our cause, for which I am eternally grateful."

She paused to acknowledge the applause of the principal, the cooks, and the teachers, who were all delighted to be associating with a figure of such importance. It was really their president they were clapping for, but she was so close to him that the prestige blurred together.

"Three years after that," Ms. Belova continued, "I was honored with the title of Children's Rights Commissioner."

More applause. She motioned for her audience to be quiet. She wanted them to save their energy for the star attraction.

"This autumn, I visited each of the four annexed regions of Ukraine, and what I saw there was truly dreadful."

It didn't escape Valentyn's notice that, as she said these words, Ms. Belova rubbed the inner corners of her eyes, right next to her nose. As if on cue, tears flowed. What a neat trick, he thought. He'd have to remember that for the next time Lilya picked a fight with him. His mother always took his side whenever he cried.

"And so I have decided, despite my many responsibilities, to set up special centers for children and adolescents," Ms. Belova went on, "in order to give them the special attention they need. We will be sending teams to Ukraine, to reach out to orphans and children abandoned by their parents."

She paused again, inhaling deeply. Her audience held its breath.

"A few months ago," she continued, her voice solemn, "the president signed a decree simplifying the process of obtaining Russian citizenship for Ukrainian minors considered to be orphans. Thanks to our hard work and the dedication of our workers, thousands of children have already been lucky enough to find new families—wonderful parents who can give them the education and love they were deprived of in Ukraine. And in the weeks and months to come, even more children will be settling in their new motherland, from Crimea to Siberia, for we are going to save them all, and our fellow Russians are already lining up to adopt them."

Another pause. Her serious face lit up.

"I will humbly admit that I didn't have to stand in line," she said, turning to Valentyn, her eyes overflowing with love.

"I met Valentyn during a recent trip, and how could I resist such an adorable face? He is like the children to whom you've devoted yourself so admirably, and bears his burden with the greatest courage: Valentyn cannot speak. But my heart, like yours, cares nothing for handicaps. It's my very great pleasure to introduce to you the boy I'll be adopting in three days, and whom I already love as a son."

Valentyn tried to free his hand, but she was holding it so tightly that his fingers hurt. She kissed his cheek, then drew him to her breast as the photographers jostled one another for close-ups. The flashes blinded him as Ms. Belova shifted her grip to the back of his neck, forcing him to look at the cameras.

It was noon. Cordelia studied the photos on the screen.

"You're sure that's him?"

"Positive, and I'm not going to ask his mother for a second opinion. It would kill her."

"Do you love me?" Cordelia asked.

"I do."

"Then prove it. Promise me we're going to give her son back to her."

"You must admit, that's a strange way for a person to declare their feelings."

"Ah, well. It's my way."

Vital felt a sudden rush of inspiration, ready to do anything to prove himself.

"If the adoption's set to be formalized in three days, then the countdown has begun," he said. "Once he's a Russian citizen, there won't be anything we can do."

"Why not?" Cordelia asked, aghast.

"Because on paper Veronika will no longer have parental rights. Valentyn won't be her son anymore; he'll be the son of a famous woman who's very close to the president. It'll take a miracle for us to get Valentyn back at that point. No Western country will accept a kidnapped child, and it will be impossible to bring him directly from Moscow to Ukraine."

"But it's the Russians who kidnapped him, dammit!"

"That will no longer be the case, as far as Russian law is concerned."

"Well, then, let's leak it, cause a public scandal before it's too late!"

"No good. It's all public already. Those photos taken at the press conference? Belova shared them to her Instagram account immediately, and there was no scandal. That kind of staged event just feeds into the regime's propaganda. And who cares about the fate of a single child these days, anyway?"

"We do," Cordelia replied. "What do we know about this monstrous woman?"

"Not enough. But while you were sleeping, and because I love you, I called Janice. She's putting together a file on Belova, who people are already calling Bloody Mary. She's even promised to put her colleagues at *Haaretz* on the case if need be."

"A file isn't going to help us bring Valentyn home."

"No, but it's a start. An operation like this requires serious preparation, and I don't have any contacts in Russia, only enemies."

Cordelia logged onto the Group of 9's private forum.

"What are you doing?" Vital asked.

"Calling in reinforcements."

"I'd still rather have showed you my feelings in a different way, you know."

Thirty minutes later, the response to Cordelia's call popped up on the forum. Maya, who owned a travel agency in Paris, had a commercial visa that would allow her to travel to Moscow. By the time they'd gathered the materials she asked for, she'd already booked her flight. She'd be landing in Moscow just before 7:00 p.m. While she was in the air, Cordelia was assigned to find the addresses where the "package" might be picked up: residence, school, office, and the place where the adoption ceremony would be held. All information that would save them precious time once Maya was on the ground.

"With time so tight, we'll have to improvise," Cordelia explained. It was the exact opposite of Vital's philosophy.

The gasoline provided by Danylo was turning out to be a godsend. Veronika and Lilya would reach Chonhar in an hour, provided that they didn't run into any militiamen on the way.

"Don't stay on the E105," Lilya advised. "Take the back roads. I'll direct you."

"Is that the way you came?" Veronika asked.

"No, I cut through the fields. We can pick up Papa's bicycle on the way. But I left it near a place that brings back bad memories."

"Your father can buy a new one," Veronika said. "For whatever he uses it for, anyway."

Lilya looked at her mother curiously.

"What *is* your situation with Papa, exactly?"

"Are you going to tell me what we're doing in Chonhar?" Veronika retorted.

"Okay, okay. Touché."
"Pay attention to where we're going, please."

Lilya devoted her full attention to the roads. They were just outside Novooleksiivka now, and she showed her mother how to avoid driving through the town, which Lilya wouldn't have set foot in again for anything in the world. As they passed the tiny village of Sal'Kove she spotted a familiar farmhouse, the woman in front of it busy hanging laundry out to dry. Lilya lifted a hand to wave to her, then thought better of it.

"Do you know her?" Veronika asked.

"Yeah. She's pro-Russian."

"But she helped you."

"How do you know?"

"You were going to wave to her. It's what she did for you that counts, not her beliefs."

Veronika slowed down. Soldiers had set up a checkpoint a hundred yards ahead, barring the road.

"Turn around. We can come back another time," Lilya said, regretfully.

But the question she had asked about the state of her mother's marriage had awakened something in Veronika. She didn't want to give up on anything from now on. Giving Lilya a wink, she continued on toward the barrier.

Curtly, the soldier manning the checkpoint asked for her papers and the reason for travel. Veronika replied in the same crisp, authoritarian tone.

"Two of your men have been hospitalized on my ward at the clinic in Rykove. They were injured fighting the fire at the munitions depot that was shelled. Surely you must know about that. And as if I didn't have enough to do, Officer Ilyevich, the regional commander, has sent me for more bandages and salve, as we don't have enough to treat their burns."

"Why didn't Commander Ilyevich ask us directly?"

"Because my colleague in Chonhar would have told you they didn't have enough supplies either, but I'm the head nurse. Now, if you prefer, I can turn around, and tell Commander Ilyevich that you're taking matters in hand. As I said, I've got plenty of my own work to do."

"The girl's a bit young to be a nurse," observed the soldier, leaning down to look in the car window.

"She's my daughter. She helps me at the clinic."

He handed back Veronika's papers and gestured to his colleague to let them through. The gearbox made a cracking noise as Veronika shifted into first. The engine rumbled, and the car set off.

"Did you think you were the only one who knew how to lie?" Veronika asked, glancing at her daughter's astonished face.

"Ilyevich? How on earth did you find out his name?" Lilya asked.

"It was on his office door when we went to ask him about Valentyn's disappearance. And it's a name I'll never forget."

Cordelia rose and went out to the garden for some fresh air. Valentyn's predicament had affected her deeply. She imagined how she'd feel if anyone touched a hair on her brother Diego's head. She still woke up drenched in sweat sometimes, from the same nightmare always the same. Reliving the morning she'd discovered, in a dorm room in Boston, the lifeless body of her brother's girlfriend Alba, a diabetic, whose life was lost due to high insulin prices.

"What's wrong?" asked Vital, wheeling his chair down the ramp leading off the porch.

"Nothing. Just wanted a cigarette."

"I don't see you smoking."

"I changed my mind."

"About us, or the desire to smoke?"

"You're an idiot," Cordelia said, smiling sadly. "Is she pretty?"

Vital stared at her, perplexed.

"Valentyn's mother," she clarified.

"Oh. Yes, I think she's very pretty."

"What is she to you?"

"When I woke up to find myself in a hospital bed," Vital paused, then went on, "and couldn't feel my legs, Veronika took care of me."

"For a long time?"

"Two years. She was amazing, but not an easy person. Your character is just as good as hers, I can assure you."

"What's wrong with my character?" Cordelia retorted.

"Nothing. You're not jealous, are you?"

"You are *such* an idiot. No, but it makes me want to kick Bloody Mary's ass—*all* the Russians' asses—even more."

"You can't think like that," Vital said. "Most of the soldiers were drafted; they didn't have a choice. And as for the civilian population, they're victims of the Putin regime too. Millions of Russians have left their country and are living in exile, and a lot of the ones who stayed are rejecting the war and the government's ideology. Like us, they're just waiting to be liberated. Dreaming of the day the dictator falls."

"If you say so. Let's go back downstairs. I've had a message from Janice, and she'd rather speak to us directly on the phone."

"Call her from out here. That way you can smoke. Since that's the reason you came outside, and all."

Cordelia kissed him on the lips.

Meanwhile, in Tel Aviv, Janice wanted a cigarette too. And since smoking was prohibited in the *Haaretz* building, she'd leaned out the open window of her office to light up.

"It's worse than I thought," she said. "The accounts given by parents, doctors, and teachers are terrifying. In Kherson, fifty-eight boys and girls ranging from newborn to four years old were kidnapped from a nursery school right in the middle of the city. An armored vehicle and a pickup truck surrounded the building, and a dozen masked soldiers with assault rifles stormed the premises. Three buses were waiting out front with the curtains drawn. They used those babies like human shields and sent them across the Dnieper aboard barges carrying rocket launchers. And the horror doesn't end there."

"I don't know if I want to hear any more," Cordelia murmured.

"We can't close our eyes to what's happening, or make excuses for it like people did after World War II, claiming they didn't know what was going on. Everyone needs to know what the Russians are doing."

"Go on," Vital said.

"The staff of another nursery school, worried about what the occupying forces might do to their little ones, had hidden them in the crypt of a church. The clergy were taking care of the children, discreetly bringing food, smuggling in bedding and cans of milk under their robes, drying laundry on the heating pipes. Until the day their well-kept secret was betrayed by a collaborator who wanted to score points with the thugs newly in control of the city. The Russians ransacked the church and eventually they found the children. They put snipers on the roofs of the buildings around the church and forced the priest to return the children at gunpoint. On the day of the raid, Maria Belova went to the site and was photographed putting a baby into a soldier's arms."

"Her cruelty is just . . . endless," said Cordelia, so angry she could hardly get the words out.

"And Valentyn isn't the first child to fall into Belova's clutches. Last year she adopted a teenage girl kidnapped from Mariupol. Bloody Mary was all over the Russian social media app Telegram, bragging that while Evgenia might have missed her friends at first, and the apartment she grew up in, so much so that she'd expressed pro-Ukrainian sentiments when she initially arrived in Moscow, she came to appreciate the comforts of her new home very quickly.

"Belova has a lot of supporters. One woman affiliated with her organization, Olga Druzhinina, claims to have adopted four children between the ages of six and seventeen, all kidnapped from the Donetsk region. They live in Siberia now, 1,600 kilometers from their homes. Druzhinina says she's proud that her new family is like a microcosm of Russia: 'Our country has taken four Ukrainian regions, and I, four children.' She also says she's in the process of adopting a fifth. She ends her statement by saying that no one can blame Russia for taking back what rightfully belongs to them."

Cordelia muted the speaker, handed the phone to Vital, and lit a cigarette to calm herself down.

"Do you have any other information on Belova?" he asked Janice.

"Yes, and none of it is good. She's convinced Putin to accelerate the deportation program. A sped-up naturalization process has been put in place by the Russian government; the kids get their new nationality, complete with passport, like some bizarre trophy, in a matter of only a few days. Russian officials are taking journalists with them on visits to the host families where, with the cameras rolling, they give toys to the little ones and clothes and phones to the teenagers. The mayor of Donetsk, who was appointed by Moscow, had himself filmed with a bunch of children, telling them that they were home now and surrounded by friends. Belova and her deputy for the Moscow region have assured the press that it takes only a few weeks for the children to be so transformed as to be unrecognizable, and they've spoken proudly of creating so many new little citizens. As soon as they arrive in Russia the children are put into schools where they're taught what a glorious thing it is to be Russian—and also that Ukraine never existed. That the land has always belonged to Russia. The number of children deported from Ukraine in the past year has reached figures not seen in Europe since World War II. Sixteen thousand according to official reports, but investigators believe it's at least double that."

"Which investigators?" Vital asked.

"One of my friends is a journalist assigned to the International Criminal Court. He was the one who told me that an investigation was underway. Forcefully moving children from one country to another with the intention of obliterating their home country can be considered genocide. The trial should quickly result in the conviction of both Vladimir Putin and Maria Belova for crimes against humanity. That won't change what's happened to these children and their real families, but the hope is that anyone dreaming of shaking Putin's and Belova's hands might think twice once they're officially recognized as war criminals."

"Have you been able to get your hands on any of the trial documents?"

"No. Why?"

"To get Bloody Mary's address."

"For that, all we need to do is take a deep dive into her social media accounts. She's created quite a cult of personality around herself, with an enormous following. Given the urgency of our situation, I've been in contact with Noa. By cross-checking the decor that appears most frequently in the background of Belova's selfies against data held by Israeli intelligence, she's managed to locate her. Ms. Belova lives in an enormous place on Ostozhenka Street, which is the most expensive street in Moscow. I've already sent the information to Maya."

"Did Maya tell you she was on the way to Russia?"

"We are all on the same forum, you know. I still have more to tell you. Noa has gotten hold of some images recorded by security cameras during a Russian military raid on an orphanage in Kherson. The children kidnapped from there were trotted out in front of the press with great fanfare. That raid was made possible by the fact that Belova's network includes so many collaborators in occupied regions. They're the ones who provide lists of hospitalized children and addresses of schools and orphanages. I'm sure I don't have to tell you that, if you manage to bring this little boy home, his family will have to be evacuated as quickly as possible."

"I'd thought of that, yes."

"I'll send you more information as soon as I can. For now, this is the best I can do."

Vital and Janice hung up.

"What else did she say?" Cordelia asked Vital.

"Nothing you'd want to hear, except that Noa has joined our operation. Come on, let's go back downstairs. We've got a lot of work to do."

The reunion with Sobaka happened at lightning speed. The fisherman opened his door, the dog bounded toward Lilya, there was an exchange of looks while Sobaka wagged his tail, and the fisherman smiled at Veronika and closed the door. Lilya folded down the passenger seat of the car and whistled for Sobaka, and he jumped into the car as if he owned it. Veronika knew Lilya had been traveling with a dog, but to admit that would mean betraying Stefan's confidence. So she got behind the wheel and started the car in silence. A silence that stretched out for thirty minutes.

"Well? Say something!" Lilya burst out at last. "Are you mad at me?"

"No."

"Is that all you're going to say? 'No'?"

"No, I'm not mad at you for bringing home a dog. You could have told me about it before, instead of making some big mystery out of it. Of course, I would have said that life was complicated enough already without taking on a new pet, so I guess you did the right thing by keeping it a secret."

Lilya tried not to laugh. She'd never heard her mother contradict herself with such honesty.

"Mama, what's going on with you? You're not acting the way you normally do."

"I haven't had any news about your brother. How do you expect me to act?"

"Neither have I, but I'm right here with you, and you're right here with me."

Veronika reached over to ruffle her daughter's hair, something Lilya hadn't let her do for a long time. Today, though, Lilya smiled.

"So I've told you everything about my journey," Lilya said. "What was the stuff you wanted to tell me?"

"Well, for one thing, the friend from Kyiv I told you about is doing everything he can to rescue Valentyn."

"Artëm gave me his word he'd bring him home too, and he's actually near where Valentyn is, at least. 'Doing everything he can' doesn't actually tell me very much about what your friend is up to."

"My next confession is that I ran away too," Veronika said. "I went to see my friend at his home, while you thought I was working at the clinic."

"You went to Kyiv? Are you nuts?"

"Says the girl who risked her neck crossing the border into Crimea. You've got some nerve!"

"I guess we're even," Lilya said, smiling again.

"I guess we are."

"And no more secrets between us," Lilya added.

"Agreed."

"No, you have to *promise*."

"I promise," Veronika said.

"Okay, then go on. I noticed the look on your face when we were talking about the surgeon, you know."

Veronika pulled the car over, though she didn't turn off the engine for fear it wouldn't start again. Holding the brake pedal down firmly with her foot, she turned in her seat to face Lilya.

"I swore there wouldn't be any more secrets, so I guess I have no choice but to tell you this. Your father's not at the front anymore. He was wounded. Nothing serious, I promise, but it was enough for him to be demobilized. The injury healed quickly and he's fine. But he doesn't want to come home. He's living in Lviv now."

"Alone?"

"I don't know."

"Why doesn't he get in touch with us?"

"He calls me occasionally at the clinic to ask about you."

"But he doesn't call *me*!" Lilya cried.

"The mobile networks are down a lot. We have landlines at the clinic."

"Why the hell are you trying to make excuses for him? He came back from the front and abandoned us!"

"You could just as easily say that I abandoned him. You aren't the first person to complain that I spend my life at work. Your father loves you both deeply, believe me. I just don't think he knows how to tell you what's happened. Maybe because things aren't clear in his own head, or in mine either."

"You've been lying to us. Both of you."

"I was wrong," Veronika said. "I wanted to protect you, because I still saw you as a little girl."

"When are you going to realize that I've changed?"

"I have realized it. Otherwise I wouldn't be telling you all this."

"Good. Well then, now you can let me go out and see my friends without asking permission first."

"Don't push it, my dear. Well! You've just learned that your parents are in the process of separating, that your father is doing very well, that he's moved to Lviv and is writing a book. I'll tell him that you know everything, and then he'll call you, I'm sure. Plus you have a dog in your life now. The day isn't turning out so badly after all, is it?"

"Do you think Sobaka is a good name for him?"

"I'll ask him what he thinks of it as soon as he's finished licking the windows of my car and slobbering on the back of my neck," Veronika replied dryly, putting the car back in gear.

When the press conference was over, the entire staff had gathered for a buffet lunch. Ms. Belova, who had somewhere else to be, had excused herself, leaving Valentyn to represent her—but not before taking away his pencil just in case anyone asked him any questions, and instructing her assistant to keep a close eye on him. Valentyn didn't understand why all these people were gazing at him with such admiration, even offering him sweets. In his life before, adults had never paid this much attention to him. The principal insisted on taking him into a classroom to introduce him to some children his own age. There, he met a little girl in a wheelchair who made him think of Cosima, from his school back home. By midafternoon he was exhausted, and the driver came to pick him up.

On the way back, the assistant informed Valentyn that he'd start at his new school on the morning after his naturalization, pushing his enrollment back by a few days. This, the man said, was because Ms. Belova didn't want his old name to appear on the school register. In the meantime, he'd study at home in the mornings and could do what he liked in the afternoons. And since he seemed to have hit it off with Anatoly, the butler would keep him company. This schedule suited Valentyn very well, for as luck would have it, Evgenia spent her mornings studying at home too.

Maya's plane had landed on time at Sheremetyevo Airport. She'd rented a car and driven to her usual hotel, the Kempinski. In her room, she ordered a crudités platter from room service and sat down to catch up on notes from the Group of 9.

The Group was made up of nine extraordinary hackers. Human beings, each with their own strengths and weaknesses, but brilliant coders, all of them. Maya was the member with the most field experience; she'd served for years as a courier for French intelligence, but it had been years since she'd last ventured into hostile territory, following a mission to Istanbul that had nearly gone horribly wrong. Now, in Moscow, Maya would have to improvise. She paced her room for a bit, then connected to the Group's private forum.

"I'm leaving in an hour to scout out the house where he's being kept. I'll go back early tomorrow morning and stake it out. Then I'll follow the car that takes Valentyn to school. In the meantime, I'm going to keep a close eye on everything Bloody Mary posts to her social media. It's easy to anticipate her next moves; she posts everything she does for her fans."

"Why are you telling me all this, Lastivka?"

Vital's use of his longtime nickname for Maya brought back a rush of memories. She couldn't reply.

"We're with you, don't forget," he added.

"Not in Moscow, you aren't," Maya retorted. "Just find a way to get me out of Russia with the boy. I can't handle everything myself."

"I'm already on it," Vital replied. "You'll take the train to St. Petersburg. Not the high-speed Sapsan, though; they check passports before boarding. But my sources tell me that isn't the case for the Nevsky Express. Nothing high-speed about *that* train but the name, by the way."

"And you're sure your sources are reliable?"

"Moving on," Vital continued imperturbably, "the ferry from St. Petersburg to Helsinki stopped running when Russia attacked Ukraine, but there's a Finnish company that's still organizing Baltic Sea cruises. Their ships make their final stop in St. Petersburg every other day, leaving at 7:00 p.m. You'll dock in Finland the next morning."

"And we'll be able to board the cruise ship even though Valentyn doesn't have any papers?"

"I may not have any friends in Russia, but I've got some good ones in Finland. I'll arrange it so you can board inconspicuously using the crew gangway. I'll confirm that with you soon."

"I'd feel better if you could confirm it before I've got a child on my hands."

With that, Maya disconnected. There was no need for Vital to add that Cordelia shared her worries.

In Moscow, Maya looked thoughtfully at the bug she held in the palm of her hand. The size of a penny, it could infiltrate a Wi-Fi network if placed within the signal receiving zone. She put the bug in her pocket, wondering if the hacking equipment she'd brought with her would be of any good for a child-recovery operation. Then she called reception and asked for her car to be brought around.

Maya had never minded danger; on the contrary, she adored it. She'd always loved taking risks, feeling the adrenaline course through her veins. She was a finely honed athlete and a daredevil who didn't feel fully alive unless she was pushing her own limits. But driving through the Moscow night, she wondered if maybe she hadn't gone too far this time. This mission could easily land her in a Russian prison.

She found a place to park on Ostozhenka Street around fifty yards from Maria Lvova-Belova's address. The spot was reserved for deliveries, but there were few, if any, likely to happen at this hour. Security cameras were installed on either side of the gate used by drivers before dropping their bosses off in front of the immense building, and Maya could see other cameras trained on the street. People might have displayed their wealth in the old days by showing off their silver collections, but today in Moscow, living in an ultra-secure residence was the ultimate show of prosperity.

Maya didn't get out of her car. If she was filmed in front of Belova's residence, it would give investigators plenty to track her with once the plan shifted into action, with facial recognition software easily able to compare her face to those of all foreigners arriving in Moscow by air in the days preceding the rescue.

She started the car again and drove slowly past the residence, snapping pictures discreetly with her phone.

Valentyn ate dinner in the kitchen with Evgenia, who told him that their other brothers and sisters were at boarding school and only came home every other weekend. She'd been sent to the school too, at first, but Ms. Belova had decided to bring her back to live in Moscow. Evgenia was the oldest of the siblings and sometimes accompanied Madame to evening events, as required. During dessert, Evgenia asked Valentyn how his day had been. He loved listening to her talk, watching her lips and eyebrows move. He picked up the pen he'd swiped from a classroom, but it would have taken too long to tell her everything that had happened that day, so he settled for writing *fine* on a sheet of paper and then asking her the same question. Evgenia's answer, though, was even shorter than Valentyn's had been: she simply shrugged her shoulders and left the table.

In the hallway, Valentyn paused for a moment in front of the door to Evgenia's room, then kept walking. He was too tired to play with the toys Ms. Belova had brought him, so he got in bed, and as his eyes drifted shut, he recited in his head:

My name is Valentyn Khodova. I'm going to escape one day soon . . .

He fell asleep before he could finish the sentence.

22

On the morning of the second day, Cordelia and Vital ate a breakfast served by a beaming and unusually affable Ilga, who inquired solicitously whether they'd slept well and urged them to go out for a breath of air in the garden before shutting themselves up in the computer room, then withdrew on tiptoe. The housekeeper had smiled not once but *twice* the day before, and Vital was beginning to get seriously worried.

"Janice lied to me, and I let her take me for a drive," he said morosely.

"It's 'take me for a *ride*,' and what are you talking about?"

"She claimed not to have access to the trial documents, but then she said the accounts given by parents, doctors, and teachers were 'terrifying.' Which means she saw them. Which means she lied."

"Well, then you lied too, because you told me yesterday that she hadn't said anything interesting."

"Only because I can see how much this whole thing is affecting you. You're not eating, you're having nightmares . . ."

"My love, I'm perfectly capable of looking after myself. It's just that I feel too . . . *small*, sometimes. And now that you have my confession, are you going to fill me in on what Janice told you?"

Vital recounted their conversation and the statements made by Maria Belova and Olga Druzhinina, her deputy for the Moscow region. In an attempt to soften the horror, he saved the "good news" of the court proceedings against Putin and Belova for last. Cordelia listened in silence, clenching her fists so tightly that her knuckles turned white.

"Call her back right now. I'll talk to her."

Vital thought it better for the conversation to take place on the private forum. As they descended to the basement, questions whirled in his head.

"You *were* able to access the trial documents, weren't you?" was the first thing he wrote.

The screen remained blank for a moment. Then:

"Yes. But I promised not to share them. It would mean betraying my source," Janice replied.

"What's in them that's so confidential?"

"The identities of the people who agreed to testify, for a start. Most of them live in occupied territory. They're risking torture and imprisonment for having supplied that information. Putin's regime doesn't tolerate dissidence."

"Okay, then without giving names, what are the basics we need to know for the mission?"

"Vital, I don't know why you're so determined to save this child in particular, when the same thing is happening to so many others. Hundreds have been taken from basements in Mariupol, and orphanages and schools in separatist regions, and the cellars of bombed-out buildings, and even right off the streets. That young girl I told you about, the one Bloody Mary likes to promenade around like a dog on a leash, was one of them. The Russians are making these children believe that their parents have abandoned them, that they don't want them anymore. They're *using* these kids to spread their ideology. They're making a business out of them, paying the families that take them in, with no concern for whether they're good parents or not. What else do you want to know?"

"Why didn't you tell me all this yesterday?"

"I haven't forgotten what Noa said to us once: 'Save a child and you save humanity.' But, at the risk of repeating myself, why just this one boy, when there are thousands suffering the same fate?"

"What do you suggest we do?" asked Cordelia.

"The Russian government has created a file of host families, with the names of all the children and their addresses. You can imagine the value of that information for the Ukrainian parents hoping to get their sons and daughters back someday. There's a copy of that file on Maria Belova's computer. You're running the show, so it's up to you whether you tell Maya to do what needs to be done. I've got to go; I'm late for a meeting and my boss is in a terrible mood."

Vital hesitated for a moment, then glanced at Cordelia, who looked as dismayed as he felt.

"I think we both agree that Maya doesn't seem to be in top form at the moment," she said. "Should we flip a coin? Loser tells her about Janice's suggestion."

"I already have my doubts about her ability to bring Valentyn home in three days. For her to attempt a hack of this magnitude... it would be suicide."

"Listen," Cordelia said firmly. "My grandfather was a committed republican who spent his youth fighting the Franco regime. And when the war in Spain was lost, he crossed the Pyrenees to join the

French Resistance. And I've got his blood flowing in my veins." She paused for a moment, her face glowing with pride, then went on.

"After the war, he became friends with a Castilian Jew who'd survived the camps. Isaac was his name, if I'm remembering it right. Isaac was convinced that Israel didn't exist, that it was a Nazi invention to attract Jews to a new ghetto and then send them all back to the camps. That drove my grandfather crazy. He showed Isaac photos from when he was a little boy in Tel Aviv, documentaries about kibbutzim . . . but Isaac didn't budge. Now, in his defense, his time in Dachau had made him suspicious of Germans, to say the least. Of course it had. But my grandfather found it unbearable that Isaac was unable to find peace of mind. And so, one day, he decided to take his friend on a trip. Even when they arrived in Jerusalem, he saw that Isaac's mind was still closed. He begged him to make an effort. They spent three days exploring the city, dined in the best restaurants, went to the Wailing Wall. And at the end of that time, my grandfather asked Isaac if, having experienced so much beauty, he wanted to take advantage of the Law of Return and settle in Israel. Isaac thanked my grandfather warmly for all the trouble and expense he'd gone to, then said that the Nazis had plenty of money and resources to have put on such an elaborate charade, and that he'd be coming back to Spain to escape the fate of all those who had clearly fallen into the Germans' trap and would be victims of the raids that were coming sooner or later. I never met Isaac, and I don't know if the story was true—my grandfather had a hell of an imagination—but I've never forgotten the moral of the story: it's no good giving in to pessimism."

"Great. So you'll talk to Maya."

"I didn't say that," Cordelia retorted, taking a British pound coin out of her pocket. "Heads or tails?"

In an attempt to clear her head, Maya started her day with a jog. The sun was rising over Moscow as she ran across the Bolshoy Moskvoretsky bridge spanning the Moskva River, then through Zaryadye Park.

She was sweating, her cheeks on fire, her muscles burning. She slowed, afraid she'd pushed herself too far, fearing a pulled muscle. She sat down on a bench to catch her breath and catch a few rays of sunlight, other joggers paying her no attention as they passed.

Back at the hotel she took a long shower, deciding she didn't have enough time for a visit to the sauna. Then she dressed, wondering, as she surveyed herself in the mirror, who she would write to, who would miss her, if this mission landed her in prison. She had let women into her life in moments of weakness, but the relationships had invariably ended. *She* had always ended them, the way you do when you're really trying, unsuccessfully, to break up with yourself.

Shutting the door behind her, Maya stepped into the elevator with her solitude.

Traffic was light, and ten minutes after the hotel parking attendant had handed Maya her keys, she was at her destination. A café on the corner opposite the Belova residence made a perfect lookout. Maya parked, went inside and ordered a cup of tea, and settled herself on a bar stool at the café window.

An hour passed. The residents of number 26 set off for their offices, passing household employees on their way in to work. A street sweeper chugged past the gates. Two nannies emerged, each escorting a child to school. Neither of them matched the photo Maya had on her phone.

At nine o'clock the gates opened to admit an SUV, a luxurious, gleaming German model that left again shortly afterward. Seeing a female silhouette in the vehicle's back seat, Maya grabbed her keys and was about to dart back to her own car and follow the SUV, but as it passed the café window, she saw that there was no child in the rear of the vehicle with the woman, only an adult man.

Maya spent another two hours watching the comings and goings at number 26. There were delivery drivers and more domestic workers, but no sign of Valentyn. The morning was already feeling very long. Maya had opened her laptop so as not to arouse suspicion, but she could tell the barista was starting to wonder about her. Maya wasn't a regular, and soon someone might start asking questions she didn't want to answer. In the end she stowed her laptop in her bag, bought a croissant, and went back to her car to make a call.

"It's noon and Valentyn still hasn't come out of the building. Doesn't look like he's going to school. If Bloody Mary's keeping him prisoner here, I don't see any way of getting our hands on him."

"He has to come out at some point, surely," Vital said optimistically.

"I think I saw Belova drive past with a man. Her husband, maybe."

"Was he dressed like an Orthodox priest?"

"No, unless priests wear suits."

"Then it was her assistant. Vadim Azarov's his name."

"How do you know?" Maya asked.

"Social media, as usual. He shares all of Belova's posts on his Telegram page."

"Spare me the condescending tone, will you?" Maya snapped. "You think this Azarov is corruptible?"

"I wasn't being condescending. And as for Azarov, maybe, but not when it comes to Belova. He worships her unconditionally. Who else works for her directly?"

"The household staff . . . there's her driver, but I wasn't able to find out anything about him before I came here. I really did leave Paris without preparing properly. I don't see how to save Valentyn in such a short time."

"You've got two whole days," Vital reminded her.

"If this were a hack, I'd be done in a flash, but rescuing a child's a different story. And I'm on my own out here."

With a finger, Cordelia slid her coin toward Vital.

"I might have a way of bringing in reinforcements," he told Maya.

"What kind of reinforcements?"

"He's bound to secrecy," said Cordelia, taking the phone from Vital, unable to watch him beat around the bush anymore, "but I'm not. My fiancé was so bored without me that he joined the IT Army."

"You're engaged?" Maya exclaimed.

"We're literally getting engaged as I speak, unless he says no. Just a formality."

"Congratulations to you both."

"Thanks, I'll pass it on. Now, in a nutshell, my fiancé's superiors are prepared to send in the heavy artillery to back up our mission, but there's a quid pro quo."

"Meaning?"

"Tens of thousands of children have been deported from Ukraine to Russia, and finding them is a priority for the Ukrainian government. They're going through the photos of these kids and cross-checking with pictures supplied by the parents—when the parents are still alive. Tracking them down is painstaking work, but the Russians have a file of all the addresses where they're being held."

"Where is this file?"

"On a server no one's been able to identify yet, but there's a copy on Bloody Mary's computer."

"You're joking."

"You wanted a hack. I'm handing you one on a silver platter."

"*Unreal*," sighed Maya.

"Wait, you haven't asked me what I meant by 'heavy artillery' yet. To start, we've got the plans for Belova's building. Our friends in the IT Army hacked the architectural firm that designed it. She's in the penthouse, which has a large bay window. We can also geolocate her SUV in real time, and I can tell you that right now she's visiting the building site of a military school where teenagers will be enrolled as soon as they're old enough. Young people are worth their weight in gold at the moment; Putin's running out of cannon fodder, and the Wagner troops recruited in Russian prisons aren't exactly in vogue anymore."

"What else?" Maya asked.

"A detailed description of the theater where a hundred children, including Valentyn, will undergo an adoption and naturalization ceremony on the day after tomorrow. The guests will include one Very Important Person, if you catch my drift."

"And that theater's going to be guarded like a fortress, I bet."

"Not necessarily. Russians don't have any reason to be on high alert right in the center of Moscow."

"What about the extraction?"

"Vital's working on it as hard as he can."

"I'll have to think about it," Maya said.

"Think fast."

It had rained all morning. Lilya was listening to music on headphones in Stefan's room. Mr. Vasylyk had fired up his still again and was producing as much firewater as he could in his workshop, while his wife had invited all the neighborhood women to a lunch at which she could regale them with her exploits, completely forgetting the fact that she'd been asked to keep things understated. Veronika was back at work. She checked her watch constantly, poking her head into the reception area again and again. She hadn't forgotten Artëm's request for her to be patient, but she wasn't managing very well.

It was a strange afternoon. A little girl had come into the clinic for her weekly physiotherapy. This was the first time Veronika had seen her since Valentyn's abduction. Her father, who'd brought her in, had the hazy look of an unhappy man who'd given up. His daughter, though, was his complete opposite: her pale face was fine-featured and open, raindrops streaming from her bangs, which framed large eyes full of promise.

She gazed for a long time at Veronika, then pushed herself up on the armrests of her wheelchair, rising to her feet through sheer upper-body strength.

"It's because of me," she said.

Her father looked up, wondering blearily what ridiculous thing his daughter was saying now. She reached for her crutch and limped toward Veronika.

"It's my fault they took Valentyn," she insisted.

Her father pulled at her wrist, urging her to sit down again and be quiet. Calmly, Veronika gestured for him to step back, and Cosima told her everything. Valentyn had pushed her to the gym exit. Then he'd turned around to face the men in black, to hold them off long enough for her to escape.

"You can't blame yourself, Cosima," Veronika said gently. "His father and I raised him that way. I'm proud of him."

"I wrote him a letter," the little girl said, "but I don't know where to send it."

"You can give it to him when he gets home. He'll like that, I'm sure."

"When is he coming home?"

"I don't know. Soon, I hope."

"All right, come on, don't bother the lady," Cosima's father said. "It's time for your session."

Cosima obeyed and they went off together.

Maya drove slowly past Maria Belova's residence again, one hand on the steering wheel, the other typing a command on her laptop computer, which was open on the passenger seat. A list of nearby Wi-Fi networks appeared. She took a screenshot and parked a bit farther down the street, partly straddling the sidewalk. The image she'd taken showed some thirty networks; many others were out of range. The only way to find out which one was Maria Belova's would be to go up to the top floor of her house and scan the most powerful signals. In other words, to walk right into the lion's den. Not very likely.

She sent a message to the mansion, determined to gain the upper hand in the negotiations with the IT Army. If Vital's superiors wanted their file, they'd have to send her the plans for this house, which was the size of an ocean liner, and they'd have to do it immediately.

Cordelia sent the plans ten minutes later, along with a brief message:
They trust you.
They don't have much of a choice, Maya replied. *And they should really be worried about* me *trusting* them.

Now it was Vital's turn to call Maya, and they studied the plans together. Beyond the wrought-iron gate, a driveway circled the building, leading to five service entrances in back, each with its own staircase used by the owners' domestic employees, and to a service elevator for deliveries and maintenance staff.

"The main lobby is guarded by concierges. You need a security badge to get in the back way, probably the same badge that opens the main gate. The card-reader models are shown on the plan, but they could have been changed since then," Vital said.

"Oh, sure. I'll slip in the gate behind a maid and follow her around to the back. Once we're at the service entrance, she'll step aside politely to let me in first. Then I'll go up to the top floor and plunk myself down on the landing to break into Maria Belova's Wi-Fi network, while being filmed by every security camera in the place. Sounds *terrific.*"

"Or you can slip in through the basement, find the cable control box, and connect that way. If you can get access for the IT Army, they'll do the rest."

"And if I run into anyone in the basement, shall I tell them I'm there to fix the furnace?"

"I'll understand if you want to back out," Vital said.

"It's not a question of what I want, it's about what's possible. I'll call you back later—the boy's just come out of the building."

23

It would have been ridiculous to keep you in your room all day in such beautiful weather! But, if you-know-who asks where you were this afternoon, you don't need to mention our little escapade," Anatoly said with a wink.

Valentyn had no intention of telling Ms. Belova's assistant anything whatsoever. He was happy to be strolling through the streets of Moscow. Everything looked bigger here than it did at home. Brighter. The sun gleamed on glass facades, the sidewalks were wide and the intersections busy, restaurant terraces full and inviting. And there were the beautiful luxury cars, vehicles he'd only ever seen in books.

"We could go to the park, but I'll admit I find slides depressing, and swings are even worse. And as for the birds that poo on your head—no, thank you!"

Anatoly made Valentyn laugh. The butler's joie de vivre had survived everything, even life's worst setbacks.

"You know what I like best?" Anatoly went on. "Books! And something tells me we have that in common. Don't you find that books always make things a little bit better?"

Valentyn nodded in agreement.

"And as luck would have it, one of the most beautiful bookstores in the world—*my* world, at least—is right nearby! And the children's book section is enormous! But before we go there, how would you feel about a cake? I know a fantastic place."

A rental car with a ticket on the windshield, parked a hundred yards from Maria Belova's residence, would draw police attention and set law enforcement on her trail, but Maya didn't have a choice. She left the car on a pedestrian side street.

Pacing herself carefully, she followed Valentyn and the man with him at a distance of some twenty yards. When they sat down at a café terrace, she chose a table of her own, ordered a cup of tea, and watched them. The man, a friendly type, by the looks of it, talked almost constantly, waving his hands around enthusiastically, while the boy devoured a pastry with seeming contentment.

After a while, the man asked a waiter for their bill. Maya had already paid hers. Putting the rescue plan into action right there in public was tempting, but too risky. Valentyn might be frightened and struggle. Maya couldn't afford to bungle this mission, and she also had to fulfill her contract with the IT Army to make sure they'd help get the boy out of Russia. So, she waited a beat, then left the terrace soon after Valentyn and his escort.

Anatoly pushed open the door of a bookstore and stood back to let Valentyn enter first. After a moment, Maya followed them inside. She lingered near the register, getting a feel for the place, put on her headphones, and made a show of choosing a stuffed animal from a shelf. Then she called Vital.

"I need information to give the boy so he'll trust me."

"His mother's name is Veronika," Vital supplied. "His sister is Lilya, and they live in Rykove. But you already knew all that."

"That won't be enough to convince him, and I don't want to risk his being afraid of me and reluctant to come with me. Ask his sister to tell you something only the two of them would know."

"Well... that's where things get a bit complicated. His mother and sister don't know he's in Moscow."

"You're kidding."

"They think he's still in Crimea and are depending on the resistance fighters there, who promised to free him."

"How long are you going to keep lying to them?"

"I just haven't been able to find the right way to tell them."

"Do whatever you need to, Vital, but I need that information, otherwise I can't make a move."

Maya hung up. She looked thoughtfully at the stuffed animal she was holding, then at Valentyn, who was deeply absorbed in a book. She felt a rush of admiration for him, for the strength of character and imagination that were carrying him through this whole crazy ordeal. Something softened in her heart, and a wave of determination rose inside her. She couldn't abandon this mission. She knew that now.

Using the tip of a fingernail, she popped a stitch in one of the stuffed bear's seams, slipped the bug from her pocket deep into its stuffing, then pulled on the thread to close the tiny hole she'd made. Then she took the toy to the register and bought it, paying for it in cash.

Calmly, she made her way toward the children's section and chose a book from the shelf, then another, and another. Next, she turned smoothly to Anatoly.

"Excuse me," she said to him, in her best Russian. "I'm having dinner at the home of some friends tonight, and they have a little boy about your son's age. I have no idea which of these books to buy for him; can you help me decide?"

"You really think we look alike?" Anatoly asked, chuckling.

"Well . . . I'm no expert on faces . . ." Maya said, as sweetly as she could manage.

"I don't have any children of my own, and so I'm probably not the best person to give advice. I'd suggest that you ask my nephew what he thinks, but—"

Valentyn shot Anatoly a dirty look. Not for lying—he quite liked the idea of having an uncle—but because this stranger didn't need to know about his mutism. He looked at the book he'd chosen, then held it out to Maya.

"*The Old Genie Hottabych!*" Anatoly exclaimed with delight. "A classic, that one—you can't go wrong!"

"You've done me a huge favor," Maya told Valentyn with a smile. "I'm so grateful."

She glanced back and forth between the book and the stuffed bear she held, and her face lit up.

"I know!" she exclaimed, as if struck by sudden inspiration. "Since you so kindly gave me your book, it's my turn to give you a gift. Here." She offered him the little bear. "Choose a name for him carefully, and he'll bring you luck."

Valentyn frowned dubiously, unhappy at being treated like a little boy in front of Anatoly.

"You don't like him?" Maya inquired, putting on a sad expression.

"Of course he does," Anatoly put in. "That's very generous of you, and we hope you'll have a lovely day. Where is that accent of yours from, if you don't mind me asking?"

"France."

"Ah, Paris," the butler sighed. "Is this your first trip to Moscow?"

"No, I come here often for work. And in fact, I'm going to be late. Thank you again," she said, waving the book at them, and left the store.

Outside, she walked up the street a short distance and then hailed a taxi, like any tourist would.

Cordelia came into the computer room. She looked in better spirits, but Vital knew that determined expression all too well.

"I haven't made up my mind about anything yet," he said.

"Well, since you don't want to hear what I think, maybe you'll listen to Ilga," Cordelia said. "I'll ask her what she thinks tonight at dinner."

"That's diabolical!"

"If Veronika means that much to you, you need to keep her informed," Cordelia retorted. "Maya feels the same. You have nothing to blame yourself for, unless you keep putting off telling her the truth. Then she'll never forgive you."

"What difference does two days make?"

"It'll change everything if Maya fails, because you'll have been letting Veronika live in false hope. If you can't bring yourself to tell her the truth tonight, do it tomorrow. But no later."

Cordelia's phone vibrated. She glanced at it, then answered on speaker.

It was Maya. "You can tell your friends that I've fulfilled my part of the contract," she announced.

"Were you inside the building?" Vital asked anxiously.

"No. But the bug's in place. I'm in my car. I just got into the Wi-Fi network in Bloody Mary's apartment."

"Have you been able to trace her computer?"

"Not yet, the signal's weak. I'm scanning the IP addresses."

"Can you give us access?"

"There isn't going to be any hack until I leave Russia. Your friends can thank me for having done so much already, in such a short time. Tell them the keys to Belova's computer are my life insurance, and they can have them as soon as I'm in a safe place."

"What's your status with Valentyn?"

"I have an idea. And don't forget, I need all the details about tomorrow's ceremony."

"You'll have them before you get back to your hotel," Cordelia promised.

Anatoly had taken the heat for the outing with Valentyn. Maria Belova had given him a ten-minute lecture, while Azarov, who preferred the title of "confidential secretary" to "assistant," drank in every word, smiling as she chastised the butler for his rashness.

Anatoly hadn't tried to defend himself. There was no point in explaining that the boy had been languishing alone in his room; it would have only made things worse. When Maria Belova had finished screaming at him, Anatoly made sure to specify that the decision to go out had been his alone, and Valentyn wasn't to blame. Finally, he apologized, assuring Ms. Belova that it wouldn't happen again, and retreated to his office, outwardly dignified but deeply humiliated.

Then Maria Belova took her anger into Valentyn's bedroom.

"Vadim had given you orders not to leave this room, and yet the concierge saw you going out with Anatoly this afternoon. I'm not happy about this at all," she said, raising her voice further. "What if something had happened to you; how would I have looked when word got out? You'll be able to go to school on Thursday, where you'll meet new people—everyone's going to want to be your friend, believe me. Don't you think you should be a bit more grateful? Look how I'm spoiling you—you have everything you need to entertain yourself here, and I'm quite sure you've never had so many toys in your life. If you want to benefit from the wonderful life I'm offering you, you'll need to learn obedience."

Valentyn nodded. Maria Belova turned on her heel and left the room. Valentyn heard the key turning in the lock.

He spent the rest of the afternoon playing with his new toys. At dinnertime, the housekeeper unlocked his door and escorted him to the kitchen. Evgenia was already at the table.

"Good or bad day?" she asked. "I heard some commotion."

Both, Valentyn wrote, putting the stuffed animal down on the table.

"Is that your teddy bear?"

Valentyn pushed it toward her. Evgenia picked it up and examined it from every angle.

"He's not in very good shape. Does he have a name?"

Valentyn shook his head.

"Shall we find one for him?"

Tears filled Valentyn's eyes, but to cry in front of Evgenia was unthinkable. So he did the only thing that could keep him from weeping and pulled his notebook toward him. In shaky writing, he explained that he was too big to have a teddy bear, and that he'd gotten it for her.

Evgenia smiled, but before she could thank him, Valentyn pushed back his chair and went to bed without dinner. The girl finished her applesauce, then looked at the bear. She didn't really want it; its seams were loose and it smelled musty. Picking it up gingerly with her fingertips, she dropped it into the garbage with distaste and left the kitchen.

Night had fallen over Rykove. Lilya stopped by the clinic to say goodnight to her mother. She was still sleep-deprived and wanted to get to bed early. Veronika's shift didn't end until midnight, but she promised to come up to Lilya's room to kiss her when she got home. Tomorrow was another day, and maybe they'd hear something from Artëm.

As she was crossing the parking lot, Lilya felt the pager buzz in her jeans pocket. She'd spent the day with Stefan and wondered what he wanted to tell her now. The evening was cold and threatening rain. Lilya quickened her step; the message could wait until she was home.

At around ten o'clock, the surgeon came into the break room and sat down next to Veronika.

"Well, I was wrong," he announced.

"About what?" Veronika asked.

"You're not the one attracting the patients. It's dead as a doornail out there tonight."

"I have to say, I don't mind it."

"Just out of professional curiosity," the surgeon said, "how are you? I was watching you earlier with the little girl who lost a leg."

"And?"

"The way you spoke to her—I couldn't hear what you said, but her eyes looked so terribly sad, and I don't know how you did it, but afterward, she seemed... different."

"I don't remember," Veronika said.

"Yes, you do. You have some special gift, I'm sure of it. I should be taking notes."

"I guess I use a certain tone when I speak to the patients," Veronika said. "Hey, do you want to get some fresh air?"

"Why not?"

The surgeon rose and pulled out Veronika's chair, then opened the door for her.

The asphalt, wet from the rain, gleamed in the darkness. The moon shone brightly in the sky with its scudding clouds. Veronika reached up and unpinned her hair, then put her hands in her pockets and looked at the surgeon. He looked different in the evening light.

"What kind of tone do you use when you speak to them?" he asked, stammering slightly.

"Kindness. It's essential in life," she said, stepping a little closer to him. "It's not instruction manuals that make you a nurse, it's love."

"Ah," he said, blushing. "You... you don't find me... unattractive?"

"I've always found you very elegant."

"Then you really are hopeless, my dear."

Slowly, tentatively, he bent and kissed her.

In her hotel room, Maya studied the confidential report Cordelia had sent her. According to the information provided by the

IT Army, the adoption ceremony would be held at the Rossiya Theater, a modern venue that had the look of a congressional building in miniature.

Maya examined the photos of the theater's interior: the lobby where patrons clustered around a bar, the gallery running along three walls of the auditorium, the rows of seats facing the stage.

She wondered if Vital was trying to make the job easier for her out of friendship or because he didn't trust anyone but himself. He'd indicated on the plan where she should park her car so it would be out of range of the surveillance cameras, and there was an X marking the artists' entrance, which, a note informed her, was usually guarded only by a theater employee who tended to abandon his post frequently, since he was also a stagehand. Security would probably be tighter on the day of the ceremony, though, given the importance of the occasion. This wasn't the first time an event like this had been held at the Rossiya, and the routine was always the same. The children waited in the wings, their adoptive parents in the auditorium. In the orchestra pit, the musicians played a few measures of a symphony each time a child was called onstage, the parents rising and joining him or her as the orchestra instilled the moment with appropriate pomp. The lucky child then received a passport, to be brandished with pride in front of the cameras, before thanking the Russian government for its generous gift of a new life. More photos, more applause, and then the next child took the stage.

Maya had rarely read anything more repulsive. She closed the file. She needed a strong drink, and maybe a one-night stand. She decided to go down to the hotel bar—but first she'd stop by the business center to print out the credentials supplied by the IT Army.

Anatoly had waited for everyone to go to bed before emerging from his office. He might have still been in there if his appetite hadn't been stronger than his wounded pride. In the kitchen, he prepared himself the kind of soul-soothing snack tray such an awful evening deserved. That bastard Azarov had finally gotten what he wanted.

Tossing out the caviar tin he'd just emptied, he caught sight of Valentyn's stuffed bear in the garbage. Seeing the memento of such a magical afternoon thrown away like so much rubbish cut him to the heart. Maybe later Valentyn would change his mind, and if he didn't, Anatoly decided, he would keep the bear and give it to the boy when he grew older, in remembrance of the afternoon's rebellion they had shared.

24

Lilya had slept late. Getting out of bed, she went and tapped on her mother's door, but there was no answer. She'd wanted to let Veronika know that her friend from Kyiv had been in touch last night, needing information that only she and Valentyn would know. Lilya had thought the message strange, but it had given her hope that Artëm was about to take action. She'd talk to Veronika about it tonight; that is, if her mother took the time to come home between shifts.

Valentyn buried his nose in the pile of clothing someone had left on his bed. It was the same outfit he'd worn to the press conference. The shirt had a clean scent that reminded him of his mother ironing in the kitchen, singing off-key at the top of her lungs.

He dressed, hoping Evgenia was coming to the theater with him. Ms. Belova hadn't said anything to him about what they were going to do there, just that it would be an important occasion in his life, and that nothing would be the same afterward. He could feel his anxiety rising. He'd always been embarrassed, on school presentation days back home, by not being able to recite a piece in front of all the parents like everyone else.

But Evgenia wasn't in the car, and neither was Ms. Belova. She wouldn't be arriving at the theater until curtain time, the assistant said. Small talk over drinks bored her just as much as emcees' speeches did.

"Here. This is your passport," the assistant said, handing Valentyn an envelope. "When you're bigger, you'll be able to travel with it. In the meantime, keep it safe in your jacket pocket and *don't lose it*. The others will be receiving their passports on stage, but you're different—you're one of the privileged ones. I hope you're proud of that."

Valentyn didn't respond, just slipped the envelope into his pocket and looked out the window at the city flashing past.

The driver dropped them off behind the Rossiya Theater. Azarov led Valentyn toward the artists' entrance.

He'd never been backstage at a theater before. Everything was a mess and it smelled strongly of dust. Valentyn looked up. There was a kind of walkway suspended in the air.

"That's the catwalk," the assistant told him, proud of his insider knowledge.

Ropes dangled from a platform near the ceiling, which was so high it was almost invisible.

"Those are called flies," Azarov explained.

Children were playing on the cables that covered the floor, pretending to be tightrope walkers, others playing hide-and-seek behind painted scenery panels, until they were all called to order by the staff. The stage manager, who was smoking a musty-smelling cigar, was in an awful mood; apparently, the mechanism controlling the main curtain was jammed again. Every time the man shouted, it sent him into a new coughing fit.

The assistant was making a call on his phone, and Valentyn took advantage of his distraction to creep onstage and peek through a tiny gap in the curtain. The big auditorium was filling up with people coming in and finding their seats. He did a quick mental calculation: sixty seats multiplied by sixteen rows; that made nine hundred and sixty places, not counting the extra folding chairs. He wished he weren't quite so good at math. Back at school there had never been more than about forty parents on presentation day. He pressed his palms to his hot cheeks. The noise of the auditorium was overwhelming.

Meanwhile, Azarov was panicking. He couldn't see the boy. He looked around wildly, shoving his way through the groups of children, calling Valentyn's name. Finally, he spotted him, standing as if paralyzed, his fists still gripping the curtain.

The fury on Azarov's face made Valentyn even more anxious. His heart pounded hard, *too* hard, and he felt a wave of nausea. The theater spun around him. His knees went weak, and he crumpled into Vadim Azarov's arms.

The assistant carried him back to the room where the master of ceremonies was having his hair done. The makeup artist had Azarov put Valentyn on the sofa, then knelt down next to him, talking to him gently and telling him that everything would be all right. Valentyn opened his eyes, and the young woman handed him a glass of sugared water. All the great actors had stage fright, she reassured him. She'd even seen some of them vomit in the wings before they went onstage. And he would only need to be out there for a few minutes.

But Valentyn didn't want to hear a word of it. He shook his head adamantly, trying to make them all understand that he wasn't budging from this sofa.

"How much longer are you going to carry on with this ridiculousness?" the assistant snapped impatiently.

The makeup artist entreated him to show some kindness—a word Azarov had forgotten the meaning of, in his obsession with power.

"Fine," Azarov sighed. "Tell me what you want and I'll give it to you, but you have to stop these shenanigans."

Valentyn took an eye pencil from the makeup table and scrawled a single word on the mirror in capital letters: ANATOLY.

Maya made her way down the dressing room corridor. She'd snuck into the theater via the unguarded artists' entrance. She slipped into an alcove near a freight elevator, neatly concealing herself behind a stack of boxes filled with props. Two members of the theater staff stood talking at the foot of the stairs; a rack of costumes for the performance of Stravinsky's *The Nightingale*, set to take place that night, formed an ideal shield. And if anyone questioned her, Maya would claim to be a journalist; she'd say everything had to look as authentic as possible in her profession, so she'd come to report on the happiness of the children attending today's ceremony. Her forged credentials as a reporter for the ultraconservative French magazine *Valeurs actuelles*, whose support of Putin was well known, would supply the final touch.

At last, the stagehands finished their conversation and walked away. Maya quickly climbed the stairs to the catwalk. From there she could see the whole stage, left and right, and, since there was no scenery, she could even see into the wings. She scanned the groups of children backstage for Valentyn.

Nearly every seat in the auditorium was full now, the last late arrivals hurrying to their places, gawking at the VIPs in the first few rows. This, Maya knew, was a ceremony designed to reinforce support and boost the morale of a population oppressed by a dictatorship, and she found it all unspeakably terrible.

The butler arrived just in time. The stagehands had managed to unjam the mechanism, and the curtain would be rising shortly. Anatoly wished he'd had time to change his clothes before coming to the theater, but since he'd be remaining in the wings it didn't really matter that much. Besides, getting one up on Azarov this way was worth all the sartorial elegance in the world. He took special delight in asking Azarov to keep his distance, so as not to traumatize Valentyn even more, as the boy was still quite pale. Less so, since Anatoly's arrival, but still far from having the rosy cheeks of an excited child on the brink of the greatest experience of his life. And if he kept making that mournful face, Madame wouldn't be happy at all.

"I'll try and repair the damage. In the meantime, go and wait over there," Anatoly ordered. "No, farther. Farther. In fact, if you'd leave the wings entirely, that would be perfect."

As Azarov disappeared from view, Anatoly turned back to Valentyn, his expression kindly, no stranger to tantrums and ready to do whatever it took to soothe the boy.

"Now," he said, "here's what I propose. It'll probably be a little while yet before your turn, but staying in this room is only going to fill your head with unhappy thoughts. But if you come and stand with me in the wings, you'll see for yourself that what you're about to do won't be so bad after all, I promise. You'll be the fifty-eighth one sworn in, according to the list I took off that fool Azarov. So, if you haven't changed your mind by the time they get to number fifty, I'll take you for ice cream instead. You'll get an almighty scolding afterward, and it'll be the gulag for me, but a promise is a promise. What do you say?"

Valentyn didn't know what a gulag was, but he figured it must be even worse than the boarding school. Anatoly was taking an enormous risk to help him, and his mother had always taught him that trust went both ways.

Since his arrival in Moscow, his thoughts had been occupied by Evgenia, and with all the new toys in his room, he hadn't had much time to think about his family except as he was falling asleep at night. Anatoly made a wonderful uncle, but all Valentyn wanted was to feel his mother's arms around him, to squabble with Lilya, to be in his family home again.

Reluctantly he rose, took Anatoly's hand, and walked toward his destiny.

"I see him," Maya whispered.

The wireless earpiece she wore connected her to Vital in the computer room in the mansion.

"Can you get near him?" Cordelia asked.

"I don't know. He's with the same man as yesterday, the one who acted like some kind of adopted uncle."

Maya quickly descended the stairs, pausing as the master of ceremonies emerged from his dressing room and went past her on his way toward the stage, and ran to reach Valentyn before it was too late. She passed a chaperone, who ignored her completely; there were only four of them responsible for the dozens of children milling around on either side of the stage.

Ms. Belova's assistant hadn't been able to resist returning to the wings. He stood some distance away from Valentyn and Anatoly, cracking his fingers menacingly. Anatoly gave the man his steeliest glare, then bent down to Valentyn.

"Don't move. I'll be right back."

The butler advanced on Azarov, wearing his most fearsome expression. Maya took advantage of the moment to emerge from her hiding place behind a pillar and step over to Valentyn.

"Your mother's head nurse at the clinic in Rykove," she said, the words tumbling out. "Your sister's first name is Lilya. She went to Crimea to save you and brought your friend Mykolai home. He's telling anyone who will listen that you were a hero at the boarding school, that you even took down that thug Guzenko. Lilya also told me about the little game the two of you play at meals and the jar of sweets in your room. I've come to get you and take you home. Please, trust me and *come with me*."

Valentyn didn't react. He just gaped at Maya, wide-eyed.

The orchestra began to play. The children stood to attention. The sound of violins filled the Rossiya Theater. The curtain rose slowly. Maria Belova had just taken her seat in the middle of the third row.

"What's happening?" Cordelia demanded.

"It's too late," Maya said. "The symphony of monsters has begun."

25

At Maya's use of the word "monster," a memory of the matron at the boarding school flashed suddenly into Valentyn's mind. His face changed, the light coming back into his eyes. He seized Maya's hand.

Together, Valentyn and Maya walked past the line of children to where the chaperone was standing. In her best Russian, Maya asked the man where the bathrooms were. He pointed her in the right direction, then turned his attention back to the little boy who was set to go onstage as soon as the master of ceremonies had finished his opening speech.

Clutching Valentyn's hand tightly, Maya guided him into the corridor leading to the artists' entrance. They were only a few yards from freedom when a voice called out.

"Where are you going?"

Valentyn stopped short and turned. Anatoly stood there, visibly trying to put a name to Maya's familiar face. Recognizing her as the woman with the stuffed bear, he rushed to reclaim Valentyn.

"Who are you?" he demanded angrily.

"A Good Samaritan taking this boy back to his mother."

"What are you talking about? That's absurd!"

"Stop and think. You'll be held accountable one day."

"What mother are you talking about? The boy's an orphan!"

"No. He has a family. A mother, a father, a sister!" Maya insisted, raising her voice now. "He was kidnapped, like most of the children here—taken from schools, hospitals, the ruins of buildings you're bombing. How can you support the horror playing out in this theater? Is there enough humanity left in you to look reality in the face?"

Anatoly stared at Maya, his eyes burning with fury and shame.

He knelt down in front of Valentyn. "Is it true? Do you still have parents?" he asked, his voice quivering.

Valentyn looked at him so trustingly that the butler was seized with a fierce desire to do something greater than himself, to accept a truth that would cleanse him of all the weaknesses, the failures, the resignation. Putting his hands on Valentyn's shoulders, he looked deeply into his eyes. He breathed in, bit his lip, and, softly, apologized.

"I'll never be alone again—I'll always have my memories of you for company. It's not enough of an excuse, but when you're older, just remind yourself that they fed us all on fear and hatred in order to enslave us, to bend us to their will, and maybe you'll be a little less angry with me. By then, all of this will be in the past. I'm an old Turk who's lost his roots, but you . . . you have to go, before you forget who you are."

With great dignity, Anatoly glanced at his watch, then turned to Maya.

"He's expected onstage in less than an hour. You have that long to get as far away from here as possible. Good luck."

Pulling Valentyn with her, Maya ran out into the parking lot. Flinging open the back door of her car, she shoved him inside, then got behind the wheel.

"Put your seatbelt on," she ordered.

Valentyn didn't answer. She glanced in the rearview mirror, saw that the belt was fastened, and threw the car into gear.

They drove toward Leningradsky Station. Maya looked worriedly at the dashboard clock.

"When does the next train leave?" she asked.

"In an hour," replied Vital, in her earpiece. "But it's a slow train and you won't reach St. Petersburg until after the ship has left, meaning you'd have to hide out until tomorrow evening. Take the train after next; it's a fast one."

"I hate to be a pessimist, but surely the authorities will have closed down the station by then," Cordelia said.

"I'll drive it," Maya said.

"You might just make it, if you put your foot down. But don't get arrested for speeding . . ."

"Can you think of a better way to transport a child who the whole country's about to be searching for?" Maya retorted.

Vital was silent. Maya could feel the noose tightening around her neck.

"What do you mean, disappeared?" the assistant gasped.

"He isn't here or anywhere else; that's the exact definition of a disappearance," Anatoly answered, straight-faced.

"How the hell did he get away from you?"

"If you hadn't come backstage again, I wouldn't have had to leave him alone. And it only took him half a second to slip away."

"He and Madame are supposed to be on that stage together in fifteen minutes, in front of the press and hundreds of people. Do you have any idea what kind of hell you're going to pay if she's subjected to that kind of humiliation?"

"Need I remind you that *you* were the one responsible for that child?" Anatoly snapped. "All I did was come to your aid. And now it's probably time for me to leave, since, remember, I wasn't invited."

"And you've searched the whole theater?" asked the assistant, who was beginning to have serious concerns about his future.

"As much as I could, given my, ahem, girth. I even asked for help from the staff—who weren't very cooperative, by the way. I'm sure he's hiding somewhere around here; this place is a real labyrinth. I almost got lost myself. He'll show up sooner or later, but as for when . . . that, only he knows. I must say, none of this would have happened if you hadn't terrorized the boy."

"So what do we do, then?" asked Azarov, who was truly panicking now.

"If I were you, I'd inform Madame as soon as possible. She's got access to resources we don't, and given the urgency of the situation . . ."

"You're enjoying this, aren't you?" Azarov snarled.

"You've got me all wrong, my dear fellow. One day you'll regret being so unfair. I came running when you called for my help, didn't I? Now, go find Madame, and hurry!"

Azarov left the wings at a run, tore through the gallery, and burst into the auditorium, dashing down the aisle to the third row and gesticulating wildly at Maria Belova, who eventually realized, from her assistant's frantic expression, that she'd have to leave her seat.

Politely excusing herself, she edged past her seatmates to join

Azarov, who led her toward the gallery. She was seething with rage, but the sight of the ushers posted nearby prevented her from making a scene.

"Have you searched everywhere?" she asked, her tone icy.

"Yes, absolutely everywhere, but this theater is a real labyrinth," said the assistant, borrowing the phrase from his archenemy.

"And you're sure he can't have left the building?"

"Positive. There's only one exit and it was well guarded," Azarov lied.

Ms. Belova rubbed her chin, thinking. The situation was serious, but not desperate. Anatoly hadn't been wrong; Bloody Mary had resources at her disposal that others did not.

"How much time before I'm expected onstage?" she asked.

"Fifteen minutes, but I can ask them to stall for time . . ."

"No," she said, her tone utterly glacial now. "Don't draw attention to the situation. No one can know. Just get me another one."

"Another what?"

"Another *child*, idiot!"

"I—I beg your pardon?" stammered the assistant.

"Oh, you'll be doing plenty of that later, make no mistake. In the meantime, find one that looks like him. You have his passport?"

Azarov gulped, his Adam's apple moving up and down like a malfunctioning elevator.

"I gave it to him, as you instructed me to," he faltered, his face white.

"Then just use the replacement boy's. We'll deal with the bureaucratic issues later."

"What about the parents who were going to adopt the other boy?"

"If they still get up even though their names aren't called, give them enough money to make them leave cautiously. And if the first boy comes out of hiding, make him disappear for good."

Maria Belova went back into the auditorium, while the assistant ran for the wings, more determined than ever to fulfill this new mission, which he knew was his last hope.

The car was stuck in the traffic that habitually clogged the ring road encircling Moscow. Valentyn took advantage of the opportunity to undo his seatbelt. Sliding over, he tapped Maya on the shoulder.

"I know," she said, gripping the wheel. "Luck's not on our side."

Valentyn dropped his new passport onto the passenger seat.

Maya opened it, then closed it again.

"Yes, but no," she said, looking back at Valentyn. "With the name listed on it, it wouldn't do us much good. The police will be looking for you by now. Come on, put your seatbelt back on, traffic's moving a bit now. Breathe. We'll find a solution."

She was already angry at herself for having made a promise that would be so difficult to keep. Just then, her phone buzzed.

"The situation has changed," Vital said in her earpiece.

"Problem with the ship?" Maya asked.

"No, but you'll be glad to know that no one's looking for you."

"Why not? Has the Kremlin been bombed?"

"Not yet. But Bloody Mary's just posted some photos on social media that are surprising, to put it mildly. Since you're stuck in traffic, have a look at what I just sent to your phone."

Maya reached for her phone and opened the file, her eyes widening as she saw the pictures of Maria Belova onstage, kneeling down in front of a small boy who vaguely resembled Valentyn. The caption boasted of her having a new son.

"She's not going to contact the police," Vital said. "Valentyn doesn't exist for her anymore, and if he were to reappear after what she's just pulled, she'd have a very hard time explaining that away. You can enjoy the rest of your drive in peace."

"See?" Maya said to Valentyn. "I told you we'd find a solution."

Six hours. A race against the clock, all the more dangerous because Maya couldn't risk being pulled over for speeding. The tires of her rental car ate up the miles, but never fast enough. She had to stop twice for gasoline, and once at a rest area bathroom when Valentyn began shifting around uncomfortably in the back seat, his stomach upset from too many sweets.

At 6:30 p.m. they finally reached St. Petersburg. The city glowed in the rosy light of a sunset that would stretch late into the evening.

By 6:45, Maya was weaving her way through traffic to the accompaniment of blaring horns. The GPS, confused by her efforts to avoid the city center, directed her toward the Fontanka River, where she narrowly avoided hitting a truck on her way across the bridge, then accelerated even more.

"Shit, shit, *shit!*" she cried. "We're going to miss it!"

"How far out are you?" Cordelia asked in her earpiece.

"Ten minutes, and it's almost seven o'clock!"

"Step on it. I'll take care of the rest," Vital ordered.

They crossed the Neva. To reach the expressway that led to the port, they had to negotiate a crowded roundabout. Maya swerved sharply, then yanked on the parking brake. Tires squealed and the car went into a drift. Maya was an expert driver, and the rental car's engine wasn't lacking in horsepower. Valentyn, in the back seat, was tossed around like a puppet with its strings cut. He clung to his seatbelt as best he could, enjoying the wild ride.

7:10 p.m. The ship was still docked, the main gangway just being raised, the crew preparing to cast off. Abandoning the rental car in the port's parking lot, Maya seized her bag with one hand and Valentyn with the other and ran for it.

At the dock entrance, a customs officer stepped from the guardhouse.

"Vital!" Maya snapped. "Shit, you said there wouldn't be any checks, and we've got an officer heading straight toward us!"

"Keep cool. Do you have Valentyn's passport?"

"Yes," Maya said.

"Any cash?"

"Yep."

"Stick 200 euros in your passport and beg him to let you board."

She managed to slip the money between the pages of her passport right before they reached the barrier. The customs officer opened her passport, pretended to study her visa while he tucked the money into his jacket pocket, then examined Valentyn's passport suspiciously.

"It's all my fault," Maya lamented. "I wanted to show him the Hermitage Museum and we're horribly late. It's the end of vacation—he starts school again tomorrow. We really *must* get on the ship, *please!* It's going to leave without us."

And before the customs officer had time to notice that the two passports were from different countries, or wonder why a Russian child traveling with a French national would be attending school in Finland, Maya had taken out her keys and was pointing toward where she'd parked the rental car.

"The rental is paid up until the weekend—it's yours. Drives beautifully, and I just refilled the tank."

The customs officer eyed the Audi. Then, without a word, he carefully took the keys from Maya, handed back the two passports, and waved them past the barrier.

Maya and Valentyn walked toward the gangway. An officer on deck waved his arms, urging her to hurry. Following a call from Vital, he'd pretended to find a problem that required the gangway to be lowered again, delaying the ship's departure—to the great chagrin of the ship's Finnish captain, who prided himself on his punctuality. Soon the officer was escorting his newest passengers to a cabin, advising them not to come out until the vessel had reached the Gulf of Finland.

Maya clung tightly to Valentyn's hand as they crossed the deck, as if she were afraid of losing him.

All Valentyn's fear had gone. They'd reached the ship. The sea was calm, the breeze gentle.

It was a white night, so Valentyn couldn't see the stars, but he imagined them looking even more beautiful than they had from his garden at home in Rykove.

He was happy to see the Russian shore receding into the

distance, and even happier to know that another shore would come into view at dawn, just as Maya had said it would. She'd kept her promise.

His name was Valentyn Khodova. He was free. And he was going home.

26

Veronika and Lilya were having dinner in the kitchen. When Lilya mentioned the message she'd received on her pager the previous evening, Veronika marveled once again at this courageous daughter of hers, so fiercely determined to never give up. She found her eyes filling with tears.

The phone rang. They listened to Vital's words without daring to believe them at first, and then with confusion at how and why Valentyn was currently on a cruise ship en route to Helsinki. Then Maya entered the conversation. The ship had entered Finnish waters. Cordelia had already arranged everything. A medical plane would fly Valentyn to Lviv, where Cordelia would personally go to collect both him and Maya and bring them back to the mansion tomorrow night.

"Here, it's for you," Maya said, handing the phone to Valentyn.

He pressed it to his ear, keeping his gaze firmly fixed on the horizon.

Valentyn listened to his mother telling him how much she loved him. As soon as Veronika hung up, she'd pack her bags, and the minute the sun rose tomorrow, she and Lilya would be on their way to meet him in Kyiv. She already knew the way.

Tomorrow, Veronika promised, she would hug Valentyn close.

The three of them would sleep in the same room together. Nothing and no one would separate them again.

"Your papa will be coming to see you too," she told him. "He's back from the war and he's just fine. Your sister's right here with me. She's crying a lot, but it's because she's so happy. I'm crying too, so I'll give her the phone. I love you so much, my precious boy. So much. The nightmare is over now. I'll be with you soon, sweetheart. I love you. Just a few more hours and we'll be together."

Valentyn drew in a deep breath. His chest felt hot and there was a prickling in his throat. Another breath, a breath of freedom. His face lit up, and for the first time, Veronika heard her son speak:

"Mama."

Epilogue

At the same time as Maya and Valentyn were disembarking in Helsinki, the head of the Wagner Group bit the hand of the dictator who had made his bloody reputation. As his troops advanced on Moscow, liberating the roads in the occupied zone, Danylo drove toward Kyiv, sirens wailing.

The surgeon had obtained false papers for them. If they were stopped, Lilya, lying on the gurney, would play the role of patient.

Before leaving Rykove, Veronika had promised the surgeon she'd return as soon as Ukraine won the war—but the surgeon had replied that it was time for her to think of herself. If the children liked Kyiv, and if she still wanted him, he'd find a teaching post in the West. And he thanked her for having given new meaning to his life.

The stuffed bear with its bug tucked inside remained in Anatoly's desk drawer. The butler's office was next to that of Maria Belova, the Wi-Fi signal strong. The IT Army had already been able to access the file of stolen children on her laptop and was working to repatriate them.

Valentyn and Maya reached the mansion at around 9:00 p.m. Lilya launched herself at her brother so fast that she actually managed to hug him before their mother did.

The rest of the night was a celebration. Valentyn presided over the table, Veronika and Lilya on either side of him, frequently covering him with kisses. Maya was exhausted but happy; Ilga took off her apron and danced with Danylo. And Vital and Cordelia quietly luxuriated in their new engagement.

At around midnight, Vital slipped down into the computer room for a moment. Turning on his screen, he read a message that made him smile.

> Well played.
> Congratulations,
> Noa

COMMUNICATION TERMINATED - 00:00 GMT.

Author's Note

On February 24, 2022, Vladimir Putin launched his war against Ukraine. Since the conflict began, 32,000 Ukrainian children have been abducted by Russian forces—sent to reeducation camps, stripped of their identities, nationalized as Russians, and placed with adoptive families.

These crimes are the result of a systematic state-run deportation program orchestrated by Maria Lvova-Belova, whom Putin appointed as Russia's Commissioner for Children's Rights.

This mass abduction of children led to the indictment of its principal perpetrators by the International Criminal Court for crimes against humanity. While the officially acknowledged number of deported children stands at 32,000, the true figure is likely twice as high.

I never knew my paternal grandparents, as both were killed at Auschwitz. Growing up, when I asked my teachers why nothing had been done to stop the camps, invariably the answer was *we didn't know.*

When I learned about the large-scale systematic deportation of Ukrainian children, I decided to write a novel about it. That way, those who will read it will not be able to say *we didn't know.*

Acknowledgments

To

My parents

Pauline, Louis, Georges, and Cléa

My sister Lorraine

Susanna Lea, Léonard Anthony

Antoine Caro, Marie-Odile Mauchamp,
Elsa de Saignes, Miguel Courtois

The whole team at Éditions Robert Laffont

Mark Kessler, Carole Delmon, Lauren Wendelken,
Thérèse Coen, Una McKeown

Gabriella Page-Fort, Ryan Amato, and the whole team at HarperVia

Tina Kover

Sarah Altenloh

Rémi Pépin

Audrey Sourdive, Xavier Baur

Bibliography

Yale Humanitarian Research Lab, Kaveh Khoshnood, Nathaniel Raymond, and Caitlin Howarth, "Russia's Systematic Program for the Re-Education & Adoption of Ukraine's Children. A Conflict Observatory Report," February 14, 2023

Andrei Kourkov, *Journal d'une invasion*, Éditions Noir sur Blanc, 2023

Heidi Levine, "What I've Seen in Bucha," *Washington Post*, April 8, 2022

Sarah El Deeb, Anastasiia Shvets, and Elizaveta Tilna, "How Moscow Grabs Ukrainian Kids to Make Them Russians," series of articles, Associated Press (AP), October 13, 2022

Emma Bubola, "Using Adoptions, Russia Turns Ukrainian Children into Spoils of War," *New York Times*, October 22, 2022

Robyn Dixon and Natalia Abbakumova, "Ukrainians Struggle to Find and Reclaim Children Taken by Russia," *Washington Post*, December 22, 2022

Jennifer Hansler, "Report Says Russian Government Is Operating Network of Camps Where It Has Held Thousands of Ukrainian Children Since Start of War," CNN, February 15, 2023

Helen Sullivan, "Thousands of Ukrainian Children Put Through Russian 'Re-Education' Camps, US Report Finds," *The Guardian*, February 15 and 21, 2023

Bibliography

Sabrina Tavernise and Emma Bubola, "Why Russia Is Taking Thousands of Ukrainian Children," *New York Times*, March 3, 2023

Marc Santora and Emma Bubola, "Russia Signals It Will Take More Ukrainian Children, a Crime in Progress," *New York Times*, March 18, 2023

Ed Vulliamy, "We Had to Hide Them: How Ukraine's 'Kidnapped' Children Led to Vladimir Putin's Arrest Warrant," *The Guardian*, March 18, 2023

Carlotta Gall and Oleksandr Chubko, "The Russians Took Their Children: These Mothers Went and Got Them Back," *New York Times*, April 8, 2023

"An Arctic Welcome: Russia's orphan listings have abruptly increased in number. In their midst, Ukrainian children are listed for adoption, too. Some have already been placed with families in the Russian Far North," *Meduza*, June 2, 2023

Messaging Codes

A = 6	F = 7	K = 15	O = 0	S = 5	W = 111
B = 8	G = 9	L = 4	P = 9	T = 7	X = 25
C = 0	H = 4	M = 2	Q = 9	U = 17	Y = 3
D = 0	I = 1	N = 17	R = 12	V = 11	Z = 5
E = 3	J = 7				

001: Yes

002: No

003: Maybe

004: OK

20: Mom/Mama

21: Me

31: Fine

34: Am

35: Was

38: Leave, go away

044: I just left

045: Good night

065: Good news

072: Bad news

123: I miss you

189: I'm on the way

303: Get ready to answer the phone

308: I'm busy

312: I'll talk to you later

315: I'm going to bed

Messaging Codes

318: I don't feel good

322: Stop

372: What are you doing?

378: Are you serious?

390: Where are you?

393: When?

395: How?

404: Forget it

434: You've misunderstood

440: I'm tired

450: It hurts/I'm in pain/I'm having trouble

470: Wait

475: Am across the street

490: I have something for you

502: Do you need something?

505: Try to call me

513: Call me in an hour

540: Don't forget!

550: I need you

911: Important

911: Urgent, hurry up

A Note from the Cover Designer

When I read the story, I understood that the cover had to convey both the devastation of war and the resilience of the human spirit. The contrast between the destruction and the solitary figure moving forward symbolizes hope in the midst of chaos. At the same time, I wanted to reflect the colors of the Ukrainian flag through the use of yellow against a blue-toned background, emphasizing courage and the will to endure.

—Pedro Viejo

About the Author

MARC LEVY is the author of twenty-six novels. His work has been translated into fifty languages and has sold over fifty million copies worldwide. Several of his novels have been adapted for the screen. *Le Figaro* newspaper commissioned a nationwide poll asking the French to rank their favorite authors; Marc Levy and Victor Hugo tied for first place. Born in France, Marc currently lives in New York City.

About the Translator

TINA KOVER'S translations include Anne Berest's *The Postcard*, a *Library Journal*, *NPR*, and *TIME* Best Book of the Year; Antoine Compagnon's *A Summer with Montaigne*; and Négar Djavadi's *Disoriental*, winner of the Albertine Prize and the Lambda Literary Award, and a finalist for both the 2020 National Book Award for Translated Literature and the PEN Translation Prize.

Here ends Marc Levy's
Symphony of Monsters.

The first edition of this book was printed
and bound at Lakeside Book Company
in Harrisonburg, Virginia, in December 2025.

A NOTE ON THE TYPE

The text of this novel was set in Carré Noir, a typeface designed by Albert Boton in 1996. A native of France, Boton was working as a carpenter at his father's workshop when, while installing new windows on a city building, he discovered a graphic design agency on the very last floor. His encounter with the designers sparked Boton's interest in type, and he promptly left the workshop to strike out on his own. After attending evening classes at the École Estienne in Paris, Boton joined several French design agencies of repute. In 1981, he became the head of the type department at Carré Noir, whose name inspired this elegant typeface.

HARPERVIA

An imprint dedicated to publishing international voices,
offering readers a chance to encounter other lives and other
points of view via the language of the imagination.